Twilight's Hidden Truth

THE WINDS OF CHANGE TRILOGY
BOOK TWO

RACHEL VALENCOURT

MARMONT PUBLISHING

Cover Design—Milblart Art

Editors—Ann Leslie Tuttle, Jenna O'Malley, Gail Delaney

Chapter Image—Watercolor flower@Freepik

Section Image—Goldenborder by yodafunkyo@Pixabay

Format Designer—Dawn Baca

 Created with Vellum

Dedicated to every mother dreaming of a better future for her children, especially my own mother, who taught me that even my grandest dreams were within reach.

Blurb

In the 1970s suburbs of Los Angeles, Twyla Cameron's life is about to take a dramatic turn. When cultures collide in her tranquil neighborhood, the peaceful façade of Twyla's life begins to unravel. Experience this unforgettable coming-of-age tale that immerses you in a world marked by self-discovery, intrigue, and cultural shifts.

Twyla seems to be the perfect daughter in a perfect family. Yet, beneath the surface, her world is falling apart. The sudden arrival of a greaser gang disrupts the community's peace, thrusting the Cameron family into a heated conflict with these newcomers. As tensions escalate, Twyla's once stable life transforms into a whirlwind of change.

As her brother is drafted into the Vietnam War, challenges intensify to plunge Twyla into the era's chaos. Amidst these trials, she crosses paths with the charismatic celebrity racer, Caleb Silverson. Is he her key to happiness, or will an unexpected opportunity entice her into a Hollywood lifestyle of sex, drugs, and rock'n'roll? Will Twyla emerge with her identity intact, or will the tumultuous winds of change sweep her into a new, unrecognizable life?

Seen through Twyla's captivating eyes, this enthralling novel unfolds as an inspiring saga of survival, love, and closely guarded secrets.

Discover the second installment in the *Winds of Change* trilogy and prepare to be swept away into the dynamic 1970s and 1980s. This family saga unfolds against the backdrop of the sun-kissed beaches of Mexico and travels to the vibrant allure of the Sunset Strip, inviting you on a mesmerizing journey of one girl's hopeful heart.

Prologue

Twilight

As I drove down the winding road leading to Mom's cabin, I couldn't help but notice the dogwood trees were in full bloom. The white petals of the trees shimmered in the gentle sunlight. Mom liked to say these blooms could brighten even her darkest days.

Over the years, Mom and I had weathered many storms together, yet sometimes, I felt a distance we couldn't quite bridge.

It's hard to believe forty years have slipped by since I stepped out from under the protective wing of my parents' home. Years brimming with failures, victories, and everything in between. Leaving the nest at just seventeen wasn't always easy, but the journey has been an incredible ride, shaping me into the person I am today.

The sight of Mom's old cabin brought a wave of comfort as it emerged from the embrace of the firs and pines. Nestled in the California mountains, the surrounding woods reminded Mom of her childhood in the wilds of Washington state.

These steadfast giants, much like Mom herself, stood as silent witnesses to the relentless march of time, their unwavering resilience a source of inspiration. The dogwoods, with their hopeful blossoms, echoed her childhood vow to return to the woods—a promise rooted in the towering forests of the Pacific Northwest.

"Mom, are you ready to celebrate Grandma's ninetieth today? You seem a world away," my daughter Starla asked as she looked over at me with questioning eyes.

"I hope Grandma feels well today."

"You know her. She always feels good when it's party time. The real question is, do you think Dad will be on time to pick up Sebastian at the airport?"

"Of course not, he's always late. Seb's been in this family long enough to know how your father is. He'll probably grab a bite to eat at the airport lounge while he waits. They'll be fine, trust me."

"You're right, Mom, as usual." Starla looked at me with a knowing smile.

"I wouldn't have it any other way, and the kids are excited to see their Great Grandma Dawn. Right, kids?"

"Right, Mom," Delaney and Brooke shouted in unison.

At eight and ten years old, those girls were the light of my life, and essential links in the chain that joined our family's maternal side, I thought to myself as I smiled back at them in the rearview mirror.

As I stepped into Mom's quaint home, a robust wood-burning fireplace crackled with the same untamed energy as the matriarch of our family. Its radiance against the honeyed wood interior complemented Mom's fiery personality. Her gray eyes fixed on mine and reflected a lifetime of unspoken words. Her hair was expertly styled and tinted to resemble the rich auburn of her childhood.

"Mom, it's almost summer and you're still running the fireplace?"

"Just to take the chill off, it was brisk this morning." She moved toward the stove to break apart the embers with her fire poker, sending a cascade of sparks dancing upwards before they disappeared into the chimney.

"Uh huh, well, happy birthday. Ready to celebrate your ninetieth today?" I gave her a quick hug and kiss on the cheek.

"Just about, but there's something we need to do first," she replied, her voice laced with quiet resolve.

Starla enveloped Mom in a big hug, "You look lovely, Gramcracker."

At forty, my daughter radiated a youthful energy, which sparkled in her emerald-green eyes. Her golden-brown hair fell in gentle waves, complementing the subtle maturity of her face. Clad in a sleek leather jacket and chic trousers she moved with a confident grace. Her red motorcycle boots added a rebellious edge to her otherwise conventional outfit, hinting at the free spirit that danced beneath the surface.

"Starla, look at this, it was my Aunt Hatt's. From her younger days." Mom pulled out a long cigarette holder, striking a sassy pose. "I love the Roaring Twenties theme you picked for tonight. You know me too well." Mom's eyes twinkled with amusement as she pretended to puff on the cigarette holder, an echo of a bygone era that perfectly matched the night's theme.

"Hey, Starla, grab that box. I've got a gift for you," Mom said with a knowing smile.

That look was one I recognized, and it made my stomach flutter, knowing how sly Mom could be when she was up to one of her schemes. She pointed to a worn-out cardboard box in the corner.

"A gift for me on your birthday, Grandma?" Starla questioned. Curiosity lit up her face as she opened the box. "What is it?"

"Everything you'll need."

"What do you mean, Grandma?" Starla asked.

With a tender smile, Mom clarified. "It's what you need to write the story of my life."

"Are you sure you're ready to let all of this go? You should be the one to write it. Or Mom. She's the writing professor," Starla looked with a puzzled expression.

"I'm sure. You're the one for the job. Are you up for this?"

"Of course, Grandma. I'mhonored."

"Good, now, come over here and help an old lady up the stairs. We have a party to attend."

THAT EVENING, AS I SETTLED ONTO MY NIECE'S PORCH, THE sky transformed into a canvas sprinkled with glittering stars, their light casting a magical glow over the poolside party below. The blend of laughter and the rhythmic pulse of music drifted up to me, wrapping me in a cocoon of comfort and reflection. Dozens of people, both friends and relatives, whirled around, their silhouettes lit by the flickering glow of fairy lights.

My thoughts drifted back to the unexpected exchange between Mom and Starla earlier today. Mom's box of memories.

What secrets did it hold, and why had she chosen tonight to share them?

Despite my apprehension, the party proceeded without incident. A nostalgia laden night, chock full of cherished family stories and clinking champagne glasses. As I soaked up the pleasant night breeze, I watched Mom, a force of nature in a glittery purple skirt suit and matching sequined shoes, navigate the dance floor. The brilliant colors of her clothes mirrored her vivacious energy. Like tinkling wind chimes, her laughter mingled with the lively show tunes, music from her childhood, and her eyes gleamed with vitality of someone who had truly mastered the art of living. That twinkle, which had captivated so many people over the years, hid a complexity only a daughter could begin to understand.

It hasn't always been an easy path with a mom so enigmatic. She could be like a tornado, unpredictable and challenging, yet undeniably captivating.

In many ways, I was very similar to Mom. We both left home at a young age, determined to make it on our own terms. Maybe that's why Mom and I had so many disagreements. Our relationship was a delicate dance between two strong-willed women. While our shared desire for independence provided us with resilience, it also led to some misunderstandings. Her feisty ways mirrored my own resilient soul.

"Mom, look at Grandma. She's like a shooting star. I can't wait to start writing her life story," Starla sat in the chair next to me, admiring the matriarch of our family.

ONCE THE PARTY HAD ENDED, STARLA'S FAMILY, MY HUSBAND, and I returned home, still buzzing with elation from the festivities. The mysteries of the day were far from over. I had my entire family home for the weekend, and I wanted to enjoy every moment of it.

"It's not that late, Mom. Let me put the girls to bed, and we'll start going through Grandma's box. It's warm enough to sit on the balcony. Should we both have a cup of hot cocoa?"

Tucked away in a lush forest embrace, my home was a rustic haven of serenity. My husband and I had recently moved to the mountains to be closer to Mom and we lived just a few miles away from her. Our home had a natural finish, and a large deck that reached out like an open invitation to inhale the fresh, pine-scented air. An outdoor fireplace added a welcoming ambiance, promising a cozy evening under a canopy of stars.

My husband called out from the kitchen, "I'll get the hot chocolate and keep your husband occupied. The men are going to sit by the fireplace with a glass of whiskey." At sixty, he was a man of stature; his commanding voice spoke of strength as reliable as the oak trees in the distance. Time had broadened his middle, but it suited his solid frame. His once full head of hair had given way to a receding hairline, and his intense blue eyes still held a gaze as penetrating as ever.

"Now *that* is a perfect plan," Sebastian, my son-in-law, agreed, his British accent adding a touch of precision to his words. "But only if it's Scottish Whisky, not the American stuff you're fond of." Amusement danced in his deep-set brown eyes; his dark hair was just starting to show the slightest hint of grey at his temples.

"Easy there, son, them are fighting words. Just for that,

you can get the drinks while I join my wife and daughter on the balcony, I'm curious to see what's in this mysterious box, myself." My husband took some time to get used to Sebastian's playful banter, but it didn't take long before they fell into their own rhythm of friendly teasing and camaraderie. Now we couldn't imagine our lives without him.

We made our way onto the balcony as Seb went to prepare the drinks. Eyeing the box, I sensed it was cradling decades of whispers and untold adventures from my mother's youth. I didn't know why, but the thought of revisiting the past sent shivers up my spine.

"I'm just wondering why Mom decided to hand it over now. She never let any of us kids rummage around her room. She was always so private when it came to the things she kept in there."

"Maybe she felt it was the right time. She's always talked about starting her memoir, and lord knows she's lived an interesting life. One thing I don't understand is why she's asked me to write it. I mean, I dabble in writing, but Mom, you teach writing for a living, for goodness sakes. Why didn't she ask you to write it?

"Maybe I'm just a little too close to home. You know Grandma and my relationship has been complicated at times."

"I know, Mom, you are too much alike. That's the problem. I'm glad our relationship is not complicated like that." Starla smiled up at me.

"Me, too." I watched as she started to rummage around through the treasure trove of letters and old photographs.

"Mom, look at this picture." Starla held a photo of my sister Rory and me dressed in matching ruffled red dresses.

"I haven't thought about that day in years. It was Grandma's fortieth birthday. That was the day everything changed."

PART ONE
Twyla Cameron

To be yourself in a world that is constantly trying to make you something else is the greatest accomplishment.

— Ralph Waldo Emerson

CHAPTER 1

You Don't Always Get What You Want

POMONA, CALIFORNIA

JUNE 5TH 1968

Twyla Cameron
Eight Years Old

"Let's turn this living room into a wooded wonderland. I can't wait for everyone to see our handiwork," I said as I launched a roll of streamers into the air. The excitement of preparing for Mom's birthday bash filled us kids with unbridled joy, our faces lit up with constant grins.

"Careful with those streamers, Twyla," Susan cautioned, skillfully dodging a flurry of ribbons. Her movements, graceful as a dancer's, contrasted with her stern warning. Her cool grey eyes and striking features were framed by dark auburn hair.

Rory and I had spent all week creating paper-mâché trees and forest animals to represent the wild woods of Washington. "Do you think Mom is going to like it?"

"I think she's going to love it," my older brother Randall responded. "She's always talking about how she misses the woods; now she can have them here for her birthday."

"Where's Daddy? Shouldn't he be helping with the decorations? Some of the trees are too tall for me to hang," Rory complained, her frustration evident on her freckled face. Despite being the older sister, her need to be the center of attention made her seem younger at times.

"Let me handle that," offered Randall, reaching for the streamers with ease. His stature nearly matched our father's. His youthful face, dotted with freckles and bearing a striking resemblance to Daddy, was complemented by his neatly combed copper hair.

As we busied ourselves with party preparations, the doorbell rang, signaling the arrival of our first guests. "That must be the Fisher kids and Chuck. Remember, dress shoes everyone! We want to look our best," Susan reminded us, her voice carrying the authority she often wielded over us younger ones.

"I gave mine away," I said, looking down at my sneakers, feeling a mix of guilt and defiance. "Lisa needed them more than I did," I defended my decision to give my shoes to the new girl in our neighborhood, hoping to spare her from the schoolyard taunts.

"Twyla, you can't give all your things away. You need them, too, you know," Susan replied.

"Grandma always says everyone helped each other during the Great Depression, and that's how they survived."

"That's true. But if you always put others' needs ahead of your own, you won't have anything left to give. Mark my words. Now go answer the door. And Rory, check if you have some old dress shoes Twyla can borrow," Susan said, tapping her fingers on the kitchen counter. My oldest sister often bossed us younger kids around, but we didn't mind. Rory and I both knew Susan would soon be heading off to college, and we'd miss her when she was gone.

By the time the clock struck five, we were all in our hiding places. When Mom walked through the door, the air exploded with joy and the sound of birthday horns. "Surprise!"

Mom stood in the middle of the chaos, five-foot-two, with a mane of fiery red hair piled high on her head. Her large gray eyes shone like moonlight, and her smile, always warm and inviting, was framed by soft freckles that danced across her cheeks, adding to her unique charm. Though not classically beautiful, she possessed an undeniable charisma; her presence radiated warmth and vivaciousness.

It was clear that she was the heart and soul of our family gatherings.

Daddy stood next to her, tall and ruggedly handsome with his salt-and-pepper hair. He hugged Mom, a look of bliss adorning his face, his eyes crinkled at the corners. I felt their love radiating throughout the house.

"Were you surprised?" Talie, Mom's best friend, asked. She had dark, mysterious eyes and long silky hair.

"More surprised than that time you jumped out and scared us on the reservation. Remember when Franny and I were out searching for huckleberries?" Mom squeezed her lifelong friend's hand in a gesture of love.

Talie and Mom's laughter joined the melody of the party, making it feel like New Year's Eve. We had a huge gathering every holiday, and this birthday celebration was as large as the parties Mom planned. People were everywhere, and I could hardly recognize our living room.

"Happy Birthday, Aunt Dawn," the Fisher kids chimed in unison. Everyone was hugging and kissing Mom while she reminisced about her time on Neah Bay with Talie.

"Where did you come from, little blondie?" A tall man with dark hair and kind eyes ruffled my hair, interrupting my observations.

"That's Twyla," Daddy came to stand next to me. "Say hello to Mr. Lockheart, dear."

"How do you do?" I smiled up at the handsome man. He looked like someone who stepped out of one of those romance movies Mom liked to watch. All neat and shiny. His hair was slick and his suit smooth and dark with a shiny clip on his tie. He peered down at me with the greenest eyes I'd ever seen.

"You can call me Uncle Charlie," he said with a smile as he pinched my cheek. His eyes somehow looked sad.

"Uncle Charlie was just dropping this off." Daddy opened a small jewelry box that held a shimmering black pearl necklace.

"Is that for Mom?" I asked.

"It sure is, now say goodbye to Uncle Charlie. Thanks for delivering this tonight." Dad turned and shook the man's hand.

"It's the least I could do."

I spotted Mom watching us from the center of the room, a concerned look on her face. The way the man looked at me made me squirm. "I'm going to go help my sister light the candles on the cake."

"Who was that?" Rory asked.

"I've never seen him before. Daddy said his name was Lockheart."

"Oh, that's their old friend from Oklahoma. He's the jeweler that Daddy bought Mom's necklace from," Rory responded.

I watched as Daddy made his way over to Mom in the middle of the room. Her eyes sparkled as she opened his gift, revealing the shiny black pearl necklace. The room erupted into cheers, and Daddy looked like he won a grand prize at the fair.

"Okay everyone, time to sing 'Happy Birthday,'" Randall called out.

Buck rolled out the cake, which was a towering master-piece of chocolate and candles, over to Mom. There were too many candles to count. Mom's cheeks flushed the same pink color as the frosting on the cake as she blew them all out.

"Happy birthday, sweetheart." Daddy took Mom's hand, and they danced around the room before she pulled herself away to cut the cake.

As the night continued, I observed Mom surrounded by love, laughter, and a whole lot of mess. Warmth spread throughout my chest, and I realized I was part of some-thing memorable. Something that would stay with me forever.

The party came to a sudden stop when Susan burst through the door, her mascara running down her face. Tammy Fisher was right behind her, appearing just as upset. My brother Randall was the first to reach them.

"What's happened? Are you both okay?" he murmured, trying to soothe the girls with his calm voice. At fifteen years old, Randall was already more responsible than most kids his age. He had a knack for saying just the right thing to make a situation better. As he looked at the two girls, both visibly upset, he gently encouraged them to share what trou-bled them.

"You know that family that just moved here from Los Angeles?" Susan's voice carried a mix of frustration and fear.

"Isn't that the little girl Twyla gave her shoes to?" Rory interjected.

"Yeah, well, her brothers act like they own the neighborhood already."

Susan sighed; her gaze focused on Randall's concerned eyes. "We were just heading down to the corner store to purchase a bag of ice, but those biker boys, they started with the catcalling. When we didn't respond, they unleashed this stream of vulgar comments. One even had the audacity to grab his privates and mimic kissing sounds at us. I've never heard such language."

Tammy clenched her fists, her indignation evident. "They chased us on their beat-up old motorcycle and we ended up running the rest of the way home. I can't believe they had the nerve to treat us so horribly. I'll never walk by their house again."

My three brothers, Buck, Bobby, and Randall, gathered around the girls. A tense silence replaced the sounds of laughter and music as they discussed the troubling incident.

Buck was the first to respond. "Well, you've got to walk by there to get to school. I'm going to go over and have a word with these fellows."

"We can't let those greasers think they can bring their city nonsense here. It's not right, and it's certainly not how we do things here in Pomona." Bobby, my middle brother, chimed in.

Randall nodded in agreement. "We've got to set things straight. We can't allow that kind of behavior in our town."

"They need to know it won't fly down here," Daddy said with a concerned look on his face.

"Don't encourage them, Ellis. Boys, I understand you're upset, but going up there isn't the solution. It's bound to turn into a fight. Violence begets more violence," Mom urged, her voice tinged with unease.

"We just want to talk to them. We're not looking for trouble." Bobby sighed, recognizing the wisdom in Mom's words.

Mom shook her head, her maternal instincts kicking in. "I know your intentions are good, but words can be as powerful as fists, and I think there's a better way to handle this. Let me talk to their mother and see if we can find common ground without making things worse."

My brothers exchanged uncertain glances, torn between the desire to protect and Mom's plea for a peaceful resolution.

"Oh, let them go. Our boys are just standing up for their sister, it's the right thing to do." Daddy took Mom's hand in his. The magic of Mom's birthday celebration had dissipated, replaced by the ominous cloud of impending confrontation.

Amid the heated conversation, I slipped away, finding solace in the quiet of my room. Posters the Osmond Brothers and the Monkees adorned the walls, but my musical crushes couldn't shield me from the burden of the situation unfolding downstairs. I sat on the edge of my bed as I grappled with the complexities of the grown-up world.

I looked up when I heard Rory's shoes clunking up the stairs. We shared a room with my side decorated in a colorful flower child aesthetic, shades of pink and yellow, Rory's side was a huge contrast with darker tones and posters of the hard rock bands she adored. Although we were opposites in every way, Rory and I were closer than any other pair of sisters I knew.

"Twyla, what's going on? Why did everyone become so serious?"

I released a breath I didn't realize I was holding and, after relating the incident, told her about our brothers' plans to confront them. Rory's brow furrowed in worry.

"Confront them? Isn't that a bit extreme? Can't they just let it go and ignore it? Last time I walked by their house, I saw those boys working on their bikes and drinking. They looked like trouble to me."

I nodded; a cold shiver trickled down my spine. "Lisa told me their Dad ran off and they moved here to live with their uncle. I don't get a good feeling about this. I can't believe something like this could happen on Mom's special day."

Rory sat down beside me. "Times are changing. Did you know they have an older sister? She's an air stewardess. I've seen her coming home looking glamorous in her fancy uniform. She's married *and* has a career. I wish I could do something like that, but Mom would never let us go anywhere if there's still a war going on."

Her words echo in the stillness. "Yes, I know about Vietnam. It's all anyone talks about. Mom is worried about the draft. It's a miracle none of our brothers have been called up to fight. I'm worried if the brothers confront those boys up the street, they could make things worse. If they get into trouble with the law, they could be sent off to Vietnam."

Rory exhaled and offered a comforting embrace. "We can't control everything, Twyla. Our brothers believe they're doing what's right. Let's not worry about it now. Like Mom says, don't borrow tomorrow's worries for today."

"You're probably right. Let's put that new record on and try not to think about it."

We found comfort in each other's presence while the Beatles played softly in the background providing a soothing soundtrack to our moment of sisterly solidarity.

CHAPTER 2

For What It's Worth

POMONA, CALIFORNIA

SUMMER 1968

Twyla Cameron
Eight Years Old

As I stepped into the kitchen the next morning, I found Susan, Randall, Mom, and Dad already at the table, their eyes reflecting the weight of the situation. The aroma of breakfast filled the air, but the usual morning hustle felt subdued, as if time had slowed down.

"Twyla, sit down. We need to talk." Mom gestured to the empty chair.

"What's happening, Mom?"

"Your brothers went over to talk to the new neighbors last night. Things got heated, and, well… it turned physical. The police ended up coming out."

My spirit plummeted. A fist fight? I glanced at Randall, who had a swollen, painful-looking black eye. "How are Buck and Bobby?" I asked.

"They are fine, dear. They went home to their apartment late last night."

"How could this be happening? I'm friends with their little sister. She's very nice." I looked at Randall with questioning eyes.

"They threw the first punch," Randall responded, his jaw clenched. "We didn't want trouble, but we won't let them disrespect Susan like that."

"Like I said before, violence is not the answer. We need to find a common ground with our new neighbors." Mom's eyes flickered with a mix of understanding and a hint of frustration.

"You know, this town used to feel like one big family. But things have changed," Susan added.

"I'm going to start dropping you kids off at school every morning, and your mom will pick you up. No more walking past that house. And Twyla, it might be best if you don't play with Lisa, at least for the time being," Daddy added.

"But for how long?" I asked.

"Hopefully things will blow over and get back to normal soon." Daddy ran a hand through his greying hair.

"Have you noticed? The Johnsons put up a 'For Sale' sign yesterday. It seems like everyone's leaving," Randall pointed out.

"Yes, I saw that. Soon we'll be the last original owners

left. The city folks are moving in fast. Everyone got scared by those riots in LA a few years back," Daddy explained.

"I remember when this was just a quiet suburb. Now, every time I look around, there's a moving truck. Our old neighbors seemed scared off by all the changes." Mom shook her head.

"It's not just our street; it's happening all over. The Smiths, the Gonzales family, they all decided to get out of Dodge. And here we are, nearly the last ones standing."

"Do you think we made the right choice to stay? With everything changing so quickly, I sometimes wonder." Mom looked pointedly at Daddy.

"This is our home. It's where we've built our lives. Yes, the neighborhood is changing, but I'm not being run out of my own town. Things will get better. You'll see"

Only they didn't, they got worse.

Soon, we were involved in a neighborhood war between the newcomers and the townies. The LA boys were edgier and more streetwise than my brothers, and the once-quiet street of Bonita became a battlefield of whispered threats and wary glances. Tensions ran high and we didn't feel welcome in our own neighborhood.

I started having nightmares and looking over my shoulder.

MOM SUGGESTED I KEEP A JOURNAL; SHE SAID WRITING helped her through rough times and it could help me too.

> Twylight's Song
> In a world where shadows linger long,
> An eight-year-old with fears so strong,
> She sings a song to escape the night,
> To find a place where dreams take flight.
> She's good at making happy songs,
> Even when things go wrong.
> In the darkest night, She's like the best nightlight.
> I wish I could find a friend like Twilight,
> She's my hero taking flight.
> In my dreams, I shine so brightly.
> Always safe, away from the fighting.

ONE DAY, AS SUSAN WENT OUT TO COLLECT THE MAIL, SHE was met by the sharp gaze of one of the neighbor girls, Gemma Layton. Her face reflected a mix of anger and defiance, and you could almost see the thundercloud gathering behind her deep brown eyes.

"I know your family called the police. Can't you fight your own battles?" Her words were a growl as she came at Susan with her fists swinging. My sister pushed back as Gemma pulled a switchblade out from the tight back pocket of her jeans.

Susan, caught off guard, put up her hands. "I'm not looking for trouble. Just trying to get the mail."

Gemma wasn't interested in words. With a sudden lunge, she swung the switchblade, narrowly missing Susan's side. Panic gripped me as I looked on in horror.

"Stop. Enough." Mom's voice cut through the tense air. She rushed out, armed with a garden hose she grabbed on the way. The water shot out, spraying Gemma and interrupted her attack. The weapon clattered to the ground, and she recoiled from the unexpected onslaught of water.

Randall appeared at Mom's side, his presence a steady reassurance in the chaos. "What the heck do you think you're doing?" he shouted, his voice a stern warning.

Gemma, drenched with her mascara running down her face, retreated a few steps, her angry expression replaced by shock. A few neighbors peered out their windows to see what the commotion was all about, but nobody stepped in to defend our family.

"You'll pay for this," Gemma spat out, casting a venomous glare before storming off.

Mom stood firm, her gaze unwavering. "This ends here. We won't tolerate this sort of violence in our neighborhood."

The violence lingered like a bitter aftertaste, leaving our once-quiet street tainted with unease. It was clear, this conflict had reached dangerous levels.

Daddy emerged from the house with a questioning look

on his face. "What's going on?" His voice, usually calm, now carried a demanding edge.

As we recounted the events of the afternoon, Daddy's face grew more and more determined. The incident marked a turning point, a stark realization, this conflict had spiraled beyond the realm of mere disagreements and had escalated into dangerous new heights.

THAT NIGHT I OVERHEARD SNIPPETS OF CONVERSATION between Mom and Daddy. The hushed tones hinted at the changes to come. "The neighborhood needs to feel safe again," Daddy asserted. "I won't be pushed out of my home. Besides, if we try to sell now, we'll lose a lot of money."

"Promise me you'll consider moving if things get any worse? None of us want to leave our home, but soon Randall will move out and it will be just me and the girls when you aren't home. I'm scared. Fist fights are one thing, but that girl had a knife."

"Don't worry, I'll take care of it." Daddy's voice was full of grit.

True to his words, the following weekend saw the arrival of a six-foot chain link fence that sprang up around our property. It stood as both a physical barrier and a symbol of our family's attempt to carve out a safe haven amid the chaos.

But this tangible barrier couldn't shield us. It wasn't just the boys anymore. The conflict had seeped into every crack and crevice of our community.

Not long after, a trip to the pound brought two additions to our family – German Shepherds named Max and Rosie. Their presence, both majestic and foreboding, patrolled the edges of our fenced haven.

That night, I was awoken by Mom, loud sounds, and the smell of smoke. "They're throwing burning bottles of alcohol at the house. You two go hide in the closet and don't come out no matter what happens. Don't come out until I come back." Mom's voice held an urgency mirroring the disorder outside.

The retaliation was here, and the night crackled with an unsettling energy. Mom's urgent whispers guided Rory and me into the cramped closet, the scent of burning wood seeping through the darkness. As we huddled together, I tried to calm the beating of my racing heart.

I lost all concept of time. The closet, once a shelter for winter coats and rain boots, had now become our refuge against the violence threatening to consume our family.

A sudden gunshot shattered the night, and fear gripped my soul.

"That sounded so close," Rory remarked with tears in her eyes.

"We need to stay hidden until Mom comes and gets us." I tried to reassure Rory, but inside was a different story.

As we huddled in the shadowy cocoon of the closet, the

distant sounds of the neighborhood at war crept towards us. Each passing moment felt like an eternity, and the silence that followed was even more terrifying. I squeezed Rory's hand, praying we'd live to see the morning.

It seemed like hours later when Mom finally opened the closet door, the hallway light revealed a bullet hole that had pierced through the wall of our home. "The police are here. It's safe to come out now."

"Mom, what's that?" Rory pointed to the bullet hole with a shaky voice.

"My God… That bullet could've hit one of you!" Mom cried out.

"We were right there… It's too close," I added.

Buck burst through the door with Bobby close behind, both wearing expressions of fierce determination: "We got here as fast as we could. No one's going to hurt this family."

Bobby added, "Looks like the police have arrested someone."

As police lights flashed, we rushed to the window and watched as the officers handcuffed Michael Layton, the head of the neighborhood greaser gang, His tough exterior was momentarily washed away by the flashing lights.

Rory whispered, "They got him. He's doesn't look so tough now."

Michael was placed into the police car, his slicked-back hair and leather jacket gleaming in the dark. He didn't look that much older than Randall. It made me wonder what had happened to him to make him so malicious.

After the arrest, things seemed to die down. Several months passed by without incident, I still looked over my shoulder and some of the kids at school bullied Rory and me. Word had gotten out that Michael had been arrested and they started calling us "the rats."

Though occasional bursts of violence and menacing glares lingered in the neighborhood, I clung to the hope that we had weathered the worst of it.

SUMMER'S ARRIVAL BROUGHT NOT ONLY HEAT WAVES BUT also a tender flourish of hope that blossomed within our family. Under the hot summer sun, we converged in our cozy backyard patio, determined to put the past behind us and celebrate our nation's birthday. The air bore traces of homemade lemonade and the scent of freshly cut grass. Plastic lawn chairs in faded orange and avocado green formed a casual semicircle, around the game of croquet Rory and I had set up.

Daddy stood proudly in the corner, grilling hot dogs and hamburgers over a dome-shaped charcoal grill, its exterior dulled from years of use. The sizzle of the grill mingled with our laughter.

"Who's ready for the world's best burger?" Daddy joked as he flipped a patty with flourish.

"Only if it's topped with your cowboy chili, Daddy," I called out, earning a chuckle from him.

Rory, croquet mallet in hand, teased, "I hope the croquet game is as good as your grilling skills. Don't forget you promised us a game after dinner."

Mom arrived with a tray of tomatoes, lettuce, and buns. "Remember, it's all about enjoying the day together. Win or lose."

"And I plan to win," Daddy teased. After dinner and games, as the sky darkened, the distant crackling of fireworks from the nearby high school signaled the celebration of our nation's birthday.

"The fireworks look so beautiful," Rory mused, gazing at the night sky.

Abruptly, a distant sound of gunfire exploded into the air, shouts and clamor echoed through the streets.

"What's happening?" Mom's brows furrowed in concern.

"They're getting drunk and firing off their guns, I hope they don't come here looking for trouble," Randall muttered, his expression darkening.

The air, once filled with the scents of joy, now carried the acrid undertones of gunfire.

Ironically, John Lennon's voice emerged from the radio, singing about peace. *Would we ever have it?*

"I'm calling the cops!" Mom shouted. "They're going to shoot up the whole neighborhood. This is the final straw. I can't live like this anymore!"

Without warning, another gunshot burst through the air, this time much closer to our home. Rory and I screamed. Mom called the police, and we huddled on the front room floor until the sounds of police cars filled the air.

"I'm going to get my gun," Daddy proclaimed.

"No Ellis, you'll just make things worse. There are too many of them."

Moments later, the presence of the police caused the neighbors to scatter back into their homes.

"We can't keep coming out here at all hours. You need to find a new place to live. This neighborhood isn't safe for your family anymore," the officer stated as he entered our living room, delivering the unwelcome advice.

"We'll see about that," Daddy responded.

"We won't come out again. We can't protect you," the officer declared firmly.

The following Friday night, when the neighbors came around looking for trouble, the police, true to their word, never showed up, leaving us to defend our home without any assistance.

The next morning, Daddy called a family meeting. The echoes of unspoken truths hung in the air as my parents exchanged solemn glances.

"We've been through a lot, but I won't let our family be torn apart by this senseless violence. Charles Lockheart has a house in Montclair for sale, and your mom wants me to buy it. We can move as soon as next month; Charles is willing to rent it to us until this house sells. For what it's worth, I don't like being run out of our home here, but the safety of this family is more important than my pride. I'm sorry it took me so long to see it."

THE FOLLOWING DAYS WERE A FLURRY OF PACKING AND melancholy. I was disheartened to leave my childhood home but relieved to escape to the proposed safety of Montclair, just one town over. It was a smaller town, and the house prices were higher. Daddy said we'd have to downgrade, but it would be worth it to keep our family safe.

The rooms of our Pomona home, once so familiar, now echoed emptiness, a stark contrast to the life we knew. The fence, once a symbol of defiance, felt more like a monument to the violence we were leaving behind. The decision to move carried hope for a fresh start, but it couldn't fully heal the scars etched in my heart.

The rumble of a moving truck interrupted my thoughts, signaling the moment to bid farewell. Through swirling dust, I stole a final glance at my beloved treehouse, now marred by scorch marks – a grim reminder of the neighbor boys' relentless attacks with Molotov cocktails. My heart felt heavy when I whispered my goodbye to the cherished memories of our old life.

"IT'S KIND OF SMALL, DON'T YOU THINK?" RORY WHISPERED in my ear as we caught a glimpse of our new home.

The house looked narrow but had a tall pointy roof, and it was painted a creamy yellow shade that reminded me of lemon frosting on a homemade birthday cake. There was a huge oak tree out front, like it had been there forever, throwing shade over the grass.

The craftsman style house, small yet brimming with a special charm, warmed my heart. "Now that Buck and Bobby have their own places, and Susan's away at that stenographers' course in Los Angeles, we don't need a big house anymore," I explained, remembering Daddy's words about the need to downsize.

"At least there's a big backyard for Max and Rosie. They are going to love it here. No more burning bottles being chucked over the fence. We can relax now," Randall assured.

We were the last three kids at home now, and we had grown closer than ever. We dreamed of a chance for normalcy, and yet, as we settled into our new home, the echoes of the past lingered.

"Hey, look, there's a boy in the tree!" Rory exclaimed, her eyes widening with curiosity.

I followed her gaze and spotted a preteen boy perched on a tree branch, his tousled hair giving him an air of uncertainty as he peered into our yard. He was tall and gangly, and I couldn't help but wonder what had brought him here.

Randall leaned forward from the backseat, trying to get a better look. "Looks like our new neighbor is quite the tree climber."

As our eyes met with the mysterious boy's from across the yard, he offered a friendly wave and a shy smile.

The boy clumsily jumped down from the tree and approached us with a warm greeting. "I'm Keith Simpson. I heard a family was moving in and came over to say hi."

Randall introduced us, "I'm Randall, and these are my sisters Rory and Twyla."

Keith nodded, a friendly demeanor about him. He reminded me of a Golden Retriever puppy I had seen at the park. "Nice to meet you all. I'm the paperboy around here. Do you think your parents will want to sign up for a subscription?"

"Come back tomorrow after we are done unpacking. Our Dad likes to read the morning paper." Randall ran his hand through his copper hair.

Keith smiled warmly. "Far out. And if you ever need a hand or someone to show you around, I'm your guy." He tapped his thumb against his chest.

A fresh chapter in our lives began, illuminated by the spark of newfound friendships and the promise of safety on the tranquil streets of our new hometown.

I still had the occasional nightmares of Rory and I hiding in the closet while our brothers fought the neighbor-hood gang, but they were starting to fade away as our new neighbors went out of their way to make us feel welcome, organizing community events and extending invitations to social gatherings. Mom continued to throw her Tupperware parties and was invited to join a local Bunco group.

In the following weeks, the echoes of the past transformed into a rhythm of laughter and the warmth of cherished traditions. Our quaint house in the heart of suburbia became the sanctuary we so desperately needed, a true embodiment of our family's quest for peace and safety.

But I couldn't shake the nagging question. Had we truly found peace in Montclair or would the threats from our past follow us, lurking in the shadows, ready to shatter our newfound tranquility?

CHAPTER 3

Tell It Like It Is

MONTCLAIR, CALIFORNIA

FALL 1971

Twyla Cameron
Eleven Years Old

As I made my way through the bustling halls of Serrano Junior High on my first day, my heart raced with anticipation. Amidst a sea of tie-dye and bellbottoms, I couldn't shake the feeling of being an outsider. Room 107 lay directly ahead and it would be my homeroom for the entire year. It was also the domain of Mr. Dougherty, an English teacher rumored to be as eccentric as he was fun, according to Keith Simpson. Intrigued by Keith's description, I couldn't wait to step inside and discover what awaited me.

"Hey, there. I'm Penny." Suddenly, a girl with a cascade

of strawberry blonde curls and an air of mischief intercepted me. "Are you ready for the savage world of seventh grade?" she exclaimed as she opened the classroom door.

I smiled at her and felt the warmth of her infectious energy. "I'm Twyla. Let's try to sit by each other."

Once inside the classroom, Mr. Dougherty's huge smile greeted me. The walls were adorned with literary posters, and words seemed to dance off the walls. "Welcome, to seventh grade Honors English class. Wait, are you two sisters?"

Penny and I looked at each other. We both had huge green eyes, sharp cheekbones, and a similar build. The only difference was that I had silky straight flaxen hair and Penny's was a mass of untamed golden curls.

"No, we aren't related. We just met out in the hallway." I looked around for a place to sit.

"Groovy. Well, grab a seat wherever you like. There's a few beanbags in the corner if you'd like to sit there. This isn't your typical classroom. I want everyone to be comfortable so they can read and create without constraint," he declared, his eyes brimming with a passionate spark. His long brown hair was tied back in a ponytail and he wore a tie-dyed shirt with a beaded red and white necklace. I'd never had a teacher quite like this before.

I found a desk nearby, and Penny took the seat next to me. "You know, we do kind of look alike. I think we are going to be best friends."

"Yeah, it's nice to make a friend on the first day of

school," I replied, feeling relieved that I had found a kindred spirit.

"Do you ever wear makeup? We should plan a makeover at my house after school. My parents just started letting me wear lip gloss *and* mascara." Penny looked at me with her huge green eyes. "I skipped sixth grade because my teachers thought I needed more of a challenge, and Mom said makeup would help me fit in with everyone in junior high." Penny pulled out a tube of cherry lip gloss and slathered it on her lips.

"Okay, girls. You can get to know each other more at lunch. Now we are going to dive into one of my favorite books. *The Outsiders* by S.E. Hinton. Did you know this book was written by a girl not much older than you? A girl from Oklahoma?"

"My dad is from Oklahoma," Penny chimed in.

"Mine, too," I giggled.

Mr. Dougherty smiled, pleased with the connection forming between Penny and me. "Well, that's quite a coincidence. A lot of people from Oklahoma migrated to the West Coast over the years. You'll read about the Dust Bowl Migration more next year, but today, we are going to start *The Outsiders.* You might find this novel particularly interesting because the author was sixteen years old when she wrote it. Now let's see how Ponyboy and his friends navigate their challenges in a world so divided."

With that, Mr. Dougherty handed out the books and we eagerly started reading about the greasers and the preppy kids. It reminded me of everything my family and I had gone through and how there were always two sides to every story. I found myself engrossed in the novel when the bell rang, notifying us it was time to find our second period class.

"Let's ditch school and go to a movie." Penny picked up her pile of books and we made our way to the door. It seemed she was trying to act older to impress me, probably to compensate for being the youngest girl in the class.

"Have you ever ditched school before?"

"No, I thought it sounded like a cool thing to say." Penny laughed.

"We can't ditch on the first day, silly. But maybe we could go see a movie after school tomorrow? I'll bring my sister Rory. She's in ninth grade over at the high school."

"It's a date. What class do you have next?"

Penny quickly became my closest friend at Serrano Junior High and together, we navigated the maze of hallways, shared secrets, and created countless memories that would last a lifetime.

THE '70s, WITH ITS UNDERCURRENT OF REBELLION, WAS ALL around us. But as a natural rule-follower and all-around 'good girl,' I often found myself in a tug-of-war. There was a part of me longing to mirror Rory and her friends, to explore the world of more mature clothing, experimentation with makeup—and boys—yet I couldn't let go of the joys of my childhood. Roller skating and Barbies still held a special place in my heart.

It seemed as if everybody in our family had a unique skill: Randall played football and slide guitar, Bobby played the sax, Susan had a wonderful voice, Buck had a knack for weightlifting and boxing, while Rory was learning to play the ukulele. I still hadn't quite discovered my calling, and to make matters worse, my fair hair stood out like a sore thumb against the auburn and red that comprised my family's coloring.

Occasionally I felt like an outsider in my own home and hoped that one day I would find something that truly resonated with me, something that would not only define my place in the family but also allow me to shine in my own unique way. I had so many feelings inside, but I often had an easier time expressing them on paper rather than saying them aloud.

I began a search to find my identity. Rory spoke of the significance of starting extracurricular activities in junior high, as they would shape my high school journey and determine which group of friends I'd have. As time passed and days turned into weeks, then months, I explored a range of activities—from cheerleading to ASB and volleyball—in pursuit of my true passion. However, these competitive endeavors didn't ignite my passion as I had hoped.

Then, one day a surprising moment came when Mr. Dougherty extended an unexpected invitation to a poetry reading. This gesture felt like a nod to my individuality, a recognition of the part of me that deviated from my family of jocks. I'd always enjoyed writing, but now someone else was praising me for something that felt so natural. *Maybe my passion could be writing and not something physical?*

"Explore your voice, Twyla. Your poetry is good. You should come to Café Luna tonight and read it to my writing group." Mr. Dougherty's encouraging words interrupted my epiphany.

"I have Girl Scouts this afternoon, but I'll ask my parents if I can come after." I couldn't wait to tell Rory I was invited to speak at a poetry reading. She was always getting to do so many cool things in high school, and now I was hopeful to have found something I could call my own.

When I skipped into the kitchen later that afternoon, my Girl Scout vest adorned with badges and my hair neatly tied in a bow, I froze at the sight of Rory hunched over the sink while holding a singed bra.

"Rory. What are you doing?" I felt my eyes grow broad in astonishment.

Rory looked up, her chin smeared with soot. "Hey, Twy. Just freeing myself from the tyranny of undergarments."

I blinked. "Mom's going to freak. Why are you doing that. You were so thrilled when Mom took you to buy your first bra and now you want to burn it?"

Rory grinned, the rebellious gleam still in her eyes. "It's a statement, sis. A protest society's expectations. Plus, it's hot as hell in those things. I want to be free. More like Cher and Joan Jett."

I wrinkled my nose. "Protest? You're thirteen."

"Never too early to make a statement."

Rory smirked, setting aside the bra. "I can't believe you still attend Girl Scouts. The girls at my school are throwing rowdy parties, playing spin the bottle, and other stuff."

"Spin the bottle? Daddy will kill you if he finds out." My cheeks flushed.

Rory laughed. "Welcome to the seventies, sis. It's not for the faint of heart."

I nervously twisted the ribbon on my vest. "I thought you hated all that stuff. Did you kiss a boy at one of those parties?"

Rory tousled my hair. "My sweet sister, I'm in high school now. You wouldn't understand, but I can be whoever I choose to be. If I want to be a tomboy who listens to heavy metal and rebels against society by burning my bra, then so be it. You can choose to be a boring little Girl Scout making friendship bracelets and following all the rules, but I know you'll grow tired of that baby stuff soon."

I hesitated but decided not to take the bait, I quickly changed the subject. "Guess what? I've got some news for you."

Rory grinned. "Do tell, sis. Did you win another citizen-ship award?"

"No, as a matter of fact, my cool teacher, Mr. Daugherty, invited me to a poetry reading at Café Luna. It looks like you aren't the only one getting to hang out with older people and do cool things. Wanna come with me?"

Rory's eyebrows shot up, and for a moment, the rebellious fire in her eyes flickered with curiosity. "A poetry reading? Mr. Dougherty invited you? Groovy, now you're stepping into my territory. Maybe there's hope for you yet." She affectionately ruffled my hair as she slid down from the counter.

I grinned, a sense of sisterly love bubbled up from within. I knew she only teased her favorite people. "Yep, and he said it's an open mic night. I was going to read the poem I wrote about what happened in Pomona."

Rory leaned back, crossing her arms. "Impressive, little sis. Maybe you've got a rebel streak in you after all. Alright, I'll tag along with you to Café Luna. But only if you solemnly vow not to tell Mom about the bra thing and help me clean up these ashes." Rory winked at me as she motioned to the sink and the mess that had once been her training bra.

"You got it. But can I have your other bra? One of us might as well get some use out of it." We both burst out laughing as we tidied up the kitchen before Mom got home from another one of her Tupperware parties.

LATER ON THAT EVENING AT CAFÉ LUNA, PEOPLE OF ALL ages and races mingled with coffee in hand. Their attire was a kaleidoscope of the era's fashion - from hip huggers to paisley shirts and platform shoes. I felt a deep desire to be part of the action. Soon it was my turn. My heart raced and I hoped I could get up and speak in front of this room of people of all ages.

It's all happening. I thought to myself as I took a deep breath.

"I am a whisper in the wind, unheard but strong, A girl lost in echoes, where she doesn't belong. In the streets of Pomona, where shadows dance, I navigate the chaos, giving fate a chance."

My voice started out soft but grew stronger with every word.

"Weeks of struggle, trying to fit the mold, But I am a story waiting to be told. In the alleys of violence, where darkness resides, I search for the light, where my true self resides.

"A quiet heart, fragile yet bold, In a world of secrets, stories untold. I paint my existence in hues of love, Yet, through the storms, I'll choose to rise above."

As I recited the final lines, the room fell silent. Thunderous applause erupted, shaking the walls of Café Luna. Mr. Dougherty beamed with pride, and a sense of accomplishment washed over me.

As the applause subsided, Mr. Dougherty leaned in and whispered, "Twyla, your words give an energy that goes beyond the pages. It's too late for this summer, but you should apply to this creative writing camp. It's taking place in Oklahoma and next summer's special guest is none other than S.E. Hinton. If you work hard, you could earn a spot. I'd be happy to write you a recommendation letter."

"I'd like that, Mr. Dougherty. Thank you. Do you really think I have a shot?"

"Absolutely, you have a talent for writing and words. Don't let it waste away," Mr. Dougherty responded.

I ran over to share the news with Rory.

"That's great, Twy. I hope you win it, but let's blow this pop stand. I've got a hot date with David Cassidy. If we hurry home, we can catch *The Partridge Family*."

As we walked home, I couldn't help but reflect on the excitement I felt when I read my poem to everyone. Normally, I didn't like speaking in front of a group of my peers, but something about reading my own poetry to an older audience had given me a new feeling of strength,

I sensed that this reading would mark the beginning of a new chapter in my life. Writing had become my refuge, offering solace amidst the chaos of the world, and providing me with a means to express my emotions and experiences, including those involving violence. Through poetry, I discovered an avenue to navigate my adolescence, transforming my complex feelings and experiences into something that might resonate with others. Until now, I hadn't realized that writing could also be my calling.

As we walked home, I became lost in my own thoughts, fantasizing about winning a place in the writing camp in Oklahoma. I hoped Mom would let me go.

"Do you think I could I be a teacher when I grow up? I want to inspire others, like Mr. Dougherty has inspired me."

"Of course you can, Twy. You definitely have the grades for it."

"I'm going to the library tomorrow to do some research on it. Want to come?"

"You really are a weird little sister. Who wants to spend their weekend at a boring old library?"

Once more, I couldn't help but feel like the outcast in my family. I was the only kid without red hair and the only one sporting glasses, the weirdo who loved spending time at the library. But despite her teasing, I knew that Rory loved me, just as I had come to realize that teaching and inspiring others was my true calling.

"WAKE UP KIDS, IT'S TIME FOR SUNDAY SCHOOL. WE MAY have given up our home in Pomona, but we're not giving up our little church in Pomona. There are still plenty of good people left in that town."

"Mom, you know those kids that fought with us in Pomona? I'm sure they have their own side to what happened on Bonita Street," I interjected.

"I'm sure they do, but how they handled it was not acceptable. Violence is never the answer, no matter where you come from. Now, you kids are going to be late for Sunday school. You can pray for those greasers if you like."

"I will, but you shouldn't call them greasers. They are just kids like anyone else."

"Perhaps you're right, lovebug. It's easy to label people rather than try to understand them. I'll call them young folks from now on. Does that make you feel better?"

"Won't you and Daddy come with us to church today?" I looked up with inquisitive eyes.

"Sundays are the only days I get your Daddy all to myself. It's important we have our grown-up time alone together."

As my siblings and I shuffled off to the bus stop, our Sunday best clinging uncomfortably in the heat, I couldn't help but reflect on how much things had changed over the last several months. Our first year living in our new home-town had passed by quickly. I had become passionate about my writing and had grown a few inches, my slim frame started to fill out. It appeared we had found the perfect small-town haven away from all the violence that had plagued us in Pomona.

My oldest three siblings were all married and living on their own now. Susan had fallen in love with a young law student. Upon graduating from stenographers' school, they married, and now she was working at the Los Angeles Cour-thouse. Buck and Bobby had married a pair of sisters and it seemed as if everyone was living their happily ever after.

Randall started his senior year at Montclair High and was our ticket to cruising around town—well, on the rare occasions his car decided to play nice. He fancied himself a mechanic, but that car spent more time up on blocks than running. So much had changed, but one constant in our lives was Sunday Bible School.

Our church was in Old Town Pomona, a blend of weathered buildings and the distant echoes of lively chatter broke the silence as we made our way to the old church house.

The exterior of the church stood with humble simplicity, fashioned from weathered wooden clapboards that bore the marks of time's passage. Despite the signs of wear, it retained an enduring charm, each weathered plank whispering stories of bygone days. Its bell tower, a prominent feature, rose majestically against the backdrop of Pomona's clear skies, often heard ringing on quiet Sunday mornings, calling the local community to service.

"Do you think anyone got mad when we moved away?" Rory whispered.

"No, I think anyone at church this early is here to worship. You don't have to worry about anyone from our old neighborhood causing trouble in God's house," Randall responded.

Like my brother predicted, the churchgoers welcomed us warmly, as always, guiding us to the front rows. From our seats, we mingled with the congregation, an eclectic group of people whose diversity faded beneath the unifying banner of faith. The wooden pews creaked, and we absorbed the vibrant energy dancing through the air.

Gospel music swirled around us, alive with devotion.

The organist's fingers danced across the keys, producing melodies that echoed with the soul-stirring rhythms of heartfelt worship. The songs were alive, reaching into the depths of our souls and pulling forth of praise.

As the reverend stepped up to the pulpit, his voice was a thunderous cascade of words raising above the music.

"Brothers and sisters, as we navigate these changing times, let us cling to the enduring peace of Christ. As the world shifts around us, the Word of God stands firm. Jesus tells us, 'In this world you will have trouble. But take heart. I have overcome the world.' *He* has triumphed over the world's chaos, offering us a sanctuary and a place of refuge."

The music gained momentum, and the air crackled with an energy that transcended the physical boundaries of the building.

Rory nudged me, her eyes widening with a combination of awe and disbelief. "Twyla, look at them."

The congregation swept up in the moment, bodies swayed, hands reached towards the heavens, and exclamations of "hallelujah" reverberated through the room.

In the midst of this passionate display, we found acceptance. In that sacred space, social class dissolved, and the lines dividing us in the outside world blurred. It didn't matter if you were a greaser or a prep, black or white, we were part of a congregation bound by something more profound than our differences.

As we left the church, Shelby, one of our old neighbors,

ran over to Randall. "Randall, I want you to meet someone. She lives in your new town."

"We live on Harvard Street now, over in Montclair."

"I know. This is my cousin Maya. She lives around the corner from you."

Randall's face turned red as he reached out to nervously shake the girl's hand. "Hi, Maya. I'm Randall."

"I think we established that." Shelby laughed. "You guys are going to the same high school. Isn't that right, Maya?"

Maya looked as transfixed on Randall as he was on her. "That's right."

"Okay. Randall, our bus is here. Time to go." Rory motioned for our brother to join us at the bus stop.

"Nice to meet you, Maya. Maybe I could walk you to school sometime?" Randall sheepishly joined us, a love-struck grin on his face.

"I'd like that," Maya stammered.

Once we were on the bus, Rory and I started questioning our brother. "You like her. Your face is red and flushed."

"No, not Shelby, it's her cousin I like. She's that Maya girl… the pretty girl who lives around the corner," Randall responded. "Do you think she likes me back?"

The city bus pulled up, interrupting our conversation. We boarded, leaving behind the Pentecostal church and its welcoming congregation.

"You should *drive* her to school. Girls like a guy with a

car. When will you have it running again?" Rory flicked her auburn hair over her shoulder.

"Soon. I just ordered the last part. I'm putting it in as soon as the parts store calls to say it's ready."

"That's what the girls like. A man with a car." Rory repeated.

THE FOLLOWING MONTH, I STOOD BY MY BEDROOM WINDOW and watched Randall pull into the driveway in his hunter green Mustang. The first thing he did after getting his car running again was take out Maya on a date to the drive-in, and they had been inseparable ever since. I wondered about the things they talked about and what they did together. I could see something was different with my big brother.

"When are you going to bring your new friend home to meet the family?" Mom asked one afternoon.

"I can bring her home Sunday night, but I need to tell you something."

"What's that?"

"Maya is the smartest, sweetest girl I've ever known, but she looks different than we do."

"What do you mean?"

"Well, she's mixed race." Randall ran his hand through his copper hair.

"I know Randall, I'm not blind. I've seen her family around the neighborhood. Her mom brought over that cherry pie when we moved in. Is that what you've been nervous about?" Mom asked.

"Sometimes we get stares or remarks. It bothers me we can't just be like a normal couple."

"Son, where I grew up on the reservation, we knew skin color was a small part of who we are. It's the heart, the spirit inside that defines a person. In our family we value a person's character above all else. Your dad's mom grew up with people calling her half-breed, and that's not how we are. Hold your head up high when you are with Maya and ignore those ignorant people. You're tougher than them. You have Cameron blood running through your veins."

"Thanks, Mom. I wished everyone looked at it the same way you did."

"Her skin color doesn't matter one iota to me or the rest of our family. What matters is the love and respect you have for each other. Remember, love is love."

Her words seemed to lift a weight off Randall's shoulders, and his usual bright smile returned. "Thanks, Mom. I want you guys to love her as much as I do."

Mom chuckled softly. "I'm sure we will."

THE LAST DAY OF SCHOOL WAS SOON UPON US AND RANDALL had invited Rory and me to go to the burger joint with him and Maya. I was so thrilled about spending time with them. As we stopped at Andy's Burgers, it's Americana charm immediately welcomed us with the promise of salty french fries and cold milkshakes. The walls, adorned with posters and neon signs, created an ambiance of nostalgia from the 1950s. The aroma of sizzling burgers wafted through the air, mingling with the sound of Elvis tunes coming from an old jukebox.

As soon as we sat down and placed our order, I heard hushed whispers and stifled chuckles coming from a cluster of high school students, their eyes darting towards Randall and Maya with poorly veiled curiosity and judgment. "What's their problem?" Rory motioned over to a group of high school kids who were making a spectacle of themselves.

Randall and Maya, however, were in their own world. Maya, with her dark curly hair and peace sign necklace, laughed as she playfully fed Randall fries. They were a picture of young love – free and unbothered by the stares of the obnoxious students that laughed and pointed.

Randall and Maya's happiness was infectious, and I found myself smiling along with them. During the ride home, I approached the subject of the high schoolers. "Hey, guys, what was with all the whispers back there? Those kids were downright rude."

Randall glanced at me, his eyes reflecting a fusion of understanding and weariness. He took a deep breath before answering. "Some people in this town hold on to outdated ideas. They think races shouldn't mix."

"It's not always easy, but we're choosing love over hate.

We're not going to let anyone else define who we can or can't be with." Maya's face glowed with determination.

"It can be frustrating, but we're not going to let it bother us. Mom and Dad like Maya and it shouldn't matter if our skins are a different color. We are the same where it counts, in here." Randall tapped his heart.

Maya beamed at my brother, and it was like they were the only two people existing in their own little world. I felt an array of emotions. Anger at the injustice they faced, admiration for their courage, and a surge of protectiveness toward my brother and his new girlfriend.

"I'm sorry you have to deal with this, you guys deserve better." Suddenly the skies opened up and it started to rain. A clash of thunder mirrored the anger I felt inside. Anger towards those jocks at the burger joint.

"Why didn't you kick their asses? You're bigger than those kids," Rory, always so feisty, chimed in.

Randall smiled with a weary but appreciative expression. "I don't want to fight anymore. After all the fighting in our old neighborhood, I want a peaceful life with my best girl."

He smiled over at Maya as we pulled up into our driveway. I tried not to think about the people at the burger joint whispering and giving dirty looks. My brother was falling in love, and that's what was important. Even though I sometimes felt left out, I liked Maya and the bubbly atmosphere she brought into our home whenever she visited.

Once home, we found Mom sitting in the living room,

her eyes locked on a letter clutched tightly in her hands. The world suddenly felt smaller, as I wondered what bad news the letter had brought to our doorstep.

"What's going on, Mom?" Randall's voice showed concern, mirroring the unease etched on all our faces.

Mom looked up, her eyes glistening with unshod tears. "Sit down, all of you."

The air was thick with tension. She took a deep breath, trying to steady herself. The silence was heavy, and I could almost hear the rapid beat of my heart.

"I just received this," she said, holding up the letter. "It's a draft notice. Randall, you've been drafted to Vietnam."

CHAPTER 4
Have You Seen the Rain
MONTCLAIR, CALIFORNIA
JUNE, 1972

Twyla Cameron
Twelve Years Old

I could practically hear the wheels turning in Mom's head. "I can't lose you, Randall." Mom's voice trembled with desperation. "Not after what happened to my brother Bobby in Okinawa. I can't bear the thought of history repeating itself. You'll have to run away to Canada until all the war is over. Or maybe you can go stay on the reservation?"

Just then, Daddy entered the front door. "I left work as soon as I heard." He rushed to Mom's side and grabbed her hand in his.

"Oh, Ellis, what are we going to do? We can't let him go to war. We were talking about Canada or Neah Bay?" Mom looked deep into Daddy's eyes.

Her words settled around us like pebbles dropping into a still pond, their ripples spreading across the surface. Randall met her gaze with a combination of surprise and disbelief.

"Running away?" Daddy echoed, his voice carrying the strain of the impossible.

"Mom, I can't run away. I must do my part. I can't abandon everything. I want a life to come back to."

"Now that Randall's turned eighteen and graduated from high school, there's nothing we can do to stop this. Running away won't solve anything, Dawn. We need to face this head-on. Hiding out in Canada or attempting to disappear on Neah Bay won't make the war disappear, and we'd never see Randall again. He wouldn't be allowed to come back. Not ever."

The conflict played out in the lines etched on Mom's face, the silent exchange of glances between her, Daddy, and Randall. The front room became a battleground of conflicting feelings, each person wrestling with their own version of fear and duty.

"I want you safe," Mom whispered, her eyes welled up with tears that she wouldn't allow to fall. "I lost my brother to World War II. Our family almost didn't survive it, and I couldn't bear the thought of it happening to my son, too."

A heavy silence settled over the room, broken only by

the sound of my own beating heart. I bit my lip, torn between my loyalty to my country and the undeniable fear of losing my brother to war.

Randall sighed, breaking the silence. "Mom, I understand how hard it must have been, but running away isn't the answer. I must face this, for Uncle Bobby and for all of us. I'll be careful."

Mom slumped down heavily onto the sofa, defeated yet resolute. Randall stood by the front door. His eyes glued to the draft notice he'd picked up off the floor. The radio played in the background, and I could hear a dog barking somewhere in the distance. Time seemed to stand still.

Beside me stood Maya, her fingers intertwined with my brothers as a single tear drop trickled down her face.

"I don't want to lose you, Randall," Maya pleaded, her voice barely above a whisper. "It's so dangerous. Promise me you'll come back in one piece."

"I promise, but you know I can't sit this one out. I have no choice." Randall sighed, and his shoulders drooped in despair.

Fear tightened its grip around my chest, and I tried to hold in the tears threatening to spill. None of us wanted Randall to go away to Vietnam. I'd grown up with stories of how Uncle Bobby never came back from World War II, and I was afraid the same would happen to my big brother.

"I suppose there's nothing we can do?" Mom looked up at Daddy with questioning in her face.

"We'll make it through this together. Randall, you'll

write to us as much as possible, won't you? Let us know you're safe."

"I'll write. I promise. And I'll come back as soon as I can," Randall nodded, a somber expression on his face.

The room was engulfed by a heavy silence. The draft notice, crumpled in Randall's hand, was like a shadow cast upon our family, unwanted, it threatened to engulf our newfound stability.

As Randall leaned against the doorframe, Maya whispered, "Walk me home?"

He turned to her, a sad smile on his face. "Of course."

I could see the pain etched on Mom's face as they left the house.

AS THE DATE FOR RANDALL'S DEPARTURE DREW NEARER, A heaviness draped itself over our family. Susan and her husband returned home often from their apartment in Los Angeles, and my eldest brothers, sensing the impending separation, orchestrated family gatherings nearly every weekend.

The Sunday night before Randall's departure our house filled with the aroma of Mom's famous spaghetti, and the familiar melodies of Paul Anka floated through the air. Our family gathered, their smiles were forced and carried an unspoken sadness.

Buck, Bobby, Susan and their spouses were all dotted

around the front room. My nieces, Lacey and April played nicely together, content to be in their playpen. Randall's expression held a mélange of bravery and worry, and Maya's forced laughter, while sweet, seemed quieter and subdued.

Susan's new baby Lacey was quiet and content, while Buck's daughter April was starting to walk. Lacey's big, innocent eyes were forever observing the events going on around her, while Susan took charge of baking dessert, barking orders like she always did.

That night we sat at the table, the feeling in the air was somber and suffocating. The clinks of silverware against the plates were like whispers of the changes about to come.

The vinyl records played, and the stories flowed. Bobby's jokes felt forced, Buck told stories about his work as the foreman of Daddy's construction company, but his words lacked their normal enthusiasm, and Susan's bossiness seemed even more pronounced. Lacey and April, however, stayed peaceful, like tiny beacons of calm during uncertainty. Oblivious to the storm threatening our family.

Rory and I treated our nieces like they were the most precious dolls in the world. We cooed and played with them until they couldn't keep their eyes open any longer, falling asleep with their tender thumbs nestled in their rosebud mouths.

The warm glow of the kitchen lights cast shadows on the walls, creating an atmosphere mirroring the emotions in my heart. We reveled in the joy of being together, but the impending departure of Randall the next morning hung over us like a heavy cloud.

As the last record ended, the room fell into a quiet pause. It had been a Sunday night infused with bittersweet moments. I didn't want it to end.

In that moment, Randall rose from his seat, drawing the gaze of everyone in the room. His handsome face, a combination of determination and vulnerability, sought out Maya who was quietly sitting in the corner of the room, lost in her own thoughts.

"Maya," his voice carrying the burden of the world on his shoulders. "I know we haven't known each other that long, but we've grown close these last few months and it's made me realize, I want to build a life with you when I return from Vietnam." Randall dropped to one knee.

Maya's eyes widened; the room's somber ambiance interrupted by the sincerity of Randall's words.

"It's not much, but it belonged to my grandmother," he continued, taking a small sapphire ring from his pocket. "I want you to marry me. I want to leave for war an engaged man. Maya, will you say yes? Will you wait for me?"

A collective gasp engulfed the room, all our attention now directed onto Maya. Her gaze shifted between Randall's face and the small ring he clutched in his fingers.

We all held our breath as Maya, tearful yet resolute, whispered a profound, "Yes."

A wave of relief and joy swept through, dispelling the lingering heaviness. Randall slid the ring onto Maya's finger, sealing a pact amid the warm glow of the kitchen lights, and loving smiles of our tight-knit family.

"This calls for a toast. Buck, open the bottle of champagne in the fridge."

As the champagne flowed and laughter mingled with our sadness, the undercurrent of anxiety couldn't be ignored. And the collective heartache lingered beneath the surface.

Rory and I, caught in a maelstrom of grown-up conversations, exchanged happy yet cautious looks. The small glass of champagne Mom let us have created a sense of wonder and a tickle that bubbled up from my core. It was like drinking pure sunshine, but this fleeting joy couldn't quite dispel the sadness that settled over our hearts.

As the night wore on, the somber celebration continued.

"Time for bed, you two." Mom grabbed Rory and I in one of her big bear hugs. "Tomorrow is a big day, and it's a long drive to Monterey. We are going to see your brother off when he reports for duty. It looks like Maya will be riding along with us to say our goodbyes." Mom's voice broke on those last words, and she pulled a handkerchief out of her dress pocket to blow her nose.

She never cried in front of Randall, but when she was alone, I could hear her soft sobs echoing through the house, carrying the weight of her fears and worries. Her eyes were ringed red, but she simply blamed it on her allergies.

In the quiet moments before sleep claimed us, I couldn't shake the sensation of dread from our impending separation. I clung to the idea our family's love would somehow act as a shield, protecting my brother from the dangers lurking in Vietnam. I tried to find solace in the shared moments and unspoken tenacity that would carry us through the impending separation awaiting in the morning.

CHAPTER 5
No Sunshine When He's Gone
FORT ORD, CALIFORNIA
FALL 1972

Twyla Cameron
Twelve Years Old

F ort Ord was located on the central coast of California, I found it intimidating, a place that seemed to swallow up young men like my brother, transforming them into soldiers. It looked like a world of strict routines and stark buildings, overshadowed by the looming reality of war.

The atmosphere was brimming with tension and pride as we gathered to see Randall off. The military base buzzed with activity as soldiers in uniform moved around purposefully and the distant sounds of commands echoed through the air.

Around the base, military trucks and Broncos rumbled along paved roads, their engines a constant growl in the background. Soldiers were moving about, working, training. There was a sense of urgency in everything they did.

Despite all this, there was beauty here, too. The hills around the base were green and rolling, speckled with wildflowers and chaparral. The ocean wasn't far away, and on clear days, you could see the blue expanse from certain parts of the base, a serene contrast to the rigid discipline of military life.

Mom stood close to Randall, unable to conceal the worry etched across her face. She seemed to have aged ten years overnight. Her tiny hands clutched a small bag, packed with sandwiches and necessities, her attempts to mask her concern betrayed by how her fingers fidgeted with the edges of her dress.

"I packed some extra socks for you, Randall," Mom said, her voice trembling. "I heard it's important to always keep your feet dry. There's also some extra sandwiches for the road and a thermos of hot coffee in case you get cold."

"I'm proud of you, son, but you be careful, don't be a hero. Promise you'll come back in one piece," Daddy added.

Randall, looking so handsome in his Sunday best, reached out and shook Daddy's hand. "I'll be back before you know it. It's just training for now. I'll write and let you know when I'm going to be leaving the country."

Maya, standing beside them in her little yellow miniskirt and platform shoes, reached for Randall's hand. Her eyes glistened with unshed tears. "Take care of yourself. And write to me as soon as you can. I love you so much."

"I love you, too. I promise, I'll be back soon, and we can start planning our wedding." Randall squeezed her hand, his gaze shining with love.

Rory, tried to hide her emotions behind a tough exterior as she punched Randall lightly in the arm. "You better come back soon, big bro, or I'll have to start driving that Mustang of yours."

Randall chuckled, tousling Rory's hair, "You two take care of Mom and Dad for me."

Mom pulled Randall into a tight hug, I could see it took everything she had not to break down in front of her youngest son. "You take care of yourself, Randall, and don't you forget where home is."

"I'm not going to be like Uncle Bobby. I'll be coming home, Mom."

Daddy saluted him, a gesture that felt both formal and deeply heartfelt. "Make us proud, son, but be safe."

With a final look at the family, my brother stoically announced, "I guess it's time to report for duty."

"We'll be here, waiting," I called out, my voice stronger than I felt. And with that, Randall turned and walked towards his future, leaving us clinging to the hope and promise of his return.

RANDALL'S LETTERS SOON STARTED ARRIVING REGULARLY. IT didn't take long before he was through basic training and had shipped out for Southeast Asia. Every day after school, I would rush home and head straight for the mailbox. Each week, without fail, a new letter awaited us. They varied in length—some shorter, some longer—but they all carried the same precious message. He was safe. He was alive.

Opening those letters became a family routine. Mom would carefully slice open the envelope, and we'd gather around the kitchen table, eager to devour every word he had written. His words transcended the paper, bringing him closer to us despite the miles that separated us.

In those letters, he wrote of his life, his comrades, and the places he had seen. He'd recount the challenges he faced, the camaraderie he cherished, and the dreams he held onto. It was as if each envelope contained a piece of his heart, a fragment of his presence, we clung to in his absence.

Mom put together care packages with fresh socks and all of Randall's favorite snacks. It was a small thing she could do to let Randall know he had a home here waiting for him when he was able to return.

As the weeks stretched into months, we found ourselves entrenched in a new rhythm, relying on Randall's letters like lifelines, each word a precious thread stitching together our fractured hearts, keeping us tethered to him from across the miles.

Until one day, the letters stopped.

We didn't hear anything for weeks, my parents looked exhausted from worry. Daddy would come home from his work on the construction sites with his shoulders slumped under the strain of the unknown.

"Any news from Randall?"

Mom didn't respond, just continued staring out the window. Dinner remained untouched on the table. Rory, in the corner of the room, delicately placed a needle on the vinyl record. The melancholy strains of a song filled my ears, wrapping around the room like a bittersweet caress.

"I can't believe we haven't heard from him in so long. You don't think anything happened?" Rory questioned.

"He'll be back," I said, my voice scarcely a whisper, my eyes on the notebook in front of me.

Mom turned, her gaze meeting mine. "I hope so."

"He promised, Mom. We must believe in him," I replied, my hand moving across the paper, pen scratching out my sentiments.

Rory was reading the back of one of her Doors albums, her eyes searching for solace in the lyrics of the song. "Music helps, doesn't it? It's like a friend who understands without saying anything."

Mom finally spoke. "I miss him so much. The house feels empty without his laughter."

"We all miss him, but we must keep going. Randall wouldn't want us to lose ourselves in grief." Daddy, now

76

seated at the table, searched the newspaper for news of the war.

"It's like my brother Bobby all over again." Mom admitted, her eyes welling with tears.

"Don't even think that. We will see Randall again. I can feel it," Daddy responded.

The music filled the void as we each tried to cope in our own way.

"I wrote something today," I confessed, looking at my family. "It helps me to put everything out on paper."

"Read it, Twyla," Daddy encouraged.

I opened my notebook, and the words flowed like a bridge between our pain.

In whispers where shadows gently blend, Change's gentle breeze, like a whisper in the wind, I know we'll find our light.
Together we'll stay behind, hearts burning so bright, as we keep the home fires alight. Through echoes of war, we'll keep our love shining in the shadows of your dreams, we'll hold on to hope, until you are in our sight.

"That's beautiful, sweetheart." Mom leaned back in her chair.

"We'll get through this together," Daddy said, his voice a promise echoing in the quiet house.

EACH DAY BECAME A STRUGGLE, A NEVER-ENDING BATTLE against the relentless tide of emotions threatening to overwhelm us. After school, my hands shook as I made my daily trip to the mailbox. I reached for the mailbox door, hoping against hope for a letter that might dispel the darkness settling over our home, but once again, there was no letter from Randall.

Days turned into weeks and one afternoon, as I approached the mailbox with a heavy heart, a glimmer of white caught my eye. I hesitated for a moment, my fingers trembling as I opened the mailbox. There, nestled among the mundane bills and advertisements, was a letter from Vietnam.

I clutched it to my chest, rushing back to the house, my heart pounding in my ears. Mom and Daddy were in the kitchen, their eyes met mine with both hope and trepidation.

"It's from Randall!" I exclaimed, breathless.

Daddy reached for the letter, and his hands steady as he carefully opened it. The room fell silent as he read aloud Randall's words, each sentence carrying the strain of a thousand emotions.

> Dear family,
> I hope this letter finds you well. I'm sorry I couldn't write for a while. Something happened that I can't write about. Just know that we faced some chal-

lenges, but I'm safe. The brotherhood I share with my soldiers has been a source of strength but can be at times difficult with so much adrenaline running through our veins, fights often break out. Don't you worry. I keep myself out of all of that and have been assigned to scout the areas to make sure everything is safe before we camp for the night. I'm always careful and have made a close friend named Dante Brown to rely on. He's a great man on my team. I anticipate returning home after this tour. It can't end fast enough. I'm ready for some of Mom's Famous Spaghetti.

I miss you all dearly. The memories of home keep me going through the toughest times. Keep sending those care packages, the snacks remind me of home and I can't wait to return and be with you all. Please take care of each other, and don't worry too much.

Love,
Randall

Relief washed over us, and Mom wiped away a tear, her voice catching as she whispered, "He's okay. Randall is okay."

Daddy folded the letter and placed it on the kitchen table, the weight of uncertainty lifting from our shoulders.

As we gathered around the kitchen table, the reality of war was heavy in the air. Randall's words, though reassuring, carried the echoes of the harsh conditions he navigated daily.

"He's a scout? Sounds risky, doesn't it?" Mom broke the silence.

"Yeah, it is. Being the first one out there, checking for trouble? It's not a walk in the park, but Randall is a smart boy with good instincts." Daddy leaned back in his chair.

Mom's frown deepened. "What if something happens? What if they run into trouble?"

"It's every parent's worst nightmare. But he sounds like he has a reliable partner and all we can do is pray for them both. God will protect them."

Skepticism colored Mom's expression. "Dante? I hope he's as good as Randall says. I can't help but fret."

Daddy nodded in understanding. "Of course, I worry, too. But Randall's trained for this. We've got to trust he knows what he's doing out there."

Mom sighed. "I just want him home already. This war is messing everything up. I want all my kids home safe, working safe jobs. Is that too much to ask? Girls, promise me you'll always choose safety over adventure. I don't want either of you gallivanting around the world like that Bishop girl. Did you hear she got a job with the airlines?"

"We heard, Mom, but I don't see the problem with it." Rory looked at me as she responded to Mom's question.

"You girls should pick careers that keep you close to home. Nothing is more important than keeping our family close."

Daddy wrapped his arm around her, offering comfort. "Our family will always be close. That's what we all want. Let's have faith and keep watching out for those letters. It's all we can do for now."

CHAPTER 6
Dreams
MONTCLAIR, CALIFORNIA
WINTER 1972

Twyla Cameron
Twelve Years Old

"This war is awful. We need to bring our boys home soon. We just can't win this thing; it's gone on too long." Mr. Dougherty started our lesson each day by watching the morning news. He had a nephew fighting in the Vietnam War and felt it was crucial for us to be informed.

As the TV droned on, casting a flickering blue glow over our faces, a sense of a never-ending nightmare enveloped me. "It feels like a never-ending nightmare," I echoed, the weight of uncertainty pressing down on me. The classroom, usually a place of learning and laughter, transformed into a space of concern, reflecting the shadow that the war cast over our nation.

"Twyla, that reminds me, there's something I want to talk to you about. You remember that writing camp we discussed last year? Well, pack your bags. You earned a spot, this is your chance to soar."

"Oh my gosh. I can't believe it," I squealed with joy. "I have to ask my parents for permission." I hadn't even told them I'd entered the writing contest.

"Do you think your mom will say yes?" Penny whispered.

"She's just got to," I responded.

I worried about letting Mom know, because of how she felt about all of us sticking close to home. I kept my fingers crossed that she wouldn't mind me leaving the state for just one short week. It was Daddy's home state, after all. Surely, I could convince her to let me go.

After school, I burst through the front door, the acceptance letter clutched tightly in my hand, my heart pounding with anticipation. The savory aroma of Mom's cooking infused the air as I found her in the kitchen, stirring a large pot of soup.

"Mom, you won't believe what happened!" I exclaimed, unable to contain my enthusiasm.

Mom turned from the soup she tended at the stove. Her red hair was as vibrant as ever and piled high in her signature beehive hairdo. She wiped her hands on her apron. "What's got you so worked up? Sit down and have a bowl of chicken soup." Mom had gone into a major nesting mode ever since Randall left for Vietnam. The house was spotless, and there were always goodies baking in the oven. As if all her love and apprehension was being channeled into Rory and I, the last two kids still living at home.

Rory loved it, but I found it stifling at times.

I waved the letter in the air, a grin spreading across my face. "There's something important I want to ask you. I got a spot at a writing camp in Oklahoma."

Mom's smile faltered, replaced by a furrowed brow. "Oklahoma? That's a long way from home, Twyla. We've already got one child away in another country, and now you want to leave, too? You're much safer at home, all my babies are growing up and leaving me. I don't want you to rush it."

"Mom, it's an incredible opportunity. I can't pass this up. You know I want to be an English teacher or maybe even a writer when I grow up. It's my dream," I pleaded, my excitement deflated at Mom's resistance.

"I know, dear. I wanted to be a writer myself when I was your age, but there aren't that many opportunities for woman writers. Focus on becoming a teacher, now that's a safe profession and you'll be able to work when your kids are in school."

"What if I don't want kids?" I responded.

"Don't talk crazy, of course you'll want kids one day. Now back to this camp business. The final answer is no. You don't need to run away to camp to be a teacher. The subject is closed. Now, finish your soup."

Frustrated with my mother, I thought about her adventures on the reservation on Neah Bay and now that I had an opportunity for an adventure, she wanted me to stay home. I quietly ate my soup, but planned to ask Daddy when he got home. I'm sure he'd take my side. He just had to.

LATER THAT NIGHT, OVER OUR STEAK DINNER, I PULLED OUT the letter and quietly passed it over to Daddy. He took a moment to read it over, a thoughtful expression on his face. "This is a fantastic opportunity, Twyla. You should go."

"I already told her no, Ellis." Mom crossed her arms, a stubborn set to her jaw. "We've got Randall off fighting a war and Susan is in Los Angeles. Now that's about as far away as I want any of my kids. Isn't there a writing camp she could go to that's closer to home?"

"Mom, the thing about this camp is that *S.E. Hinton* is going to be there. She's an important writer. A female writer. She wrote her first book when she wasn't much older than me."

"Honey, it's a chance for Twyla to get her mind off the war and Randall being gone. Both girls should experience a bit of the world and some adventure, don't you think?"

"Oh, I'm not sure, Ellis," she said, her uncertainty evident as she nervously twisted her hands together, a clear sign her resolve was beginning to falter.

"We had plenty of escapades growing up. Plus, we can

all drive to Oklahoma for a visit. Stay a few days, take our time driving home. Rory can visit the Cameron homestead while Twyla is at camp, and then the girls can stay on for the rest of summer with my brother and Daisy Mae in Hugo. How about some alone time with your love?" Daddy squeezed her hand from across the table.

"It could be like a second honeymoon." Mom giggled. Her entire attitude had done a one-eighty. I could already see the shift from a worried mother to an excited wife planning her second honeymoon.

"Absolutely. We can start it off as a family trip and finish it up with just the two of us. We can go to the Grand Canyon. You've always wanted to go there. Twyla can attend her writing camp, and afterwards, the girls can reconnect in Hugo. It would do us all some good to have a change of scenery," Daddy laid it on thick. He could be so charming when he wanted to.

I looked at Mom with hopeful eyes. "What do you say, Mom? It'll be an adventure for all of us."

She sighed, a small smile playing on her lips. "Alright, alright. Promise me you'll write to us every chance you get, and don't forget where your home is. Don't get any crazy ideas about moving far away."

"I promise, Mom." I pulled her into a tight hug.

Daddy grinned, the prospect of a family adventure bringing warmth to the room. The Cameron family was ready for a summer vacation, with Oklahoma and the promise of adventures in Daddy's home state on the horizon. Plans buzzed in the air like excited bees, each of us throwing ideas into the mix, painting our upcoming journey with strokes of eagerness and joy. It was the happiest we'd all been since Randall had gone off to war.

"No way, Twyla. Your mom said yes? That's so groovy. Your dreams are coming true. I wish my mom was that open minded."

As soon as dinner ended, I phoned Penny to share my exciting news. We had grown to be tight-knit friends, frequently chatting over the phone. Oddly enough, my parents prevented me from going to Penny's house, and her folks never let her come here. Mom mentioned something about a longstanding feud between our families; Daddy and Penny's father had even had a fistfight once. But I knew Daddy still talked to Charles Lockheart, Penny's uncle who owned a jewelry store in town. Whenever I mentioned the feud, everyone behaved oddly, and one night, my parents ended up in a huge fight. I could hear them arguing in their bedroom but couldn't make out what they were saying. After that, I never mentioned it again. It didn't stop Penny and me from talking on the phone and hanging out at school.

"I couldn't believe Mom agreed to it."

"Listen, I also have some news. You're not going to like it. We're moving to Chino Hills. Mom says she can't stay in Montclair anymore. I don't know why. Everyone is acting so weird. Do you think they'll end up divorced? They've been fighting a lot."

Silence stretched out between us, and I could almost see Penny twirling the phone cord anxiously. "Is that why you've been acting strange lately?"

"I guess I didn't hide it that well."

"I could tell something was bothering you, but moving all the way to Chino Hills? That's a bit drastic. When did this happen?"

Penny's voice, once bubbly, held a quieter tone. "It's been cooking for a while, ever since the beginning of seventh grade. I didn't want to say anything until it was official. I thought it was just grownup talk and didn't think they would go through with it. We're moving when school's out."

"Moving? Penny. I didn't expect this. This is horrible news. I'll miss you."

"Yeah, it's overwhelming. Dad says it's a fresh start. I'm okay, I guess. It's just, you know, tough leaving everything behind."

My gaze wandered to the posters on my wall, a backdrop to our countless conversations. "Who am I going to share my deepest secrets with?"

"You'll find someone. Probably a cute boyfriend in Oklahoma. Hey, it's not like we won't keep in touch. We're just a call away. We can write letters, too."

I bit my lip, a pit formed in my stomach, but I tried to sound upbeat. "Yeah, maybe. I just wish we could still go to high school together. We had so many plans. It won't be the same without you."

"It's not goodbye, Twyla. It's just a 'see you later.' We'll always be friends, no matter where we are." I wished with all my heart that this would be true, but I knew it wasn't always the case when friends moved away.

As our conversation flowed, we made plans for the time we had left together, a hurricane of feelings stirred inside me. The news that Penny was moving to Chino Hills engulfed me like a dark cloud that wouldn't go away.

Penny's voice, normally filled with exuberance, now carried a touch of nostalgia. "Twyla, we've been through so much together. Remember the time we met those boys at the drive-in, or when we tried baking cookies and burned the whole batch in Home Ec? We'll always have those memories, no matter where we end up. Besides, you are going to be a famous writer one day, so you'd better keep in touch."

It seemed like whenever something good happened in my life, something rotten soon followed. Would I ever be allowed to find true happiness and stability?

CHAPTER 7

Small Town

ROAD TRIP TO HUGO
SUMMER 1973

Twyla Cameron
Thirteen Years Old

The driveway hummed with the anticipation of a new adventure, and the metallic click of the station wagon doors echoed in the air. Suitcases thudded into the trunk; each moment echoed with the promise of a journey about to unfold on this balmy summer afternoon.

"Alright, you bunch, gather 'round." Susan's voice cut through the flurry of preparation. "I want you all to have the best time in Oklahoma and send my love to everyone. I'll keep everything in order here on the home front. Don't fret about a thing."

"Thanks, Susan." Mom ran over and gave her a big hug. "We'll call you as soon as we get to our first hotel. Now let me give my grand baby a big squeeze." Mom reached her hands out to take Lacey from Susan's arms.

"Twyla, Rory, you girls don't put up with any gruff from those cowboy cousins of ours," Susan joked.

"I can't believe I'm nearly in high school and this is my first trip to Oklahoma. I've heard so much about it, I feel like I'm going home in a way." I gave Susan and Lacey a final hug goodbye as I climbed into the back of our wood paneled Ford.

The absence of Randall and the possibility of Penny moving weighed heavily on my heart. Farewells had become all too familiar, each one leaving a scar. I promised to keep in touch with Penny, and I hoped Randall would be home from Vietnam soon. It was hard to believe he'd been gone almost an entire year now.

I was growing tired of everyone leaving me behind. Now the tables were turned. Sure, I was sad to leave my friends and family for the summer, but I was eager to start my next adventure: Oklahoma.

Growing up, I was captivated by Daddy's tales of his childhood in Hugo, and my fascination with the book *The Outsiders* only added to my excitement. With every passing mile, my eagerness for the adventure at the writing camp awaiting me there grew stronger.

Rory, sitting next to me, didn't share my enthusiasm for my venture to Camp Loughridge.

"How long is writing camp anyway? I'm going to be so bored without you."

"It's just one week, and I can't wait to meet S.E. Hinton and find out how she became a famous author. Her book reminded me of what we went through in Pomona. I want to see how she turned such a negative situation into something so inspiring."

"I can't believe Twyla gets to run off to a fancy camp while I'm stuck staying with the relatives and she's off gallivanting with kids her own age," Rory's complaining, interrupted my daydreaming.

"Enough complaining, you'll have a great summer riding horses and getting to know your cousins. Charles Franklin is only five years older than you. He's a real fun guy. You'll fit in like peas and carrots," Daddy attempted to ease Rory's frustration.

Rory huffed, her teenage disdain for familial obligations evident. "It's not the same as going away to some fun camp filled with other teenagers. Twyla gets to meet a famous author. It's not fair."

"Twyla will join you in Hugo soon enough, and this will be your summer of adventure, your chance to become real cowgirls," Daddy responded.

"You're probably right," Rory grumbled.

The car bounced along the interstate with the sun casting a warm glow. Daddy glanced at us in the rearview mirror, a nostalgic smile on his face. "Alright, kiddos, listen up. I'm going to spin you a yarn about the good ol' days."

I shuffled closer to the edge of the back seat, while Rory rolled her eyes. Daddy's stories were always a treat yet could sometimes be a little long-winded.

"Daddy, tell us about growing up in Hugo again," I encouraged him, not just because I liked his stories, but I also wanted to get back at Rory for rolling her eyes.

Daddy chuckled, his voice reflecting a time long gone. "Hugo, now that's a town that holds more stories than you can shake a stick at. Picture this. I was not much older than you two when I decided to leave my small town for the big smoke."

"What does that even mean?" Rory questioned. "Sometimes it seems like you're speaking another language."

"Let's just say there weren't many chances for a young fella back then in Hugo. So, I jumped on a freight train and headed to Seattle, with dreams as big as the Oklahoma sky.

"Were you scared?" I asked.

"A little, maybe. But sometimes, you've got to be brave and push yourself. Some folks called me an 'Okie,' but I took it as a compliment. Us 'Okies' are hard workers. I ended up joining the Air Force, met your mom in the process, and she made me the happiest man alive."

As Daddy spoke, the car transformed into a time capsule, carrying us back to the sepia-toned memories of a bygone era. The landscape outside blurred into the stories of Daddy's youth, echoing with the laughter, dreams, and hard times his family had endured because of their mixed ancestry.

After two days on the road and an overnight pit stop in New Mexico, we arrived in Tulsa, and immediately, the humidity hit me.

"Is it always this humid?" Rory whined.

"You get used to it," Daddy retorted.

The writing camp in Tulsa promised to be my haven for creativity and inspiration, but as I stepped into the unfamiliar surroundings, a sudden nervousness settled in. The camp, nestled amidst lush greenery, hummed with the conversation of aspiring young writers.

"Take care, sweet pea." Daddy hugged me goodbye, followed by Rory and Mom.

"Stay safe," Mom advised as she kissed me goodbye.

"Don't do anything I wouldn't do!" Rory yelled out the window as they continued on their way to Hugo.

I quickly realized I didn't know where I was supposed to go. I pulled out my acceptance letter and scanned it, searching for any clue about where I would be staying for the week.

"You seem a bit lost," came a soft drawl, slicing through my panic.

"Just trying to figure out where to drop my backpack," I admitted.

"I'm Jake Thornton, I help with the horses around here. Give me your grade and last name, and I'll point you in the right direction."

"Twyla Cameron, eighth grade," I replied.

"Nice to meet you, Twyla. You're with the other eighth-grade girls in the Hemingway Room. Follow me," he offered.

As we walked, I couldn't help but notice how handsome Jake Thornton was, his tousled brown hair and eyes full of mischief he was the very picture of small-town charm.

"Thanks for your help, Jake." We arrived at my dorm and a mix of relief and curiosity bubbled up inside me. "I appreciate you showing me the way."

"No problem, Twyla. If you need anything else or just want to learn a bit about the horses, you know where to find me," he said with a wink and inviting smile.

As he turned to leave, clad in tight Wranglers with his leather boots kicking up dust, he cast one last glance over his shoulder and I knew that this summer camp was going to be unforgettable, and somehow, Jake Thornton would be a part of it.

THE DAYS SOON BLURRED INTO A WHIRLWIND OF WORKSHOPS, writing sprints, and fireside brainstorming sessions. Even though it was a writing camp, there was plenty of time outdoors, swimming, and riding horses. I thrived on the connection with the other young writers, each of us sharing our unique stories, our ambitions as wild and varied as the stars above.

Everyone was in middle school, and I'd never met so many book lovers in my life. I had finally found a place where I truly fit in, and I went to sleep each night with a smile on my face.

What thrilled me the most was the opportunity to meet S.E. Hinton. The thought of diving into the secrets behind her iconic book *The Outsiders* lit me up inside like a spark to tinder, I couldn't wait to get a glimpse into her world.

Finally, the day had arrived, I woke up early and put on my favorite long skirt and brown clogs. Daddy always said it was important to make a good first impression and I was determined to do just that.

As I looked at myself in the mirror, wearing my long flowing skirt with my hair styled into a smooth, professional-looking bun, I was content with what I saw. In the few short days I'd been at camp, my skin had darkened to a golden bronze, and my green eyes glowed with anticipation.

When I arrived at the small outdoor amphitheater, I noticed Jake was sitting there with an empty spot next to him.

"Hiya, Twyla. I saved you a seat up front." He waved me over. "You look so much older with your hair up like that." His cheeks reddened.

"Don't you *ever* work?" I quipped.

"Today's a big day, I wasn't going to miss a chance to see the author of my favorite book. I wonder what she's like."

"You love *The Outsiders*, too?"

"Of course, every kid in Oklahoma has read it. Probably every kid in the nation."

Just then S.E. Hinton took her place before us and introduced herself. I was struck by how petite she was, she carried a
thoughtful expression, accentuated by her large, attentive gaze
that seemed to hold a depth of understanding. Although her
stature was compact, she carried a determined set to her jaw.
Her hair, styled in soft curls, framed her face with a gentle,
nurturing air and her entire aura exuded a quiet confidence.

I sat at the edge of my seat, prepared to soak in her
words of advice.

"Writing is about finding your voice and being brave
enough to share it with the world." Her words felt like they
were meant just for me, filling me with a rush of inspiration
and the courage to chase my own dreams. Listening to her
recount the highs and lows of her journey lit up a fire inside
my soul, in ways I hadn't anticipated.

After the session, a select few of us had the opportunity
to meet S.E. Hinton personally.

As I stood in line, clutching my dog-eared copy of *The
Outsiders*, my heart pounded, and my palms began to sweat.
Every step towards her felt like a leap towards a defining
moment in my young life.

It was finally my turn to step forward. I had rehearsed
what I would say a million times, but now words seemed to
escape me.

Momentarily speechless, my eyes filled with admiration,
I silently prayed I'd remember the question I'd prepared.
"Hello, Ms. Hinton. I-I want to be a writer or maybe an

English teacher. I want to inspire others, just like you," I said in a quiet voice.

"Please, call me Susan," she said, her smile warm and encouraging.

I closed my eyes for a moment to take a deep breath. In that brief pause, a flicker of strength began to stir within me, giving me the courage I needed to voice the question I had so carefully prepared. "Your book changed how I see certain things. How were you able to write about Ponyboy and his gang so realistically?"

"A skilled writer takes note of everything, reads widely, and writes a lot. Keep in mind that every narrative matters —all of our stories—and with practice, you'll become a better writer. you won't even be able to hold it in."

"Thank you, ma'am. Meeting you means so much to me." I looked down.

Her eyes softened, and she flashed a knowing smile. "Sometimes, you must find power in your own experiences and turn them into stories that resonate. It's about making sense of the world and leaving a piece of yourself in your writing." She reached for my copy of *The Outsiders* I was holding onto tightly.

"How about I sign that for you?"

"I'd love that, thank you."

As she signed my book, I felt a surge of inspiration. Here was a woman who, as a teenager, had penned a novel that spoke to the hearts of so many.

Dear Twyla,

Keep writing, keep striving. When in doubt, just pick up the pen and start all over again. Remember, things are rough all over, but that's where beauty and power emerge. Keep looking for your inner strength to shine forth.

— S.E. Hinton

Encouraged by her inscription, I made the bold decision to follow my passion, to be strong enough to share my writing with the world. It was a leap of faith, fueled by the hope that one day, my words could touch just as many lives.

"SUSAN IS A PRETTY COOL LADY." JAKE SLID INTO THE CHAIR across from me in the cafeteria with easy confidence.

I couldn't help but smile at his playful tone. "She certainly was. I wish I could have talked to her more. One question wasn't enough, I could have talked to her all day."

He chuckled, stirring his sweet tea. "So, you like writing I take it."

"That's an understatement. I *love* writing. Mostly songs and poetry. I haven't written any books or anything, yet." I blushed.

"I have a feeling you will. You know, the sunsets around here; they're something else. Maybe we could watch one together before you go… and you can read me one of those poems."

I tried to imagine what Rory would say when boys flirted with her. I leaned forward. "I might take you up on that. I've always had a thing for beautiful sunsets."

A wide grin broke out across his freckled face. "What about this evening? I'll show you the most beautiful spot at this entire camp. It's a local secret."

"A secret, huh? I'm honored. You Oklahoma boys sure know how to intrigue a girl." I was starting to get the hang of flirting and felt my confidence grow.

"Meet me out at the stables in about an hour?"

"See you then," I responded.

An hour later, when the sun had begun its slow descent, the sky streaked in hues of gold and pink, I found myself making my way to the horse stables, the expectation inside me growing with each step. The air filled with the scent of hay and the distant sound of horses shifting in their stalls.

Jake was already there, leaning against the wooden fence, a confident grin on his face as he fed the horses. He turned as he heard my approach, his smile widening when he saw me. "You made it," he said, as if there was any doubt.

"Wouldn't miss it for the world," I replied, my nerves settled as I took in his welcoming demeanor.

He pushed off from the fence and gestured for me to follow him. "Come on, you can ride with me."

I watched him climb onto the horse's back with ease. He

held a hand out for me, the crunch of wood chips under the horse's feet was the only sound. After ten minutes, we arrived at a small hill that overlooked the entire camp. The view from here was breathtaking, with the vast open sky stretching out above us, the setting sun casting an other-worldly glow over the landscape.

"This is it," Jake said, spreading his arms wide. "Best view in the whole camp."

I couldn't disagree. Sitting snuggled in front of him, watching the sky change colors as the sun dipped lower, I felt a sense of peace wash over me. It was a moment of pure beauty in nature.

Jake finally broke the silence, his voice soft. "I come here whenever I need to think or just get away for a bit. It's my own slice of heaven."

"It's beautiful. Thank you for sharing it with me."

He placed his hand under my chin and gently turned my face towards his.

"Twyla," Jake said, his gaze meeting mine. "There's something about you. Something special. It's like you have this light inside. You're vulnerable, but I can tell you are strong underneath."

As he leaned in, I felt a flutter of butterflies in my stom-ach, and time seemed to stand still. His lips touched mine in a delicate, wonderful first kiss.

That moment would stay with me as a symbol of youth, and the endless possibilities that lay ahead. We exchanged a few more kisses until it was time to return to camp and I drifted off into a content sleep, dreaming of the days ahead.

JAKE AND I SHARED A FEW MORE TRAIL RIDES AND STOLEN kisses over the next few days and promised to write to each other. I'd thoroughly enjoyed spreading my literary wings, but the time had arrived to bid farewell to Camp Loughridge and join Rory on the Cameron Homestead.

I made Jake promise he wouldn't come out to say goodbye on the last day. I didn't want to leave camp on a sad note.

> Dear Jake,
>
> I never imagined saying goodbye would be this hard. Meeting you was like a burst of sunshine—bright, warm, and unexpectedly wonderful. As I pack my bags and say farewell to Camp Loughridge, I can't help but wish for just one more day of laughter and adventures with you. Keep in touch and hopefully I'll see you again.
>
> Here's a little poem to hold close to your heart:
>
> In the glow of summer's embrace,
> We found our pace, a special place.
> Though seasons change and we must part,
> You'll remain a beat in my heart.

Keep smiling, keep shining, and keep this note as a reminder of our summer of sunshine.

Luv always,
Twyla

After slipping my letter to Jake into his cubby in the common area, I made my way to Camp Loughridge's pick-up area, scanning the rows of vehicles for Uncle Biggin's old truck. My mind was still consumed with thoughts of our stolen kisses when Rory came bounding towards me, her energy infectious. She enveloped me in a tight hug.

"You've changed. Just a week away and you look so grown up," her eyes sparkled knowingly.

"It felt like forever. But I guess being away from home for the first time does that to you," I responded, caught up in her excitement.

"We still have a few weeks of summer left, and I've got big plans," Rory said, a playful smirk on her face.

"What's up, Rory?"

"I've signed us up for a rodeo next week," she announced proudly.

"You're kidding." I laughed, a mix of nerves and amusement in my voice.

"Nope. I've been practicing on Firecracker all week. It turns out, I'm pretty good at barrel racing. Your job is to grab a gunnysack, stand on it, and hang tight," she explained.

"That sounds insane," I said, half-worried, half-excited.

"You'll see. Once the adrenaline hits, it's a blast."

As we drove through downtown Hugo in Uncle Biggin's old Ford, I pressed against the window, absorbing the sights of Daddy's hometown. "Your Pa used to bring his dates to that picture house there." Uncle Biggin pointed out an old theatre.

"Imagine Daddy jumping on a train right there." I motioned toward the train station.

Uncle Biggin laughed. "Your mama lasted here only six weeks before heading back to Washington. We had to chase after her. I'd never seen your Pa so heartbroken. Ever heard that one?"

"I guess Mom and cowboy life didn't mesh." Rory giggled.

"It's funny thinking of Mom as being so adventurous. Did she really take the Greyhound Bus from here to Washington all by herself? These days, all she does is stay home and bake. She's all about keeping us close," I reflected.

"Sometimes people change when they've been through things. She's probably just takin' a breather. She sure seemed fixin' to take an adventure when they left here. She called it their *second honeymoon*." Uncle Biggin threw his head back and laughed heartily, his deep chuckle echoed around the truck.

"Mom will get back into the swing of things, especially when Randall returns from Vietnam," Rory added with hope.

I quietly wished the same as we left the town's quaint streets, entering a landscape of cornfields and proud oak trees on our way to the Cameron Homestead. Soon, a gravel driveway crunched beneath the tires, announcing our arrival at Daddy's childhood home.

"This is where your Pa grew up," Uncle Biggin said, as he stepped out of the truck.

The scent of earth and a whisper of adventure filled the air. My first visit to Hugo felt significant, a connection to my roots waiting to be explored. The Cameron property sprawled over five acres of land, housing horses, pigs, and a few cows.

When we arrived, our cousin Charles Franklin awaited us. He was tending to his pigs and smoking a cigarette, a pack of Marlboro Reds poking out from his denim overalls. He had jet black hair and a handlebar mustache, his well-worn cowboy hat shaded his eyes from the harsh sun, adding an air of mystery to his persona.

"Excitin' times ahead." Charles Franklin took a drag on his cigarette before asking his question. "Are you ready to start practicin' for the rodeo?"

"Rory mentioned that, but can we start tomorrow? I might need to work up to it."

"Can ya ride a horse?" His eyes twinkled with mischief.

"She can ride." Rory giggled as we made our way into the house to unpack my bag.

"He's the family rebel, a bit rough around the edges, but he's got a heart of gold," Rory whispered to me as we entered the house. "He's going to take us to the movies tonight. Let's get ready."

A few hours later, Charles Franklin was banging on the door. "You girls ready for the pictures?" he asked.

"Be right there." I called out as Rory and I grabbed our purses.

Charles Franklin's old truck bumped along the dirt road as Johnny Cash played on the radio.

"Where are we going? Isn't town that way?" Rory pointed in the opposite direction.

"It's a surprise." Charles Franklin laughed as he took another drag on his cigarette.

We soon pulled up outside a weathered old building, its wooden exterior faded by years of sun and storms. The sign outside promised cold brews and live music. Our cousin's fondness for drinking and dancing led him to take us to the local honkytonk under the illusion that we were headed to the movies to see *Charlotte's Web*.

"Are you sure they'll let us in?" Rory asked with a gleam in her eye.

"Let's find out. This will be way more fun than that picture show." He adjusted his hat and we made our way into the saloon.

Walking into The Rusty Spur felt like a step back in time. The air was a mix of leather, tobacco, and whiskey. The jukebox played a Hank Williams tune and was the heart of the place. The walls were adorned with peeling posters of country legends. Each table and chair bore the marks of visitors who'd left a piece of their story behind.

As soon as we entered, Charles Franklin beelined to a corner table and quickly snagged us some bottles of Coke before diving into a pool game with the locals. Rory pulled out a bag of peanuts and dropped them into our Coke bottles —a trick that made us feel we were living the country life.

Surrounded by cowboys in their snug Wrangler jeans, we couldn't help but ogle a little as we excitedly hashed out our plans for the upcoming rodeo.

"I can't believe we are doing this. Aunt Daisy would die if she knew where we were." I whispered to Rory.

"Welcome to Oklahoma." Rory laughed. "I guess normal rules don't apply here."

The next day, I helped milk the cows while Daisy May worked her culinary magic in the kitchen, crafting the most delicious biscuits and gravy I'd ever tasted. I didn't have the heart to tell her we never made it to the movies and had spent my first night here at a honkytonk.

That summer of our youth, Rory and I spent nearly every hour outdoors, in the heat, riding horses, catching fire-flies, and getting to know my father's relatives.

They were kind and loving people. Daisy May was a fabulous cook and baker. She loved to spoil us and constantly worried we'd get hurt riding Firecracker, who was a spirited Quarter Horse most didn't dare ride.

The Cameron family was known for giving nicknames,

and Daddy's last living brother was called Biggin'. He had a fondness for hunting squirrels on the property and preparing them for dinner, much to the repulsion of Rory and me. We had always regarded squirrels as cute forest creatures, not suitable for a meal, but Biggin' seemed to enjoy eating them and complained they were always stealing the nuts off his pecan trees.

Beneath the vast Oklahoma sky, Rory and I soaked ourselves in the sun and explored the plains atop our trusty horses. The wind whistled past us, carrying the sweet scent of wildflowers as we embraced the thrill of the ride. Sable and Firecracker, the horses we borrowed for the summer, mirrored our enthusiasm and our adventurous hearts. Our kindhearted uncle often joined us on our trail rides.

Uncle Biggin' talked slow, and rode slower, savoring the unhurried pace of the countryside. It was a pace that clashed with our desire for speed and freedom. He trotted along on his horse named Dusty. Rory and I exchanged mischievous looks, as we silently plotted our escape from the leisurely ride with our uncle.

Rory grinned at me, "Can we pull it off today?" she whispered.

"Let's give it a shot."

I nudged Sable into a gallop, pretending to struggle with my spirited companion. With theatrical distress, I let out a mock gasp before disappearing into the distance.

Rory, always the expert rider, seized the opportunity with a casual remark, "I'd better go after her." She guided

Firecracker into a swift pursuit, pretending to chase after me.

Moments later, she was by my side laughing her head off. "This is way better than a slow ride with Uncle."

"Meet you at the old oak tree." I called out, and we both sped off, leaving Uncle far behind.

Eventually Biggin' would show up with a twinkle in his eye, playing the role of the oblivious uncle.

Our horses understood the unspoken language of rebellion and camaraderie. We had a silent pact that bound us together in the joyous pursuit of freedom on the vast plains of Oklahoma.

Charles Franklin worked around the farm all day, but derived immense pleasure from encouraging us girls to live the Oklahoma lifestyle. He was adamant we practice barrel racing every day so we could live up to the Cameron family reputation for horsemanship. We spent most of our time practicing.

When the day finally arrived, we were the only two girls brave enough to enter the rodeo.

Under the blistering sun of the rodeo arena, the three of us huddled together—Rory, me, and the irrepressible Charles Franklin. His face gleamed as he imparted years of horse wrangling wisdom. As we stood outside the arena waiting to hear our names called over the loudspeaker, my heart raced with adrenaline.

"Alright, you two," Charles Franklin declared, his voice carrying the unmistakable enthusiasm of a seasoned horse rider. "This ain't your ordinary Sunday ride. We're talkin' about an authentic rodeo. Show 'em what the Camerons are made of."

Rory grinned. "You got it, cousin. We're gonna ride like the wind and leave 'em all in the dust."

Our cousin's deep voice resonated with encouragement. "That's the spirit, Rory. Now, Twyla, don't let your sister steal all the thunder. Remember, it's not just about speed; it's about grace and control. Make that rope an extension of yourself."

I nodded as I absorbed his advice. "Got it, Charles. Wish me luck." My hands shook as I gripped onto the rope that would tow me behind Firecracker. Time seemed to stand still.

It's all happening. I thought to myself as I took my place behind Firecracker, my feet firmly planted on the old burlap sack.

The time for our grand entrance was here, Charles Franklin called after us. "Twyla, just try to hang on. Don't fall off that gunny sack and if you do, run like hell to get outta there."

I was about to be pulled at top speed through an obstacle course of oil barrels by one of the most infamous horses in Hugo.

The announcer's voice crackled over the loudspeaker, and the arena was filled with applause. "We have two cowboys all the way from California."

We rode into the arena with heads held high. The cheers

of the crowd blended with Charles's boisterous encouragement. However, a hush fell over the crowd as they registered that we were two young *cowgirls* from California. Charles, always the jokester, had entered us into the competition pretending we were boys.

The sudden silence spoke volumes about the surprise and realization spreading through the audience. The entry of two young teenage girls promised to add an unexpected twist to the event.

In the exhilarating race that followed, Rory and I navigated the barrel race with determination and flair. The roar of the crowd echoed in our ears as we showcased our freshly honed horsemanship skills, defying expectations with each daring move.

"You know, even though we didn't win the race, we really had a great time," I remarked, still feeling the excitement of the event.

Rory didn't respond because she was engrossed in conversation with a cute cowboy who would become her summer boyfriend. I didn't mind Rory spending time with her new love, because I had made friends with a local girl. Her name was Lilly, and her parents owned the store that used to be the one-room schoolhouse where Daddy went to school.

The summer of our youth flew by, leaving behind a trail of laughter, love, and cherished memories. In those sun-soaked days, we uncovered the enduring power of family ties and the untamed spirit within our wild beating hearts.

Despite the heat and hard work, we felt proud to be on the Cameron homestead. Grateful for the small-town experience, I cherished the memories made with my sister, my best friend.

On one evening, as we braided each other's hair, Rory tried to convince me to let her cut my hair like Joan Jett.

"Come on, Twyla, it'll be fun. A whole new look for California." Rory grinned, holding up the scissors.

Uncertain about such a change, we reminisced about our summer adventures in Oklahoma taking care of horses, competing in a rodeo, and experiencing our first summer of freedom.

"Remember that cute cowboy from the honkytonk?" Rory teased.

I rolled my eyes. "Yeah, yeah. You and your summer flings. What about your summer boyfriend, Michael Williams?"

"Michael who?" We both burst out laughing as Rory played Little Miss Innocent.

It had been an amazing summer. We came to Oklahoma as one set of girls and left more mature, our sisterly bonds fortified by the experiences that tested and revealed our strengths.

THE VIBRATION OF THE PLANE'S ENGINES SLOWLY GAVE WAY to the distant buzz of the airport terminal. The scent of jet fuel and the hustle of fellow travelers filled the air as Rory and I stepped off the plane in Ontario, California.

We both had deep, dark tans from our days riding horses in Oklahoma, and Rory had bleached her hair blonde. We looked more alike now that we both had blonde hair. I couldn't help but feel happy I wasn't the only flaxen haired one in the family.

As we made our way through the terminal, the familiar faces of our parents emerged from the crowd. Mom enveloped us in a tight hug, her voice tinged with nostalgia, "My girls are back. Rory, what did you do to your hair?"

"It's just a little Sun-In" Rory replied before rushing into Dad's arms. "Did you miss us?"

Dad chuckled as he ruffled Rory's hair. "Of course, sweetheart. How was your summer in Oklahoma?"

"It was amazing," I replied. "We did so much – rode horses, competed in a rodeo, and made some new friends, too."

"Rodeo? Really? You never mentioned anything about a rodeo." Mom looked pointedly at our father.

Rory laughed. "We surprised everyone, Mom. You'll hear all about it."

But our joyful reunion quickly turned sour as we exited the terminal. A trio of hippies shouted angrily at a Marine who had just returned home from duty. Rory and I watched in shock as they spat at him, their disdain evident upon their faces.

My parents rushed forward to defend the soldier, their

voices filled with indignation. "How dare you!" Mom's words rang out, her anger palpable. I felt a surge of pride for her as she fearlessly confronted the three men with long hair.

Rory looked confused, trying to make sense of the situation. We had heard about the protests getting ugly, but seeing the hatred directed towards the soldier was jarring. "Let's get out of here before a fight kicks off." Rory gently grabbed Mom's hand and we made our way to the baggage return.

"Can you imagine being drafted to fight and receiving a home coming like that? It's disgraceful." Mom's face was red with anger.

"It's worlds away from the welcome we received when we returned from World War II," Daddy added.

"Try not to think about it, girls." Mom advised.

But I couldn't help but think about it. My brother was a good person, he didn't want this war, he even faced jail time if he didn't go. Now people were targeting those who'd risked their lives.

Daddy caught my eye in the rearview mirror and deftly changed the subject. "Did you girls take to life on the ranch."

"You betcha. Can we have horses one day?" Rory asked.

"I'm working on it, sweet pea, I've been looking at land and I know it will all come together... One day."

As we pulled into the driveway, the familiar sights of home greeted us. Our parents exchanged glances, and I sensed an unspoken understanding hanging in the air. Rory, ever the perceptive one, voiced it.

"What's up, guys?"

Mom hesitated before answering,

"Girls, I have some news to share with you," Mom began, her tone serious yet hopeful. "We received a letter from Randall. He'll be home soon." Relief flooded the car as we processed the news.

"Why didn't you tell us right away?" I asked.

"We wanted to hear about your trip and all the adventures you've had, there's been too much talk of war lately." Tears welled up in Mom's eyes.

"He's not out of the woods yet, but it's a step in the right direction," Dad added, his voice laced with emotion.

"I won't relax until he's safely at home. Where he belongs," Mom added.

Rory and I hugged each other as we both cried tears of joy.

The summer had been the most exciting of my young life.

As we settled back into the familiarity of home, the expectations of high school lingered and I prayed every night that Randall would return safe and sound. I couldn't wait to get my brother back.

Randall was coming home!

CHAPTER 8

Carry On

MONTCLAIR, CALIFORNIA
SEPTEMBER 1973

Twyla Cameron
Thirteen Years Old

The aroma of Mom's pancakes filled the air as we made our way downstairs. Breakfast sizzled on the griddle, and Dad was already engrossed in his morning paper.

"Morning, girls," Mom greeted with a warm smile. "Rise and shine. First day of high school, remember?"

"Ugh, how could I forget?" Rory groaned as she got two plates out of the cupboard.

"Well, if school ain't your thing, we could sure use another hand on the construction site. Let's toughen up those tender hands," Dad teased.

"Very funny." Rory shot back.

Suddenly, the front door creaked open and interrupted our morning conversation. Rory and I turned to see a figure standing in the doorway, clad in a military uniform.

"Randall?" Dad exclaimed, rising from his chair. The newspaper slipped from his hands as he rushed to embrace our returning soldier.

"My son, you're home." Tears welled up in Mom's eyes as she, too, approached the doorway.

"They let me leave a little earlier than anticipated," he responded.

Rory and I gasped in surprise when our older brother Randall walked into the light. His face, once young and carefree, bore the weight of war. His uniform hinted at the journey that had transcended the boundaries of our suburban haven.

"Hey there, Twy, Rory," Randall greeted us with a hug, a weary but genuine smile formed on his face. "Did you miss me? I've got gifts for everyone."

The exhilaration for the first day of high school faded into the background as we hugged our brother, who had safely returned from the tumultuous depths of the Vietnam War.

"Grab a plate for Randall. Are you hungry, son?" Mom asked as she started whipping up another batch of pancakes.

"Ravenous. It's good to be home," he responded.

Randall spoke of his experiences as we opened our gifts. He gave Rory and I each a beautiful elephant shaped necklace carved from jade. He gave Dad an engraved lighter that was meticulously detailed, and Mom received a silk scarf, its vibrant colors a representation of the exotic beauty of the places he'd seen.

The air was thick with a mix of joy, relief, and unspoken worries about the future, but for that moment, we were all absorbed in the here and now, hanging on Randall's every word.

"You wouldn't believe the challenges we faced," he said, his eyes reflecting the burden of his memories. "But the camaraderie among us kept us going. You bond with your fellow soldiers in ways hard to explain."

Rory and I listened intently, pride and concern swelling up inside. Randall continued, "And the longing for home. That's what kept me pushing forward, knowing I'd eventually come back to all of you."

As he spoke, we glimpsed the profound impact the war had on him. His words painted a vivid picture of the sacrifices made, and yet we couldn't fully grasp the depth of his experiences.

Randall hesitated before revealing, "I was awarded a Purple Heart, but I left before the ceremony. I didn't want a reward for what I had to do over there. It's not something to be celebrated."

"Purple Heart!" Daddy stood up, knocking his chair over. "Were you injured, son?"

"Just a little shrapnel and an overnight in the hospital.

Nothing permanent. I'm fine. I'm completely healed. I didn't write to tell you, because I didn't want to worry you any further."

His words hit me like a ton of bricks, a heavy silence settled over the breakfast table. My brother had been injured and forced to kill people in a war I didn't understand. Would he ever be the same?

As the morning unfolded, we decided the first day of high school could wait for the real lessons shared around the breakfast table that morning. The return of Randall brought with it a deeper understanding of sacrifice, resilience, and the harsh realities of life.

"We'd better go get Maya. You two have a wedding to start planning. Let's tuck all this unpleasantness away and move on with our lives." Mom exhaled as if she were releasing all the pent-up worries she had been holding in.

"Not right now, Mom. I'm not in the wedding planning mood. We were writing to each other about eloping to Las Vegas. I need to talk to Maya about it more, but for now, can I stay here? Can I have my old room back for a while? I need to decompress."

"Of course. Your room is exactly how you left it." Mom replied.

I couldn't help but notice the sadness etched on Randall's face, and he seemed a bit jumpy. Like he carried the weight of the world on his shoulders.

The familiar walls of our home were filled with unease

and somehow felt different. It was like the air was charged with questions we weren't ready to ask. A dark cloud seemed to envelop our home and I could sense the world of emotions brewing beneath the surface of my brother's new rugged exterior.

THE NEXT FEW WEEKS PASSED IN A FLURRY AS I ADJUSTED TO a new school routine and Randall tried to find his footing back in civilian life. After that morning around the breakfast table, we never discussed Vietnam again. Randall would start shaking at the mention of war, so we stopped watching the news and watched more comedies and sitcoms instead.

Our family dinners, once lively with teasing banter and laughter, carried a more somber undercurrent. Randall's experiences left an indelible mark on him.

I watched him closely. New lines had formed around his eyes, all traces of boyishness had been erased from his face, he was still handsome as ever, possibly even more now with the depth and maturity that hardship often bestows. His laughter, when it came, had a different timbre—richer somehow, but tinged with a shadow that wasn't there before. His hair had started to gray prematurely, and there was a haunted look on his face.

Most evenings, he retreated to his room early, leaving the rest of us in a contemplative silence as he continued to navigate the challenges of post-war life.

"He'll come back around. There's always an adjustment period when coming back from war," Dad said, his tone suggested he tried to convince himself as well as the rest of us.

The walls of our home absorbed his unspoken fears and hopes and became a witness to a healing process that unfolded gradually, like the first hint of dawn breaking the horizon.

"Hey, big bro, Maya is here to see you." I knocked on Randall's door one afternoon after school, as the door creaked open, I could see my brother trembling and shaking. He rocked back and forth, tears streamed down his face.

"Not now, I can't let her see me like this." He motioned for me to close the door.

I made my way back to the living room "It's not a good time right now."

"Is he having another bad day?" she asked.

"Yes, caught him watching the news before bed, and had nightmares all night long," I confided.

"I'm going to be his wife soon. I need him to understand. I want all of him, even the broken parts. We'll face this together." Maya pushed past me and slowly entered Randall's room. Her gaze softened as she took in sight of him as he struggled with his inner turmoil. The air felt heavy with the burden of his trauma, and Maya, with a tenderness only love could bring, approached him slowly.

"Randall," she whispered softly. "It's me, Maya. You don't have to face this alone."

The trembling of his hands didn't escape Maya's notice, but she continued forward with a calm determination. She sat beside him on the bed and reached for his hand. "I know you're going through some things, something tearing you apart," Maya said, her voice steady. "But we're in this together, Randall. Your pain is mine, and we'll find a way to heal, together."

"It's too much. I don't know how to get past this." Randall, still gripped by the haunting memories, hesitated before he finally met her gaze.

"I love you, Randall. All of you. The scars, the fears, everything. We can face the shadows together."

She pulled him into an embrace, as her tears flowed freely. Love, the most powerful healer, had entered the room, and Maya, with her unconditional acceptance, became the guiding light through the darkness.

Outside the room, I silently prayed Maya's love could be a force to help mend the broken pieces of Randall's soul.

As the door to his room softly closed, I couldn't help but feel a sense of promise bloom within our home. Maya, with her love and compassion, had taken the first step in letting Randall know that it was okay to be overwhelmed. She still loved him, no matter what.

THE YOUNG COUPLE DECIDED TO HAVE A SMALL BACKYARD wedding. We were hopeful Randall would be able to move forward with the life he had planned before he left for war. The wedding day soon approached, a bittersweet anticipation in the air.

The backyard looked like something out of a fairytale, all dressed up in flowers and sunshine. I perched on a white chair and watched as Mom and Susan fussed over the last-minute details. Mom kept saying, "It's got to be perfect for Randall," her voice firm and proud.

I twisted a strand of my hair and squinted up at the archway where Randall and Maya would stand. It was draped in roses, white and pink from Mom's garden. Randall and Maya both agreed they wanted something simple, something that felt like home, but that didn't stop Mom from adding some of her personal touches.

"There needs to be a bit of sparkle in every wedding, lovebug," Mom had said as she weaved delicate strand of fairy lights through the roses. The lights twinkled softly, making the flowers seem like they were part of some enchanted garden.

Grandma Lenora arrived from Washington the other day, bringing with her three pounds of Randall's beloved razor clams. The family stayed up late into the night preparing the fritters and catching up around the dinner table. This was a cherished family tradition, dating back to the 1930s when Mom's family lived on the Makah Reservation. Amidst the laughter and shared memories, the warmth of family togetherness filled the air.

When Maya appeared, a hush fell over the crowd. She

moved down the aisle with the grace of a ballet dancer, her dress billowing around her like a cloud. She had dyed her curly hair blonde, which looked like a crown of light around her head. Amidst the festivities, Grandma leaned over to me, her voice a soft murmur, 'I hope he's put his troubles behind him.

"I know," I whispered back, a weird twisty feeling formed in my stomach.

"Look at them, Twyla," Grandma said, her hand intertwined with mine. "Look how happy your brother is. When I heard he was marrying Maya, well I can't say I wasn't worried about the road ahead, but just look at how happy she makes him."

My brother's gaze never left his bride. He looked different, taller somehow, and there was this new glow about him, his face, once dimmed by hardships, now sparkled with a resurgence of light and hope. It was as though, in the presence of his soon-to-be wife, he had rediscovered parts of himself long forgotten.

"I love you, Maya," Randall whispered.

"There's nothing we can't overcome as long as we have each other," she responded.

Everyone applauded when the groom kissed his bride.

"Let's get this party started." Buck shouted.

"Everyone can grab a plate of food from the kitchen. It's a dinner buffet tonight," Dad added.

The celebration unfolded a representation of love and resilience. Friends and family gathered, and after everyone had their fill of Mom's famous spaghetti, Buck turned on the stereo he had set up to play the songs of our era.

As Rory and I moved to the melodies, her eyes abruptly darted across the yard, catching sight of something—or rather, someone—unexpected. With a gentle nudge, she drew my attention to the figure approaching.

"Look who it is!" she exclaimed, a hint of amusement in her voice.

There, weaving through the clusters of our guests was Keith, our neighborhood paperboy. But instead of his usual ballcap and jeans, he was clad in a button down and clip-on tie. A surprising contrast to the image we were so accustomed to.

"Hi, Rory," he greeted as he approached us on the makeshift dance floor. "Hello, Twyla."

"Hi, Keith," I replied, my curiosity piqued. "What are you doing here?"

"Your mom invited me to the reception," he explained as he adjusted the collar of his shirt. He looked slightly out of his element yet genuinely happy to be here.

"That's great. There's plenty of food to go around." Rory replied.

Keith shuffled his feet as he glanced down before mustering the courage to look up at me. "Twyla, would you like to dance?"

Surprised but not wanting to hurt his feelings, I nodded and smiled. "Sure, why not?"

As we moved awkwardly to the rhythm of the music,

Keith's confidence seemed to grow. The song ended, and he leaned in, his face shining with delight. "Hey, Twy, I've got something cool to show you. Want to see my new bike? It's out in the front yard."

Intrigued, I followed him, curious about his enthusiasm. We stepped away from the lively celebration and into the quiet realm of the front yard, where his new bike stood gleaming under the moonlight.

"It's a beauty, isn't it?" Keith beamed; his hand brushed the handlebar.

Before I could respond, he turned quickly towards me, his face serious. In a swift motion, he leaned in, and attempted to kiss me, his mouth opened wide like a fish. Startled and uncomfortable, I instinctively pushed him away, my hands landed on his chest. He stumbled backward, losing his balance, and tumbled into the nearby bushes.

"Keith!" I exclaimed, my heart raced. "I didn't mean to. I wasn't expecting that. I thought you liked Rory, she's in your grade."

Keith stood up and brushed leaves from his hair, looking more embarrassed than hurt. "Sorry, I'd hoped you liked me, too. I guess I misread the situation."

Realizing he wasn't mad, I offered him a hand to help him up, a combination of guilt and relief settled in on my shoulders. "It's okay. I do like you, as a friend. Let's forget it happened, alright?"

We started to walk back to the party when a dark car

pulled up. A mysterious man got out and handed me an official looking envelope. "A message for Randall Cameron."

"I'll make sure my brother gets it. Come on, Keith, let's go find him."

Keith nodded, still a bit flustered as we made our way back towards the lively sounds of the backyard. The envelope felt heavy in my hand, its formality out of place amidst the joy and celebration of our homespun wedding.

"Hey, are you okay?" Keith asked, his voice laced with concern.

I forced a smile and tried to shake off the awkwardness of the moment. "Yeah, I'm fine. Just surprised, that's all. Let's go find my brother, okay?"

Keith nodded, and we quickened our pace, eager to rejoin the festivities and leave the embarrassing incident behind us. The backyard was alive with laughter and music, the air filled with the tantalizing aroma of food. I scanned the crowd for Randall, the envelope burning like a question mark in my hand.

"There he is." Keith pointed towards the dance floor where Randall was lost in a dance with Maya, they both looked blissfully happy as I handed him the letter. Suddenly, the color drained from his face.

"It's from Dante Brown's mother," Randall read aloud. "Dante has been killed in action." His words hit hard, breaking through the joy of our celebration. As he spoke, the light drained from Randall's face, reflecting the gravity of the news that fell upon us like a shadow. The war's dark presence now loomed over me, making me question the government's choices in Southeast Asia.

Maya moved uneasily; her expressions reflected an inner distress. In that moment, I couldn't help but wonder, would my brother ever truly be free from the nightmares of the Vietnam War?

CHAPTER 9

Sweet Emotions

MONTCLAIR, CALIFORNIA
DECEMBER 31, 1975

Twyla Cameron
Fifteen Years Old

" D o you think Randall is doing as good as Maya says he is, or she just trying not to worry Mom?" Rory asked as we experienced a moment of sisterly solidarity before the New Year's Eve celebrations unfolded.

"It's been a roller coaster for those two. Let's hope this new baby keeps him focused on looking forward and not looking back," I hopefully replied. Randall and Maya had recently welcomed their first baby girl into the world, a radiant child my brother insisted on calling Freedom Ellen Cameron.

Rory gave a small, thoughtful nod, her face taking on a serious look for a moment. "She's such a ray of sunshine, the happiest baby I've ever seen. I suppose with a new baby in the house, it's hard to think about the ugliness of war. I tell you what: If I never hear the word 'war' again, it will be too soon." Rory's gaze drifted back to her makeup kit, a clear signal that it was time to shift gears. "Why don't we talk about something more lighthearted? Sparkles or classic navy for tonight? What do you think?" Her tone was lighter as we discussed our attire for the night.

"You're right. There's not much we can do about it anyway." Everyone was worried about my brother's mental state, but whenever anyone brought it up, the subject was quickly changed, as if sweeping it under the rug and pretending everything was okay would protect Randall from the shadows of war.

"Which dress are you going to wear?" Rory asked the question once again. "Because I'll wear the other one."

I stood in front of the mirror, holding up two mini dresses. One shimmering like a starlit sky, and the other tried and true as the night itself. "I can't decide. The sparkles scream 'Happy New Year,' but the navy one is so me."

"Go with the navy, it's definitely more your style. Leave the funky sparkles to me." Rory laughed.

"I think you're right." I pulled the mini dress over my head and twirled around, admiring myself in the mirror.

"This sparkly number will be perfect with my purple

boots. Bold and bright, just like the upcoming year. Can you believe it's nearly 1976? Time to boogie and let our hair down. Let's forget about our worries for now."

"You're right, sis."

"Besides, you might catch a certain paperboy's attention," Rory added.

I rolled my eyes, a blush creeping up my cheeks despite my best efforts. "Keith? He's just a friend, Rory. And he works at the skating rink now. He's too old to be a paperboy."

Rory laughed, tossed her blonde hair over her shoulder, fluttering her eyelashes at me. "Haven't you noticed how cute he's gotten? He's changed a lot this past summer. You know, in a 'look at me, I'm not just a paperboy anymore,' kind of way."

"Maybe I've been too busy noticing other changes," I replied, thinking of Randall and Maya's new baby. Our family was growing, and there were always little nieces and nephews to babysit. Our three oldest siblings had all welcomed babies over the past year.

Rory's expression softened. "Yeah, there must be something in the water. Better not drink it." She laughed at her own joke.

Despite claiming Randall's old room, Rory was always in my room, bringing laughter and her witty outlook to every situation.

"Let's go downstairs and help finish setting everything up." I threw on my go-go boots and started making my way down the stairs. The living room adorned with festive balloons Mom had placed around the room, a kaleidoscope of colors that reflected our hope for a happy new year ahead.

Randall, dressed in slacks and a black t-shirt had just arrived with Maya and baby Freedom. He looked as good as we all had hoped. The burdens that weighed so heavily on his shoulders seemed to slowly be lifting over the years since he had returned. We all thought he'd have a set back the night we heard about Dante, yet here he was, smiling more genuinely than he had in a long time.

Dad clapped him on the back, a proud look on his face. "Randall, you've come a long way. Your Mom and I are so proud of the man you've become."

He squeezed Maya's hand, and she beamed up at him. Then, with a twinkle in his eye, he announced, "And we have more good news—Maya and I are expecting another baby!" The room erupted in cheers and congratulations, adding an extra layer of joy to the celebrations.

The living room buzzed with conversation as we all caught up, and Bobby regaled everyone with tales of his latest adventures on the road as a truck driver. The sound of children's laughter mingled with the adults' banter, creating a blanket of familial warmth.

"I also have an announcement to make." Dad broke through the noise with his southern drawl. "It's sort of a late Christmas gift for all of us, but I want you all to know that your mom and I have just closed on those five acres out in a place called Redlands. It's about a half hour from here. The construction business is going well, and with this growing family, we need a bigger place to host these celebrations. There's even enough room for horses."

"Ellis, I can't believe it. Our dream is coming true." Mom's eyes sparkled with elation.

Everyone else hushed at Dad's surprise announcement, and the warmth of the living room seemed to expand, mirroring the growing dreams of our family.

"Dad, you did what?" Rory exclaimed, her voice tinged with delight.

"Five acres? Do I sense a horse corral in the future?" Bobby chimed in; a mischievous grin spread across his face. "You know, I'll be needing a place for my own horse."

Our dad laughed, enjoying the reactions. "That's right. It's not just a place for horses. I want to parcel it out and build a house for each of my sons."

Bobby's eyes lit up, a mixture of surprise and joy illuminating his face. 'It's really happening,' he said. 'I sometimes thought we were just pipe dreaming."

With a nod and a twinkle in his eye, Dad responded, "We've got plenty of space now. What do you say?"

"Let me talk to the boss." Bobby turned to his wife Kelly and sought her opinion without words, his gaze filled with hope.

Kelly exclaimed, "You really did it, Dad! I know you've talked about this since the day I met you, but seeing it all finally happen is a little surprising. That's all."

"Us Camerons stick together, and I want all my sons close by. I thought that's what you all wanted, too?" Dad questioned.

"Of course," Kelly replied, her voice warm with affection. "We always said we'd move with you if you ever got that property. I'm happy for you, for all of us. The cousins can all go to school together in Redlands." She crossed the room and gave Dad a huge hug, sealing our joint future with a hug.

Maya, still holding onto Randall's hand, shared an amused look with him. "Looks like we're moving to Redlands dear."

Randall chuckled. "As long as there's enough room for a chicken coop."

"The house is in the planning stages. I want each of my sons to have an acre to build their own houses on with a huge corral in the middle, to join all our homes. We're all going to be neighbors," Dad proclaimed.

"Ellis, this is the best news ever. Our dreams are coming true. A fresh start for all of us." Mom's face shined with happiness. The room erupted into cheers and excited chatter at the significance of Dad's announcement. The idea of three new homes, acres to explore, and the prospect of horses and chickens filled the air with dreams yet to be realized.

"Wait until you all see it. I'm going to build a game room, a pool, and Jacuzzi, and a garden for you my dear." Dad took Mom's hand in his and gave it a kiss.

As the night continued, discussions shifted to plans for the new property. Dad's dream was becoming a reality, and the prospect of a larger space for family gatherings and celebrations filled our hearts with hope.

During it all, Randall and Maya found a quiet spot by the fireplace. Randall's face filled with gratitude. "Looks like the Camerons are building something beautiful together."

She nodded, leaning into him. "Our own piece of paradise, surrounded by family and love."

As the clock neared midnight, the elation in the room reached a crescendo. Eventually, Randall excused himself to the kitchen where a pot of Mom's meatballs simmered in the slow cooker.

"Are you okay?" I asked as I joined him for a late-night snack.

"Yeah." He grabbed a couple of plates from the cupboard. "Dad's announcement is a lot to take in. Everything's changing. Sometimes I just need a moment to take it all in."

I nodded. "Are you really happy about it?"

"I am. I think it will be good for all of us," he replied.

"I'm not looking forward to switching schools, but I agree it's going to be good. We'll all have horses and it's been Dad's dream for so long."

"Dad's always supporting our dreams, I want to do the same for him. Hey, it's almost midnight. Should we finish our food in the front room and rejoin the party?"

"I wouldn't want to be anywhere else." I smiled as I

followed him with my plate in hand. The warmth and laughter in the front room welcomed us back. The moment felt like a snapshot of our future—gathering together, adapting to changes, but always rooted in love and unity.

Finally, the countdown began. The room hushed as everyone joined together to count down the last ten seconds. As the clock struck midnight, cheers erupted.

"Happy New Year!" Susan called out, raising her glass. Throughout the room, glasses clinked, sealing the promise of a brighter future.

"Let's make a toast," Randall suggested, raising his glass as we celebrated the arrival of a new year. "To new beginnings, to our family's piece of paradise, and to Redlands," he announced.

Everyone raised their glasses, and I realized that no matter where life took us or what changes came our way, this feeling of love and togetherness would always be our true north.

CHAPTER 10
Last Child
MONTCLAIR, CALIFORNIA
SPRING 1976

Twyla Cameron
Sixteen Years Old

I woke up to the sound of Rory blasting Aerosmith on the record player. A bright and sunny morning greeted us on the day of Rory's eighteenth birthday.

"Happy birthday, sis," I said as I entered her room. She stopped brushing her hair and looked up as I handed her an envelope, still seated at her vanity table, she quickly ripped open my gift.

"What do we have here. Aerosmith tickets? Tonight? Twyla, how on earth did you ever keep this secret? Did Mom say we could go?"

"I already asked. Mom said now that you're eighteen, we are old enough to go to LA alone together."

"But you don't even like Aerosmith?" Rory questioned.

"Who ever said that? I just don't like them as loud as you want to play them." I smiled back.

"This is going to be far out. I can't wait." Rory jumped up and gave me a big hug.

Her energy was infectious as she slipped into her favorite bellbottoms and a Deep Purple t-shirt, a perfect match for her vivacious spirit. Her baby face, a striking contrast to her bold style, was framed by waves of bleached blonde hair cascading loosely around her shoulders. With a playful grin, she clipped a feather into her hair, adding an extra touch of whimsy to her look. Meanwhile, I was the sugar to her spice, always opting for more subdued styles that sometimes contrasted with her seventy's flair.

Now that she was eighteen, I wondered if we'd drift apart. Rory's crowd didn't quite feel like my scene. She had always been the tomboy rocker chick of the family, while I embraced a bohemian vibe with peasant blouses and soft colors. As we headed to the concert, I hoped this birthday excursion might bridge the gap between us, pulling us back to the closeness we once shared.

It's not like Rory would ever leave me behind on purpose, but I still wondered if she was holding back when she was around me. I was sixteen and our relationship was shifting now that Rory was about to graduate from high school.

"Come on, Twy," she urged, joy vibrated throughout her words, "Tonight, we're gonna to boogie 'til we just can't boogie no more!" Her excitement infected me, sparking my own anticipation for the night's adventures.

"Smells like Mom's cooking bacon. Let's get down there before Dad eats it all." I grabbed my shoes before making a beeline for the stairs.

We were surprised to find Dad cooking in the kitchen. He looked up from the stove and smiled at us. "Good morning, girls. Were you expecting your mom?" He laughed.

"It's good to see you changing it up. Mom, can I get you a coffee?" Rory asked.

"No dear, you sit down and let Dad spoil us today. He said he wanted to cook your birthday breakfast, cowboy style."

"What are we having, Dad?" Rory asked.

"I've got biscuits cooking in the Dutch oven, some bacon and beans. This is how we ate when we were cowboying. I bet you didn't know your Dad was such a good cook?" He dished each of us out a large plate of food.

"Ellis, you're a man of many talents. Now girls, are you ready for this concert? Airplanes or whatever their called."

"Aerosmith." I laughed.

Rory practically bounced out of her seat. "You know it, Mom. We're going to have the best night ever. Thank you for letting us go."

Mom gave us a stern look, but I could see the love in her face. "You girls better behave yourselves. And Rory, I know you are considered an adult now, but Twyla's curfew is still midnight. Dad and I will be in Redlands this afternoon, we're going to see how the building is going. Have fun but keep a good head on your shoulders. Is that clear?"

Rory smirked. "Don't worry, Mom, we'll be on our best behavior. When are those houses going to be done anyway?"

When Mom looked away, Rory pretended she was smoking a joint. I almost choked on my bacon and wondered how we could be sisters and still be so different.

"The houses are almost ready. Ours will be done next month. I want to move soon so we can enroll your sister in her new high school. You girls might have to commute for a few months, then Twy can finish school at Redlands High. I'm planning a big graduation party for you, Rory."

"Sounds like you have everything all planned out," I replied.

I do, my lovebugs. And I need you both to help keep things on track. Now, have a good time tonight, but remember to take care of each other. You know a girl can only ever count on two people in her life.

"Her sister and her daddy," Rory and I chimed in unison.

"Very funny, girls. I *do* want you to always count on each other. I'm not even going to let myself worry about you two gallivanting around Los Angeles."

And with that, Rory and I headed out the door, ready for whatever adventure the day might bring.

"Twy, you know how we are always asking Dad for gas money?"

"Didn't he give you some birthday money over breakfast?"

"Yeah, but I want to use it for other things. Hollywood can be expensive you know. I have a plan." Rory pulled into the gas station and pulled up to the pump. "Have you ever heard about resetting the pump?"

"No, what's that?"

"It's how we can snag some free gas without anyone noticing. We're going to fill up the tank halfway, you distract the attendant while I restart the counter. Just a bit of harmless fun on our way to the big city."

I eyed her with cautious curiosity. "Rory, are you sure about this? What if we get caught?"

She scoffed, waving off my concern. "Trust me, Twy, it's foolproof. You're so gorgeous the attendant won't even notice. I'll fill the tank halfway up, reset the pump, and no one will ever know. Come on, it'll be an adventure."

"If you say so." I walked over and tried to dazzle the gas station attendant with flirtatious questions while Rory pumped the gas.

"Okay, Twyla, are you ready to go?" She winked.

I paid the cashier for the second half of the gas Rory had pumped and nobody seemed to notice our little attempt at being teenage rebels.

As we sped away from the gas station, a triumphant grin adorned Rory's face and uncontrollable giggles echoed in the car.

"Don't ever make me do that again," I laughed.

"I think you are a wild child underneath all that good girl behavior. I couldn't even get Laury Johnson to try that with me."

"You are too much. Look at the skyscrapers!" I exclaimed.

The City of Angels was upon us as Rory carefully navigated the traffic to Hollywood where we spent our day wandering around, looking at the stars on the sidewalk and having lunch at Pink's Hotdogs before heading to the concert.

We arrived at the Forum in Inglewood just as the sun made its descent over the concrete jungle. The air pulsated with an overwhelming energy and we made our way toward the front of the stage. The thunderous music threatened to burst my eardrums, my eyes wide in awe while my heart raced with the rhythm of the music.

"Look, Twyla, it's those cute boys from the parking lot. Let's make our way over to them. They are right at the center of it all." Rory pulled me along in her wake. Soon, we found ourselves pressed up against the front of the stage, our bodies pushed from thousands of people surging forward behind us.

"Rory, I can hardly breath up here."

"You'll be fine, sis. Stand in front of me."

The concert's blend of thick smoke and dazzling sounds coursed through my body, my limbs felt lighter as I started to move my body to the music. My former anxiety dissipated in a vapor of the teenage high from experiencing my first live rock concert.

In her element, Rory flirted with everyone around her, scheming her way backstage.

At the beginning of the encore, Steven Tyler pointed directly at us, a mischievous grin on his face, sending Rory into ecstatic chaos while the boys cheered. I was stunned, my eyes wide as he spat beer over the crowd.

Laughing nervously, I admitted, "I wasn't expecting that."

"It's amazing! I love him!" Rory yelled back before turning to the boys. "Hey, can you lift me on your shoulders? And your friend can lift my sister?" Without hesitation, they obliged, elevating us above the crowd.

From this new vantage point, the concert felt even more magical. Despite my ringing ears and hoarse voice from singing, the rush was indescribable, like flying. But all good things must come to an end and we soon found ourselves walking back to Rory's yellow pickup truck, the night's energy pulsating within us.

As we started our drive home, Rory couldn't contain her exuberance. "The concert was insane. Did you see Steven Tyler point at us? I'm still buzzing. Hey, let's try to get you into that bar we heard about."

"It's getting close to midnight, and we should be heading home. Mom will be worried sick."

"Come on, this is our chance to check out the Sunset Strip at night. Mom's probably already asleep. How often do we have the chance to party in Hollywood? And who knows, we might even run into the band members at the Rainbow. That's where the roadie said everyone goes after the concert. It's legendary."

"Alright, you win. You only turn eighteen once, but I'm only staying for one hour. Then we head home?"

"Deal."

The irresistible allure of meeting Steven Tyler lured us to the Rainbow Bar and Grill on the epicenter of the Sunset Strip. Where the Roxy and the Rainbow collided. The bouncer eyed us knowingly. I knew he could see that I was an underage girl looking for a taste of rock 'n roll. Unfazed, Rory flashed a smile and her ID, batting her eyelashes. "Fresh from the Aerosmith concert," she declared. "Any chance the band's here?"

The bouncer raised an eyebrow but let us in, no reservations needed. Inside, the Rainbow Bar was dimly lit, thick with smoke.

As we approached, a vibrant scene unfolded—an amalgamation of hippies in bellbottoms, punks with ripped shirts, glam rockers in outrageous costumes and boys wearing makeup. I'd never seen anything like it.

My flowery peasant top and clogs suddenly felt out of sync with the tight and revealing clothing the other women were wearing, but Rory thrived in the environment. Adorned with rock memorabilia, the legendary spot in rock 'n roll history was a place Rory looked right at home. The bright, red, vinyl leather seats, dark wood paneling, and iconic ambiance created an experience beyond imagination.

"What should we order?"

"I'll have a Heimakin. That's what Bobby always drinks."

"It's Heineken, silly." Rory rolled her eyes.

As she ordered our beers I scanned the room eagerly, searching for signs of Steven Tyler or any rock band, the surreal nature of the night sinking in. However, the thought of Mom waiting up for us at home made my palms start to sweat.

The crowd grew rowdier as the night marched on, and a group of older guys kept eyeing us which made my cheeks flush.

Rory, still absorbed in her quest for rock stars, seemed oblivious to the stares we were garnering. "Rory, we should go," I said, tugging at her sleeve. "It's getting late."

"What are you talking about? We're having fun."

"Hey there, sweetheart. What's your name?" An older man approached us. He wore a leather jacket over a faded band t-shirt, low-slung jeans, frayed just right, and pointed boots that clicked against the floor. His belt buckle gleamed with rock 'n' roll flair, and he draped his arm around my shoulders.

"We were just leaving." Rory flicked her hair over her shoulder.

The guy laughed. "Leaving so soon? Why don't you stick around for a while? I can show you a good time. Both of you." He lightly caressed Rory's wrist.

For a split second, uncertainty gripped me, causing my head to swim as the secondhand smoke was starting to get to me. But with a deep inhale, I summoned my inner strength. "Back off," I asserted, pushing his arm away. "We're leaving!"

"That's right. We don't need your version of a good time. Let's get out of here." Rory looked at me.

We pushed through the crowd, leaving behind the unsettling encounter. As we walked towards the car, I could finally breathe again. I'd discovered, when push came to shove, that I could stick up for myself.

"Are you okay? He was so old. He looked older than Dad. What was he thinking talking to a couple of teens?" she questioned.

I let out a shaky laugh, trying to brush off the tension even though my heart was still pounding. "Yeah, he's a pervert trying to talk to girls our age. We'd better get home before Mom realizes we broke curfew." Maybe I wasn't as carefree or tough as Rory, but I could stand up for myself when pushed.

It was true Rory and I made quite a pair, I thought, as we headed back home. Rory didn't fret about the conse-

146

quences, and I needed someone like her to pull me out of my shell.

Even without meeting any rock stars, this night had become unforgettable and cemented a bond that time couldn't erase. As the city lights faded in the rearview mirror, I somehow knew our lives were about to take a turn into uncharted territory.

CHAPTER 11

Fast Lane

REDLANDS CALIFORNIA
LATE SPRING 1976

Twyla Cameron
Sixteen Years Old

A few short months later we were all gathered in the new Redlands house. The aroma of simmering tomatoes and garlic filled the air as Bobby leaned against the kitchen counter, watching Mom stir the pot. "You know, Mom, I think your spaghetti has magical powers," he joked as a smile formed on his lips.

Mom chuckled, her eyes twinkling with glee. "Oh, really? And why is that?"

"Because it's the only thing strong enough to pull this crazy family together every month without fail." He gestured toward the living room where laughter filled the space.

Just then, Maya walked into the kitchen. "He's not wrong, you know. I swear, all these kids ask about anymore is spaghetti night at Grandma and Grandpa's house."

Mom smiled, pride gleamed in her eyes. "It's important, keeping traditions alive. It's what keeps a family *a family*, through all the seasons. Once my parents bought their first home in Kent, Washington, Mama started the Sunday night family spaghetti night and I intend to continue it."

Bobby nodded, glancing out the window towards the sprawling property that had become our new family compound. "The new house has definitely made these get-togethers easier. Remember when we all had to cram into the tiny kitchen on Harvard Street?"

Mom laughed, "How could I forget? But I must admit, there's something special about this place. It's like we've all found a little piece of paradise here. It's so peaceful living on property."

From the doorway, Dad's voice boomed. "Peace? With this bunch? You must be joking!" His face beamed.

We turned to see him standing there, Lacey and April clinging to each leg. Dad's face was alight with a happiness that seemed to fill the room, even more than the scent of Mom's cooking.

"Yeah, but you love it, Dad. Admit it. You're happier here, playing Grandpa," Randall jested.

Dad smiled, a soft, content smile. "Maybe I am. Maybe this old dog can learn a few new tricks after all."

As the family converged in the dining room, the warmth of the evening wrapped around us like a cozy blanket, a testament to the power of tradition, of spaghetti nights, and of a family that, no matter where life took us, would always find our way back to each other.

Every first Sunday of the month, like clockwork, our growing family came together like this. It pulled us into a ritual more steadfast than any other in our lives.

Susan and Daniel, the city slickers, still clung to the vibrant, pulsating heart of Los Angeles, while the rest of us had moved to the outskirts of Redlands to start a new life. There was more open space here in the country, it was a slower paced way of life.

Ever since we'd moved here, Dad had found a new spring to his step. He'd taken on the role of Grandpa with a gusto that was both not too surprising and extremely heartwarming.

His latest project was something right out of an old movie: an antique carriage he worked hard to restore to its former glory, just for the grandkids. He even got the horses he'd always dreamt about.

When the older siblings came to visit, Dad took the little ones for rides around the coral in the center of our land. Watching them, their faces filled with wonder, hearing their laughter combined with the clip-clop of horse hooves, it was like I'd stepped into a time capsule. Simple, pure, and it reminded me of the sort of adventures I used to daydream about when I was their age.

One balmy Sunday evening, Randall burst through our front door, his eyes alive with the thrill of the day. "You guys won't believe what I have witnessed."

"Tell us, big bro," Rory urged him on.

"You won't believe it—I was at a real motocross race! And guess what? I'm actually thinking about buying my own dirt bike. I really want to give racing a shot."

Randall had started a job as a truck driver with the Alpha Beta grocery store. He, Maya and their baby girl lived in the house next door, and everything was copacetic for them. They even had a third baby due to be born at any moment.

"So, I was at the local grill after work last week, grabbing a drink with Chucky Fisher." He paused for effect, his hands animated as he spoke. "And we ended up talking with this guy sitting next to us."

"Who was he?" Dad chimed in, leaning forward with interest.

"Turns out, he's a sponsor for one of the big motocross teams." Randall's enthusiasm was contagious.

"No way! Motocross? That's intense," I said, my eyes widening in mock surprise.

"Alright, smarty pants, it gets better. We hit it off, and he offered me a pit pass to their next race." Randall's smile was wide, his voice filled with disbelief and joy.

"You went to a race?" Mom said, her eyebrows raised in surprise.

"I did, and you know what? It was incredible. The guys all camp out at the desert on the weekends, to practice."

"It sounds like you've found a new hobby." Dad reached for the breadbasket.

"Oh, Randall, what about the new baby? You can't drag three kids out into the desert," Mom chimed in.

"Why not? I've been saving my money. I'm going to buy a camper and a secondhand dirt bike. It's only hot there in the summer. We can go during the winter months, get one of those playpens to set up. Right, Maya?"

"I'm willing to give it a try, a little fresh air never hurt anyone." Maya laughed as she rubbed her belly.

"That's cool, Randall. I love seeing you excited about something again," I said, feeling genuinely happy for him.

"Just try not to crash that bike and mess up your movie star looks, little bro," Buck teased.

Dad, sitting at the head of the table, looked up from his plate with a proud grin. "Well, I always knew that boy had gumption. Motocross, huh? Sounds like a Cameron legacy in the making."

"Are you up for it, Dad?" Randall asked.

"I ride horses. I think I can probably ride one of those motorcycles. We should all give it a try. It could be fun camping out in the desert around a campfire."

Randall grinned, "What do you say, Mom? Twyla? You

guys up for doing some riding, too? It's not only a guy's sport, you know."

Mom smiled. "Well, are you sure it's safe for everyone?"

"Yes, Mom, we'll get all the proper helmets and riding gear. We'll be safe. There are even four-wheeled motorcycles for you and Dad in case you're worried about falling. It makes it easier. They call them quads," Randall assured her.

"It sounds like fun, but I'll come and be the cook and babysitter. You won't get me on one of those things. I could use a little excitement in my life, but I'll get it by watching you all," She responded.

Dad chuckled. "Alright. Twyla, what about you?"

I hesitated, imagining myself on a dirt bike, but the fervor in Randall's voice was contagious. "Sure, why not? I'll give it a try."

At first, I assumed motocross would be another passing fad. Little did I know Randall had discovered a new passion and this decision would alter the course of the rest of my life.

Once Dad and I got our dirt bikes, everyone started wanting in on the action, and our weekends turned into family bonding time as we explored trails and rugged terrains across the California deserts. The motocross bug had bitten us all.

I was surprised to find I enjoyed riding dirt bikes more than I thought I would. Out there, with the vast horizon stretching before me I wasn't just Twyla, the girl who'd rather get lost in a book or scribble lines of poetry in a hidden notebook. On my bike, I turned into a more daring version of myself – fearless, fierce, and free. It's not what people expected from me, and I kind of loved that.

And, I'll admit it – the boys who hung around the tracks weren't exactly a bad bonus. There's something about guys who share a love for racing that I found exciting and a bit dangerous. It was like we all shared a commonality, a love for speed and being surrounded by nature.

Randall's newfound passion had not only changed his life's course, but it also ignited a spark in the entire family. Our monthly Sunday dinners transformed into motocross-themed camping trips, with our desert adventures dominating the conversation whenever my brothers were around.

Not long after that night Randall talked us into trying out this new sport, we found ourselves gathered around a crackling campfire, the desert sky painted with stars.

Mom spoke up, "This is something else, isn't it? Who would have thought we'd all end up on dirt bikes? I enjoy giving the grandkids rides on my new quad. I'm glad you talked me into it, Ellis."

Rory agreed. "Next time, let's invite the Fisher family. I know they would enjoy it too."

Randall gazed into the flickering flames, "Wonderful idea, Ror. These excursions are all about being together, creating memories with family. I have something else I want to spring on everyone."

"Oh no, he has that look in his eye again," Buck interjected.

"Maya and I are going to the Baja 500 in June, and we want everyone to join us. It's going to be our next big escapade." Randall glowed as he talked about his new venture.

Dad smiled "Well, son, you have a way of steering us into fresh adventures. But I must admit, so far, this hobby of yours has been great for the family. Quality time together, a little thrill, and a lot of laughter. It reminds me of my time as a young man, herding cattle across the Oklahoma plains."

"Tell us more about this race, little brother," Buck chimed in as he took his wife's hand and settled into his camping chair.

Randall, fueled by an undeniable excitement, leaned forward, his eyes glittered with dreams of Mexico. "Picture this: dusty trails, untamed landscapes stretching for miles, and the thunderous roar of engines echoing through the desert."

Mom raised her eyebrows. "And why in the world would we want to go there when we are perfectly safe here in California? There's plenty of good riding for you, closer to home."

"Because, Mom, it's not merely a race. It's an adventure. I'm envisioning getting involved in professional racing. It's not too different than what we are doing now, but I could win some serious money. I want to take it up a notch and get more involved in the racing community."

"But where would we all sleep? It's one thing all of us

cramming into the RV, your camper and a few tents, but we'd need something better if we were going all the way to Mexico."

"Bobby has been looking at a secondhand airstream my buddy has for sale. Dad could bring the motorhome and anyone else who wants to come can pitch a tent. It won't be that different than what we do now. Just more exciting." He leaned back in his camping chair.

Susan, always the critic, chimed in. "Sounds like you and Bobby have your minds made up. What is it about Mexico that has you so excited?"

Drawing closer, Randall's eyes met each family member. "I want us all to venture there, absorb the atmosphere, and be part of something extraordinary. I know I won't win, heck, I might not even place, but it's about the journey not the destination."

"Mexico? It's a long way from Neah Bay. I've never been that far south," Mom said, still looking concerned.

Acknowledging her worry, Randall nodded. "I know, Mom. But you won't be diving into the thick of it. You'll be spectators, savoring the thrill from a safe distance. Not too different from your adventures on Neah Bay."

"We never had motorcycles on the bay. The only racing we did was by foot," Mom harumphed.

After a moment of reflection, Dad cleared his throat. "You know what? Why don't we give it a try? Let's all go and support Randall in his dream. It's obviously something important to him."

As Randall's younger sister, I felt an unspoken under-standing linger—an acknowledgement of our profound bond and the sacrifices Randall made during those difficult months in Vietnam. Maybe more than anybody else, I could see the toll it took on him and it was nice to see him fired up about a new phase in his life.

The thought of loading into Dad's new RV and venturing into the off-roading world wasn't just a family outing; it was an attempt to keep the smile firmly planted on Randall's face. The question was, would it stay there?

CHAPTER 12
Love on the Radar
ENSENADA, MEXICO
JUNE 1976

Twyla Cameron
Sixteen Years Old

In the six weeks leading up to our Baja trip, time seemed to accelerate as it propelled us toward our Mexican adventure with unstoppable momentum.

Every day was filled with anticipation and preparation. Our living room became a staging ground for gear and guidebooks, each item carefully chosen for its necessity and versatility.

As the departure date neared, the excitement within the family grew. We took turns sharing facts and trivia about Mexico, from its rich history to its diverse ecosystems. Our conversations buzzed with discussions about the Baja 500.

Now, as we arrived in Ensenada, Randall's dream, once casually discussed around a campfire in the California desert, had come vividly to life.

In true Cameron fashion, whenever one of us found a new passion, we all enthusiastically joined in. The entire family rallied around my brother and his passion, catching the infectious joy of off-roading in the desert.

"I want you to be extra careful out there, son," Dad advised Randall with a concerned tone.

"You know I always am. And did you hear, Caleb Silverson is here? He's the racer I've been following. He's part of the reason I started wanting to race," Randall responded.

Whispers among the campers circulated—an electrifying buzz surrounded Caleb Silverson, the emerging celebrity motocross racer. He had even graced the cover of *Dirt Bike* magazine, and news of his participation spread like wildfire through the motocross community, adding an extra layer of thrill to an already charged atmosphere.

Caleb Silverson, with his racing skills and charismatic presence, had recently become a sensation in the racing world. The prospect of watching him navigate the challenging terrain of the Mexican desert sent ripples of excitement throughout the spectators. His name, once a well-kept secret among motocross enthusiasts, was now on everyone's lips in the racing world, spoken with a reverential awe, especially among the girls.

"So, he's the one we have to thank for you dragging all of us all the way down to Mexico?" Mom laughed.

"That's right. Now let's do a practice ride today to warm up these muscles. You coming, Twyla?" Randall asked.

"Sure thing, Randall. Lead the way." I strapped on my helmet and revved my engine as Randall kicked his bike into gear, the low rumble of our engines blending into a chorus of readiness. As we set off, Randall took the lead, his engine humming in harmony with the desert breeze. Rory and I were both in the secondhand dune buggy Dad had bought us, especially for this trip.

Suddenly our engine sputtered and the dune buggy coasted to a stop. With a frown on my face, I tried to get the engine started again. The last thing we needed was this. "What do you think is wrong with it?" Rory scratched her head.

"I think it's flooded. Hopefully Randall sees we've stalled and comes back."

"Good luck with that. Did you see the stars in his eyes?" Rory laughed.

In the distance, the unmistakable sound of another motorcycle approached. A rider clad in full gear emerged, a helmet concealing their identity. As he parked his bike, the helmet came off to reveal a handsome face.

"Having some trouble?" he asked, a genuine smile gracing his lips.

I nodded, still processing the unexpected turn of events. "Yeah, seems like our sand car had plans of its own."

The young man chuckled. "Well, lucky for you, I happen to know a thing or two about engines. Let's check her out."

Side-by-side, we examined the bike. This rider looked to be a bit older than Rory and me. He had piercing blue eyes and longish blonde hair. As he examined the buggy, he shared insights and suggestions, his expertise evident in every move. Frustration gave way to glee as he confidently got the engine purring again.

"There you go, good as new. I'm Caleb, by the way." He was tall, nearly six-foot-three, his long, sun-bleached hair he had tied back with a bandana. He gave off that effortless, rugged vibe and looked a bit rough around the edges. His worn motocross pants were snug, and he wore them well. He had a confident swagger, the kind that comes from knowing you're good at something. He was the epitome of cool.

"Thank you so much. You really know your way around an engine."

Caleb grinned, his eyes twinkling. "Well, I've spent a fair amount of time with them."

"I'm Twyla," I introduced myself. "That's my sister Rory."

"Nice to meet you, Twyla. Just glad I could help. Where are you guys camping? Maybe I'll stop by later." He winked at me and my face flushed beet red.

"We are the burgundy and white motorhome over there. We hadn't gotten too far from camp when the engine stalled," I responded with a smile. "Feel free to stop by, but you'll have to come over and meet my Dad and brothers first. I'm here with my entire family."

"I don't think it will be a problem; I have six brothers of my own. I can handle brothers. I'll see you after dinner time." Caleb mounted his bike and rode off with a wave.

"That was Caleb Silverson. The racer Randall is always talking about," Rory squealed. "Wasn't he gorgeous? I think he likes you."

As the sun cast it's evening glow on our campsite, the Cameron family gathered around the campfire for a dinner of roasted hot dogs and beans. Randall couldn't contain his excitement as he recounted the events of the day, including our unexpected meeting with Caleb.

Dad, intrigued by the mention of Caleb Silverson, joined in the conversation. "Well, I'll be darned. Randall was telling me about him. We've seen him race on the TV. That's something else."

"Seems like Mexico is bringing more surprises than we bargained for," Mom chimed in with a playful glint in her eye.

After dinner, Caleb kept his promise and visited our camp. The glow of the campfire highlighted his easygoing smile as I introduced him to my family. The night echoed with laughter, shared stories, and ample discussion about the upcoming race.

My brothers went fairly easy on Caleb, but Buck did challenge him to an arm wrestling match. In the end, Caleb emerged victorious, but it was a long and exhilarating match.

Our conversation flowed as I stepped closer to the sleek motocross bike Caleb wanted to show me. It turned out that he was the champion from 1975 and a fan favorite to win in 1976. He'd traveled all over the US, sharing his tales of victories and the unique challenges of motocross life. Despite my usual preference for poetry over engines, his stories and passion were contagious.

"How long are you going to be in Mexico? When this race is over, can I take you out on a date?" Caleb asked with a charming smile.

"That sounds like fun, but you just focus on this race for now," I replied, matching his playful tone.

"Oh, I'm not *really* here to race. My brother is the one who wanted to come. I'm saving myself for the Motocross circuit. Some of the sponsors paid me a nice fee to come down here and get some attention on this race," he explained.

"Is that how it works?" I smiled back.

"Sometimes being a celebrity has its perks." He grinned.

"Well, I didn't recognize you. I guess you aren't as famous as you think," I taunted back.

"Alright, I can see you're going to be a tough one to

impress. What if I faked a little engine problem partway through the race and came back to take you horseback riding? Would you be impressed with that?"

"Don't you dare. You can't throw the race," I shot back.

"This Baja 500 is my brother's dream. I came along to support him and for a bit of fun. Motocross is my passion. I'm not really into these big drawn-out races, and the sponsors don't care if I win. They wanted the buzz they thought I'd bring just by being here." He smiled, revealing a genuine side beyond the celebrity facade.

"I'll be around for a few days if you suddenly become free, but seriously, Caleb, don't do anything that's going to get you in trouble," I warned.

"The only thing I'd regret is not seeing you again." He interlaced his fingers with mine as we walked back to camp. An electric tingle traveled up my arm as I squeezed his large, rugged hand and the desert night enveloped us in a cool embrace.

After we said our goodbyes and I wished Caleb luck, I lay in my lawn chair by the fire, staring up at the stars, replaying the events of the evening in my mind. Could a guy like Caleb Silverson be interested in someone like me? We seemed like complete opposites.

Recently, I'd been getting a lot more attention from the boys at school, but Caleb was so mature. I had never felt such an immediate connection to someone before. I'd had a few dates with Keith Simpson, but never anything serious. I always found the boys at school too eager to please and it wasn't attractive to me.

As the night air whispered through the desert, my thoughts drifted to how confident and fearless Caleb had seemed. His voice, the manner he spoke, the contrasts in his personality—all of it hinted at a multifaceted individual with a wealth of tales to share. I had heard that underneath his racing gear, he wore a Jesus Saves shirt, but he seemed to also have a bit of a bad boy reputation. Was it a facade, or was something more going on behind that rough exterior?

"What's on your mind, lovebug?" Mom noticed I was worlds away in thought.

"I was worrying about the safety of this race. Randall has never been involved in something as intense as this." I tried to cover for my thoughts about Caleb.

"And now she has sexy Caleb Silverson to worry about, too," Rory interjected.

"They'll both be okay. It's certainly couldn't be worse than what your brother faced in Vietnam." Mom sighed and ran a hand through her red hair.

THE NEXT MORNING, AMIDST THE RELENTLESS HUM OF engines and the never-ending spectacle of the Baja 500, the campsite had transformed into a whirlwind of anticipation. The vibrant energy of the race, spanning several days, had permeated the dusty air around us. The scent of fresh coffee mingled with the chatter of last-minute advice.

After breakfast, we got as close as we could to the start of the race and joined a lively crowd of fellow spectators, their vehicles adorned with sponsor decals and homemade signs rooting on their favorite racer. I stood beside my parents, watching as Randall made his way to the starting line. The roar of engines pierced the silence as the contestants got ready to take off. My family all shouted words of encouragement to Randall as he prepared to take off on his next big adventure.

The desert air, cool and expectant, seemed to hold its breath as moments stretched into eternity, waiting for the race to begin.

Then, in a heartbeat, the tranquil morning erupted into life with the sound of a horn, signaling the start of the race. It wasn't the dramatic gunfire many had expected, but it was enough. It felt like a call to something greater than just a race; it was a call to live, to feel the rush of life and test yourself against some of the best racers in the nation.

Randall, reacting with the instincts of a seasoned racer, twisting the throttle, and his motorcycle leapt forward, a blur of motion and intent. The ground beneath him became a blur as he navigated the treacherous terrain of the Baja desert, every fiber of his being focused on the path ahead.

Dust billowed behind him as Dad shouted, "Look at him go!" Soon he was just a speck in the distance, and we made our way back to our campsite to begin listening for updates on our CB radio. There wasn't much news of Randall, and I soon grew tired of waiting around for updates.

"What are we going to do while Randall is off racing?" I asked Rory.

"I guess we never thought that far ahead." Rory laughed. "Want to play some cards?" And we spent the rest of the day playing cards and telling stories about our child-hood adventures. Each memory, shared between laughter and the occasional sigh, painted a picture of a bond as enduring as the desert around us.

"You know, Randall always had this untamed spirit," Rory mused as she shuffled the deck of cards. "Even as a kid, he was always pushing the limits, chasing dreams that seemed out of reach to the average person."

I nodded, the image of Randall speeding across the desert vivid in my mind. "He's doing what he loves," I said, a mixture of apprehension and pride swelling within me. "And somehow, that makes waiting here a little easier. Knowing he's out there, living his dream."

As night fell, and the stars began to twinkle above us, I knew these moments of waiting, of hoping, and reminiscing was just as much a part of our adventure as Randall's race across the desert. In the quiet of the Baja night, with only the crackle of the campfire and the distant hum of the desert wind, I felt closer to my family than ever before.

Halfway through the second day of the race, I sat by the dwindling embers of the campfire, sipping my lukewarm tea, when an unexpected visitor rolled up in an old Ford. Now donning his red t-shirt and faded blue jeans, he flashed a mischievous grin that melted my heart. "Looks like I've run into some unexpected engine trouble," Caleb announced, his voice tinged with feigned disappointment.

"Oh no, Caleb. What about the fans? They'll be so disappointed," I responded.

"They'll live. I thought there might be other adventures waiting for me."

"What did you have in mind?"

"Have you ever been horseback riding? It's my second passion, next to riding bikes."

"I can ride. I've even been in a rodeo back in Oklahoma," I bragged.

"Well, you're just full of surprises. Have you ever been riding on the beach? It's a whole other experience," He took my hand in his and motioned over at his little Bronco. "What do you say?"

"If it's okay with Mom, I'll come," I went to grab my tote bag and asked Mom, who I was pretty sure would say yes.

"You kids have fun now," Mom shouted as I left to join Caleb.

"¿Quieres buy una foto for un dolarito to remember esta aventura?" the man at the horse rental asked in Spanish as Caleb and I prepared for our horseback ride.

Caleb handed the man a dollar bill, and we found ourselves posing atop two sturdy Appaloosa horses.

"You speak Spanish, too?" I asked.

"Por Quito. A worker in our family business has been teaching me," Caleb replied. The man snapped our Polaroid, placed it in a small frame, and handed it to us with a warm smile, ensuring we had a tangible memory of our scenic ride along the Mexican beaches.

"So, you rode in a rodeo before?" Caleb asked after I'd tucked away the photograph into my small tote bag and tied it to the saddle.

"I sure did."

"Then I'll expect you to keep up," Caleb spurred his horse on. The sunlit vistas of Ensenada unfolded before us, a picturesque scene of sandy shores and rhythmic waves. Guided by our horses, Caleb and I left imprints on the soft sand, knowing the tide would soon wash them away.

"This looks like a good spot for a picnic" Caleb pointed to a secluded spot on the beach, and he quickly helped me tie up my horse to a nearby palm tree.

Seated on a blanket spread out on the sand, the soothing sound of waves served as the backdrop to Caleb's tales of motocross adventures. His laughter harmonized with the gentle cadence of the ocean.

"You were right about riding horses on the beach, it's invigorating. I love it so much." I smiled at Caleb.

Caleb's eyes shimmered as blue as the sunlit waters

when he shared, "I grew up in North San Diego County. Coming down here to fish and ride horses on the beach was our family pastime before we got into biking. I love it, too."

"You really love speed, don't you? I noticed you holding back with your horse, I could tell you wanted to go faster."

"You picked up on that?"

"I've spent a lot of time around horses. I could tell you were holding back." I laughed.

"Very observant. You know, I never walked as a kid, I always ran. Once I got my first little CRF50, well that was the end of it. Every time I hit the dirt track, I feel so alive. It's more than just speed. I like pushing myself to the edge, feeling that adrenaline... Sorry, sometimes I can ramble about riding."

"Don't apologize, I love it when someone can speak so openly about their passions. I wish I was more like that."

"So, what's your passion?"

"Besides riding bikes? I love writing, I know it's a contradiction but that's what I like about it. Writing fulfills my contemplative side and riding bikes out in the desert with my family has brought out my adventurous side. I can see why you're so drawn to it."

"Writing, huh? What sort of things do you write? I'd love to read something you wrote."

"Mostly poems and songs." I blushed.

"Very deep. I could tell you had a lot going on behind those beautiful green eyes. So where do you call home?

Maybe I'll have to come by and read some of these songs," Caleb flirted.

"I grew up in Pomona and Montclair, but now we live in Redlands."

"I've been up that way. They have a county fair there every year. Can I take you to the fair when I get off the racing circuit? I'll be back in California in September."

"I look forward to it."

Caleb leaned in as he whispered, "There's just one more thing," before kissing me softly on the lips. That incredible kiss sent electricity coursing through my body, and I suddenly pulled back, a bit overwhelmed. Up to this point, my experiences had been with a few boys—kisses that were sloppy, rushed, and passionless compared to the intensity I now felt with Caleb. It took me a bit off guard and I needed a moment to catch my breath.

"I feel a little weird kissing you while you're wearing a Jesus Saves shirt, it seems a little bit of a contradiction, I mean, it's not that I don't appreciate the sentiment," I continued, a playful glint in my eyes, "but Jesus Saves and stolen kisses on the beach seem like they don't mix."

"This is my lucky racing shirt. I wear it to spread the good news. I recently became a born-again Christian. It's all new for me. I'm still finding my way. Besides, I don't think Jesus minds me kissing a pretty girl that I like." With that, he peeled off the red t-shirt, revealing a well-defined, tanned, physique that glistened in the fading sunlight. The shirt found a new home beside us, folded neatly on the blanket. I stared at him in shock.

"What? I'm just working on my tan. I promise, no more kissing. At least until our second date. Now tell me more about these songs. Any love songs in your catalogue?" He laid back and crossed his hands behind his head.

"You are too much, Caleb Silverson. I don't know what to make of you. Are you the bad boy motocross racer or the nice Christian boy?"

"I guess I'm a little bit of both. I'm human, but I try my best." He lifted his eyes to mine.

"Ever tire of traveling so much?" I asked, curious about the man beyond the racer.

"Never. It's my passion, as you now know." He ran a hand through his hair.

"Yes, you've been quite clear. It looks like it's going to be a beautiful sunset, but we should take these horses back before it gets dark." I stood up and shook the sand from my clothes. I enjoyed being close on the picnic blanket but didn't want to get carried away on our first date.

"Sure thing. Let's get you back to your castle, princess."

"You see that?" I asked as we rode back to camp, pointing to the horizon. "It's like the edge of the world meeting the sea. Makes you feel small in the grand scheme of things."

He smiled. "Small, but part of something wonderful, I hope?"

"Wonderful, but unexpected," I whispered, acknowledging the magic woven into our unforeseen rendezvous. "When I first met you, you didn't strike me as the romantic type," I teased.

Caleb grinned. "There's more to me than motocross, you know."

As we reluctantly tore ourselves away from the mesmerizing shoreline, I felt the enchantment of the evening lingering in every step. Caleb's hand in mine provided a steady anchor as we strolled back towards the campsite.

As we returned to camp I called out to Dad, "Hey, have you heard from Randall?"

Dad's eyes crinkled at the corners as he shook his head, a concerned look was on his face. "Not yet. He's probably out there tearing it up. I hope he isn't taking too many risks."

THE NEXT MORNING ALL THE RACERS STARTED STRAGGLING in. Randall didn't win, but he enjoyed the experience and had made some connections in the racing world.

"Hey, guys, I've been invited to race in a qualifying race in Rancho Cordova in September. This could be the start of something amazing." Randall's voice was filled with anticipation.

"That's wonderful, son. Keep being smart and don't take any unnecessary risks and we'll continue to support you." Dad took a drag on his cigarette.

"Hey, Twyla, what happened with Caleb? Word's out he had some engine trouble and left the race halfway through. You don't know anything about that, do you?" Randall looked at me pointedly.

"Engine trouble? Umm, no comment on the engine trouble but he did take me out on a horse-riding date yesterday and he asked for my number, so I think I've had more fun in Mexico than all the racers combined." I chuckled.

"Well, he looks like a nice guy and everything, but you should be careful. Guys like that are always on the road and have a girlfriend in every city," Randall warned.

"We'll see about that." I tried to sound confident, but Randall's words had shaken me. I was stimulated by the possibilities with Caleb, but could this all be a game to him? Only time would tell.

CHAPTER 13
Wild Side
RANCHO CORDOVA, CALIFORNIA
FALL 1976

Twyla Cameron
Sixteen Years Old

O ver the next few months, I received several calls from Caleb, each filled with tales of his adventures on the road. He spoke of breathtaking landscapes, unexpected challenges, and his love for the racing community. Postcards arrived regularly, showcasing the various cities he visited on his journey, they all ended with the same line. "Can't wait to see you in September."

The next few months of summer dragged on, but eventually the anticipation for the Rancho Cordova race in September mounted. As Randall's excitement grew, my own eagerness did as well.

Caleb's postcards and phone calls had remained consistent, and he started calling me every Friday night. We'd spent countless hours on the phone talking. He sent small gifts and souvenirs from each city he was racing in. I'm sure it had cost him a small fortune in long-distance fees. I found myself eagerly awaiting our rendezvous in Rancho Cordova.

Finally, the Hangtown Motocross event was upon us, and I was filled with fervor. What would it be like to see Caleb after all these months of separation? Would our spark still be there?

"Stop fiddling with your hair. You look amazing." At eighteen, Rory had shed her Disco Bunny phase and went fully into a Glam Rock phase. Her hair was dyed platinum blonde and cut into a shaggy mane. She embodied the spirit of her idol David Bowie. To me, she was the same old Rory, untamed and tough on the outside but sweet and thoughtful on the inside.

"Do you think it's true what Randall said about the racers having a girlfriend in every city?"

"If that's the case, your boy must be loaded because all those long-distance phone calls and gifts he sends can't be cheap. He wouldn't be able to afford another girlfriend with all his spending," Rory retorted, a teasing smirk on her face.

"You're probably right."

"By the way, did you ask him about setting me up with one of those hot Silverson brothers of his? I'm not picky. They're all cute," she added with a playful wink.

"Yes, Cal is going to be here. We're all planning to grab some pizza after the race. Oh, there's Caleb." I pointed, noticing a handsome racer making his way toward us. Caleb's gaze was as piercing as I remember. Blue, clear, and intense, they appeared to be scanning the landscape, looking for his next challenge.

"Hey there, Twyla. Fancy running into you here." Clad in his protective riding gear that shielded him from the elements, Caleb jumped the rail to engulf me in a big bear hug. "Hi, Rory. Ready for a double date later?"

"Ready and willing," Rory fired back.

"I've got about an hour while the amateurs race. Want to go for a walk?" Caleb suggested.

"Absolutely. See you later, Rory," I bid my farewells to my sister, ready for some alone time with Caleb.

"What about Randall's race?" Rory questioned.

"We can catch it from the VIP suite," Caleb replied.

"Meet me back here in an hour?"

"Sure thing, sis." I yelled back as Caleb took my hand and whisked me away.

"I know we haven't known each other for long, but I can see a future with you, Twyla," he said earnestly.

I hesitated before softly responding, "Caleb, I appreciate that, but I still have two years of high school left."

"Wait, you're only a junior? I thought you were about the graduate this year. Don't you have to be eighteen to work at a restaurant?" The shock on Caleb's face was evident.

I nervously chuckled, realizing the misunderstanding. "I work at a fast food restaurant. You only have to be sixteen to work there. I'm still navigating the halls of high school during the day, and I work most evenings and weekends serving up chicken and fries."

"How old exactly are you?" he questioned.

"Don't worry, I'll be eighteen soon enough." It wasn't an outright lie, but in truth, I wouldn't be eighteen for another sixteen months. I was afraid to say I was just sixteen, afraid to lose this gorgeous and interesting man I was falling for. "How old are you?"

"I'm nineteen in May. I suppose January is only a few months away. I'm sorry I didn't ask sooner. You act so responsible and mature for your age. I assumed Rory was the younger sister, she's so daring and rebellious. More like my little sisters." Caleb nervously ran his hand through his hair.

"Everyone thinks that. She also has that round babyface. I inherited the Cherokee high cheekbones. I don't look much like my siblings. My age doesn't change anything, does it?" I asked, searching his piercing blue eyes for a reaction.

"No. I like you, Twyla. Probably too much. You know, my parents are a few years apart, and it's working out for them," he added, taking my hand in his. "How about a good luck kiss before my next race?"

We spent the next half hour kissing passionately in a secluded corner of the stands. The misunderstanding about my age was temporarily forgotten.

"You'd better be off to your race soon." I broke away from Caleb's caress just as things were heating up. I hadn't made out this long with anyone before, and my body felt like it was on fire.

"I suppose you're right, as usual. What would I do without you?" he laughed as we both made our way to the door. "Let's get you back to your family, little high school girly."

"Don't you *dare* start calling me that." I playfully smacked his arm.

As we made our way to the stands, the gravity of our conversation weighed profoundly on my heart. I hated to mislead him, but I'd never had such an instant connection with anyone my age. They were like little boys, Caleb was different.

The lively atmosphere of the motocross interrupted my thoughts; I'd have to worry about it later. I couldn't change things now and I found Rory in the stands and directed my attention to the race that was about to start.

"Are you okay? You look all flushed," Rory commented.

"Everything's fine. I told Caleb I wasn't eighteen yet,"

"How did he take it?'

"Well, he wasn't thrilled, but he wasn't mad either. Now let's focus on the race." I tried to change the subject. I didn't want to tell Rory about the rest.

I waved at Caleb as he revved his engine, ready to hit the track. I wished him luck with a smile as the gate dropped and the racers lurched forward, the thunderous roar of their engines drowning out the crowd's cheers. The intensity of the motocross race consumed my attention, pushing aside the concerns about our age difference.

Caleb skillfully navigated the twists and jumps, showcasing his prowess on the track. As he approached the first corner, he maneuvered his position to the front of the racers, the dirt flying beneath his tires. The atmosphere buzzed with energy, and I found myself cheering for him with abandonment.

Unexpectedly, the exhilarating sound of engines and the cheers of the crowd turned chaotic as a deafening crash echoed through the air. A few of the riders collided with one another.

"Where's Caleb?" Panic gripped my heart as I frantically scanned the track for any sign of him. The crowd shared a collective gasp, as I held my breath. The atmosphere was charged with tension.

Randall rushed to my side. His face, once radiant with the thrill of his motocross victory, now mirrored the concern etched across my own face. The motocross track, which had witnessed triumphs and celebrations, now became a stage for a different kind of drama.

Time froze as the scene unfolded before me. My heart raced as the gravity of the situation became apparent.

Medical personnel rushed to the scene, and a wave of concern washed over the spectators. I made my way through the crowd, desperately searching for any signs of Caleb's condition. The air was thick with tension as the paramedics worked to stabilize him and eventually took him away to the closest hospital.

"Let's follow the ambulance. Come on, girls. Hurry up," Randall called out as he grabbed my hand.

"I'll stay back and let everyone know where you went," Buck chimed in. All my brothers and their families were here to watch Randall race, the only one missing was Susan and her family.

"Thank you, brother," Randall squeezed our oldest brother's shoulder. "Twyla, Rory, you come with me. Mom and Dad can follow in their truck."

As we made our way to Randall's vehicle, he gave me a little pep talk. "Listen, Twy, this is the risk every rider takes. It's not about if you'll crash, but when. Caleb's strong, he's got the best gear money can buy. Let's hope for the best. When I was away, I had to learn how to have faith again. It's a light in the darkest times."

I climbed into the truck next to my brother in stunned silence. This was the first time I'd heard him reference his time in Vietnam since the day of his wedding. I grabbed his hand and squeezed it, in support.

"Thank you, Randall. Let's just go to the hospital and see what they say."

Soon we arrived at the ER and navigated the sterile, dimly lit corridors of the hospital to the waiting room, the air thick with the scent of antiseptic and underlying worry. The space was a stark, muted palette with linoleum floors boasting patterns long out of style and walls painted a faded, once-cheerful yellow, now dulled by time. There amongst the worn vinyl chairs we encountered Caleb's family.

Their Nordic heritage was evident in their towering stature and waves of blonde hair, that created a sharp contrast against the room's drab interior. His parents, and brother Cal, paced relentlessly, each step echoing on the hard flooring.

"You must be Twyla. I'm Caleb's dad. I wish we had met under better circumstances. Caleb speaks highly of you." His father was a stern figure, his hands toughened into concrete from a lifetime of rigorous tree work and handling lumber, betraying the rugged life he led. He was built like Caleb and had those intense blue eyes; his head was shaved clean, and he had a no-nonsense demeanor.

"It's nice to meet you, sir. I can't believe this is happening. Has there been any word from the doctors?"

"They are still working on him. He's in surgery for a broken jaw. I'm sure he'll be alright. He's got to be."

Suddenly a doctor entered the room, interrupting our conversation. "I have news about Caleb Silverson." The doctor paused as if to gather his thoughts. "The surgery was successful, but he's currently in a medically induced coma. It's a necessary step for his recovery. You can see him now, but I recommend going home and getting some rest. We will wake him *slowly* tomorrow."

"Thank you, Doctor," Caleb's Dad responded, his voice steady despite the turmoil of emotions, while his mom quietly shed tears of relief, each one a symbol of the fear and love intertwined in her heart.

"Perhaps we should go and leave the Silverson's to be alone with their son," Dad suggested, his words a gentle nudge towards giving their family some space during this difficult time.

"It's okay, you're welcome to stay. I know Caleb would want to see Twyla when he wakes up. She's all he's talked about since they met in Mexico," Caleb's mom assured, her voice carrying a warmth that softened the sterile, tense atmosphere of the hospital.

Before she could finish, Mom carefully interjected, her voice a soothing balm in the tense atmosphere. "I can stay another night here with Twyla. We both need to be here for Caleb when he wakes up."

I felt a quiet resilience radiate from her, and it bolstered my own resolve. Looking into my parents' faces I felt a profound connection, an unspoken understanding. "Thank you, Mom," I murmured, gratitude and determination intermingling in my voice. "I need to be here. Caleb is – he's everything to me. I can't leave before he wakes up."

Rory, a steady presence of quiet support, spoke up. "I'll stay too."

Dad, absorbing our words, nodded slowly, his eyes reflecting both pride and concern. "Randall and I will drive back tonight. We have responsibilities at home, but you three stay another night in the motel. Be there for Caleb when he wakes up tomorrow. We'll leave Randall's truck for you to drive home. Is that okay, son?"

"Whatever Twyla needs. I told you I'm here for you, sis. Do you want me to stay too?"

"No, you go back to your family, but we'd appreciate you leaving the truck."

"I can drop you off at work tomorrow," Dad chimed in. "Dawn, you call the hotel and book an extra night."

"Don't worry, honey. He's a young man, and young men heal up quick. You need to lock those worries up into a box in your mind until we know what we are dealing with." Mom gave me a quick hug before making her way to the pay phone.

In that compact, hushed room, a silent pact was formed. Though the path ahead was uncertain and fraught with apprehension, one thing was resolute – we would face it together, as a family, each of us supporting the others in the ways we were best able.

The next day, as Caleb emerged from his coma, we met his mom in the hospital waiting room. She exuded a grace reminiscent of a 1950s sitcom. Her hair, a soft wave of dark blonde, framed her face elegantly. Despite the unease evident in her face, she maintained a composed demeanor, her quiet strength serving as a pillar for the family during this tumultuous time. Her presence in the room, poised yet reassuring, offered a silent promise of resilience and hope.

"Don't be shocked at how he looks," she had warned as we approached the hospital room. "The doctors are optimistic about his recovery, and the bruising should subside, with time."

Yet, as we entered the room, my heart dropped. There was Caleb, his gaze meeting mine, and a wave of longing crashed over me. I rushed to his side, my fingers entwined with his. The sight of the bandages swathing his jaw and his form propped up, sipping through a straw, sent a pang of anxiety through me, yet his eyes still sparkled with that familiar, comforting light.

Caleb motioned for a pen and paper, eagerness in his eyes. He slid the note across with that playful glint still on his face. Unfolding it, I found his untidy handwriting spelling out a question that made my cheeks flush with surprise and tenderness, *Will you marry me when you turn eighteen?*

"Oh, Caleb," I murmured, my voice a blend of affection and concern. "Let's focus on your healing first, okay? How are you feeling? Does it hurt a lot?"

Caleb's mom's voice, light yet realistic, filled the space. "He's on quite a bit of pain medication, dear. It might be best to not take his proposals seriously right now."

With a knowing smile, Mom gently ushered Mrs. Silverson out for coffee, leaving Caleb and me in a cocoon of quiet intimacy. As the door clicked shut, I turned back to Caleb, my heart aching yet full, ready to be there for him through every step of this unexpected journey.

"I was so worried about you," I stroked his arm as Caleb wrote out another note.

Don't listen to my Mom. I may be all doped up, but you will be my wife one day.

OVER THE NEXT FEW DAYS, CALEB SLOWLY STARTED SHOWING signs of improvement, and was finally released from the hospital. The road to recovery would be long, but knowing he was on the mend brought a glimmer of light to my world. I returned to high school and in the weeks that followed, the motocross community rallied around Caleb, offering support and best wishes for his recovery.

As Caleb started rehabilitation, I couldn't help but wonder if he was serious about getting married in a few short months. How was I ever going to tell him I wasn't going to be eighteen for another year?

CHAPTER 14

Being With You

REDLANDS, CALIFORNIA

EARLY 1977

Twyla Cameron
Seventeen Years Old

"I'm sorry, Twyla, I'm not going to be able to drive up tonight. I've run into some car trouble." Caleb was on the other end of the phone.

"That's fine, I'll find something else to do." I slammed the phone down and couldn't help but wonder if Caleb was telling the truth. Things progressed quickly after his racing accident, and he often talked about wanting to marry, but I kept telling him we'd have to wait until graduation. Still, this last-minute cancellation didn't sit well with me.

"Why the long face, sis?" Rory hopped up on the kitchen counter, her bare legs swinging back and forth.

"Caleb canceled on me. Apparently, he's having engine trouble," I grumbled.

"Don't you believe him?"

"I guess I do, but I've been looking forward to going to the fair all week. I've done my hair and makeup and even bought a new shirt to wear."

"We can still go. Call Keith Simpson. He's always mooning over you. I'm sure he'd jump at the chance to take you out tonight. He'd probably cancel whatever plans he already has. I'm going with my boyfriend, so we can double." Rory had a devilish glint in her gaze.

"Do you think I should?"

"Show Caleb you aren't sitting around waiting by the phone for him to call whenever he wants. You're a woman in demand."

"Ok, I'll do it." I picked up the phone and invited Keith to be the fourth on our double date. He was more than happy to oblige.

"Far out." Rory smirked.

It was true, Keith had a huge crush on me since junior high, and we had a couple of dates my freshman year. He was a nice enough guy and had matured physically from that gangly paperboy I once knew, but I ended it because he was a bit too eager and clingy. Maybe he'd outgrown it?

THAT NIGHT AT THE COUNTY FAIR, UNDER THE VIBRANT lights of the fun zone, a sense of guilt nagged at me. Keith acted sweet and was still eager to impress, even winning me a stuffed bear at the ring toss, but my thoughts kept drifting back to Caleb. Part of me couldn't shake off the feeling I was betraying Caleb's trust.

"I'm glad you called tonight." Keith looked deep into my eyes.

As the Ferris wheel ascended, I felt a pang of unease. The night was supposed to be about letting loose and having fun, but the joy was tainted by the knowledge Caleb should have been there instead.

Despite Keith's genuine efforts to cheer me up, my mind drifted back to Caleb. "I'm sorry, Keith, I'm not feeling that well. Do you mind if we end our night early?"

"No problem. Let's head back to the car and get you home," Despite my guilt for coming out with another boy, I was starting to see another side of Keith. He was considerate and understanding about me, not being in the best mood.

"Keith, you are such a decent guy and all, but I've been dating Caleb Silverson. He stood me up tonight and so I was trying to teach him a lesson. It was wrong and I shouldn't have done it." I looked up into Keith's hopeful face.

"Oh, I knew you were dating Caleb. The whole school knows. I figured this was my last chance to win you back. I guess I failed miserably?"

"You really are a good guy, but I'm starting to realize I care for Caleb more than I knew. However, I'm not sure if I'm ready to be so serious." I sighed.

"Don't fret, Twyla, you'll figure it out, and know I'm always here for you. As a friend or more." Keith caressed my hand as we drove home.

When Keith walked me to the door, the unexpected sound of an engine roaring broke the night's stillness. There, in his brother's truck, was Caleb, revving the engine and burning rubber on the street in a dramatic display. Neighbors peeked out of their windows, alerted by the commotion. Caleb looked at me, his eyes an intense blue, his hands gripped the steering wheel. The quiet night had turned into a spectacle, with Caleb's impulsive behavior at the center.

"Caleb, what are you doing here?" I asked, a blend of surprise and annoyance in my voice. I had never seen this side of him.

He jumped out of the truck, his expression filled with accusation. "I was able to borrow my brother's truck, and when I called to tell you, your mom said you went out with another guy." Caleb pointed at Keith.

"I don't have beef with you. Nothing happened, we are family friends," Keith shot back.

The front door creeped open. "Excuse me, fellas. Let's cool things down out here." Mom appeared on the porch, dressed in her robe. "Now Twyla, you need to pick one of these boys here. It's not proper for a girl to be running around town with two boyfriends."

"I'm with Caleb. Keith is just a friend. Right?"

"Of course, Twyla," Keith replied, looking down at his feet.

Caleb extended his hand with evident tension. "Heard a bit about you. Thanks for looking after my girl tonight."

Keith nodded, recognizing the awkwardness. "No problem, Caleb. I just wanted Twyla to have a fun evening; rest assured, her heart is with you."

There was an uncomfortable silence before Caleb turned his attention back to me. His gaze, usually so full of confidence, now reflected a vulnerability I hadn't seen before. "Twyla, I'm sorry about earlier. The engine trouble was real, and I hated missing our plans. Hearing you went out with another guy. It about drove me crazy. I thought I'd lost you."

A torrent of emotions churned inside me. "Caleb, I believe you. Tonight was a mistake. I'm glad you're here now, but don't ever do something like that again. Racing around the street, you could have hurt someone."

"I won't do it again." He looked deep into my eyes. "Scout's honor." He raised his right hand.

Mom, who was still standing on the porch, cleared her throat, signaling an end to the tension. "Enough drama for one night. Caleb, you're welcome to come in for a bit. Keith, say hello to your mom for me."

As Keith left with a polite wave, he said, "I'll see you at school on Monday."

"Mrs. Cameron, do you think I could take your

daughter with me to Bob's Big Boy? We could share one of those hot fudge cakes she likes so much," he asked.

"It's fine. Be home by midnight. And Caleb, don't let me catch you driving like that again." Mom gave Caleb a stern look.

"Yes, Mrs. Cameron."

Relief washed over me as Caleb's smile returned, that familiar spark returned to his eyes. "That sounds perfect, Caleb. There's nothing I'd rather do." In that moment, the tension lifted, replaced by the warm glow of forgiveness and the promise of shared memories yet to come.

CHAPTER 15

Landslide

REDLANDS, CALIFORNIA
FEBRUARY 14TH, 1977

Twyla Cameron
Seventeen Years Old

"Are you sure you are ready for this?" Caleb gently held my hand. We'd been dating now for almost six months, and finally decided it was time to take our relationship to the next level.

"I'm ready, I love you and I want this." I smiled softly. We were at the nicest hotel in town, and, after a romantic Valentine's dinner, we found ourselves making out on the hotel bed.

"I'm in love with you, Caleb, and want this Valentine's night to be special. But before we make love, there is something I have to tell you." I nervously fiddled with the hem of my skirt.

"What is it?"

I took a deep breath and let it out. "I'm not eighteen yet."

"What are you saying?"

"I just turned seventeen, but you can't be mad at me on Valentine's Day. It's a rule." I smiled at Caleb and batted my eyelashes.

"Oh, Twy, I already knew. After my accident, I went to see your dad about asking for your hand. He spilled the beans, and we had a long talk. He's fine with us dating, but marriage would have to wait until you graduate from school."

"Why didn't you tell me? I've been worried about keeping this secret."

"I knew you'd tell me when you were ready. I'd already fallen in love with you, and I couldn't stay away, even if I wanted. I'm in love with you." he confessed.

I kissed him softly on the lips. I felt a flutter inside as he removed my top and traced a line of kisses down my stomach. I let out a soft moan and laid back on the bed. "Caleb, do you have protection?"

"Yes, I picked some up on my way here, but we don't need that yet. I want to take my time with this. Your first time is going to be special." He gently started kissing my neck. A tingling sensation spread throughout my body and I felt so safe.

With Caleb, time had a way of both standing still and rushing by, each second brimming with an intensity that made everything else fade away. The trust between us had grown steadily, a silent pact that was now as natural as breathing. As I lay there, soaking in his warmth and the sincerity in his every caress, I knew that this wasn't a fleeting chapter in our lives or some schoolgirl crush.

I was in love with Caleb Silverson.

SOON, WE WERE MAKING LOVE ON A REGULAR BASIS. BEING with Caleb consumed my mind, I wanted to be with him every second.

I had always been the responsible, quiet girl who loved to read and followed the rules of society. I had big dreams for a career in writing, and Caleb had plans to take over his father's tree business. I continued to daydream about our future together during my second period gym glass.

"Heads up" one of the girls from my class shouted.

"Twyla, get in the game. No more daydreaming," the gym teacher ordered.

My body was there, on the court, but my mind was miles away, lost in thoughts of the evening ahead with Caleb, completely absorbed in the exuberance of young love.

I positioned myself under the fast-flying volleyball, trying to keep my mind on the game. As the ball flew over the net, my vision swirled. The gym, once sharply outlined by the glare of fluorescent lights and the crisp lines of the court, transformed into a blur of indistinct shapes and colors. The game's noises, the cheers and calls of my class-mates, echoed as if from a distant place.

The floor beneath me shifted, the whole world tilting off-axis. My hands, poised to return the serve, now reached out desperately for something stable. But it was no use. The cool, hard gym floor rushed up to meet me, and a blanket of darkness took hold as I fainted, out cold.

When my senses trickled back, I was greeted by the waxy smell of the volleyball court.

"Who wants to walk Twyla to the nurse?" Mrs. Ramirez asked, concern evident in her voice.

"I'll take her," Toni Garcia, my good friend from down the street chimed in.

"Can you get up on your own?" Mrs. Ramirez looked at me with a concerned expression.

"I think so." I slowly started to stand as Toni took my arm and we made our way out of the gymnasium. "Are you feeling okay? You're as white as a sheet."

"I've been fighting off this stomach bug and didn't eat breakfast." I rubbed my stomach.

The nurse's office was a cramped room at the back of the school with a couple of cots in the corner. The nurse with a calm, steady voice cut through the haze in my mind, "You passed out, Twyla. I'll call your mom, but you should be checked by a doctor, to make sure it's nothing serious."

My mind raced, a cyclone of what-ifs and maybes. I

drifted off to sleep on the cot only to be woken up a short time later by the creaking door.

"Your sister is here to collect you," the nurse called out.

Rory furrowed her brow with concern. "Mom's tied up, so she sent me. How are you holding up, sleeping beauty?"

Leaning against Rory, we made our way to her lemon-yellow truck. I sank into the passenger seat, enveloped by the familiar, comforting scent of clove cigarettes and air freshener, "I've been better."

As we drove away from school, Rory cast a worried look my way. "You're not looking that well and you've never fainted before. What is going on? Did you eat breakfast?"

The trees outside blurred as I let out a sigh. "I've been so tired lately. I think I'm fighting off a stomach bug. I've been throwing up this past week."

Rory's grip on the steering wheel tightened, her anxiety palpable. Her voice broke through my thoughts. "When was your last period, Twy? Can you remember?"

"You don't think I could be pregnant? We've been using condoms and being safe." I felt a heavy, almost suffocating tension in the air.

"You can still become pregnant even with condoms. They aren't foolproof, you know. How long has it been?"

I bit my lip, my mind racing back through the days and weeks, trying to pin down a memory just out of reach. "I can't remember my last period, Rory. Everything's been such a blur lately," I confessed, the admission sending a shiver down my spine.

Rory reached out, her hand squeezing mine reassuringly. "It's okay, Twy. We'll make you an appointment with Doctor Maybe. I'll take you and we don't have to say anything to Mom until we know for sure. It's probably a little stomach bug."

THAT EVENING, CALEB ARRIVED FOR OUR DATE AS PLANNED, but instead of going out, he carried a tepid pot of his mom's chicken soup in hand.

"Sorry it's not that hot, I hit a bit of traffic. Want me to heat it up on the stove? This chicken soup cures everything."

I managed a weak smile. "You know you didn't have to come all this way to play nurse." I pulled the blanket tighter around me.

"I wanted to see you. I'm not worried about catching anything, I'm healthy as a horse." He lightly pounded his chest with his free hand.

"Thanks for the soup. It smells amazing, but I've been feeling nauseous. I don't think I can stomach it just now."

Caleb's brow furrowed, his hand feeling my forehead. "I'm sorry, Twy. What do you think it is? Fainting in gym class isn't normal. I'm worried about you." His voice was gentle with concern.

"There's something else. I can't remember when I had my last period," I confessed, my voice barely above a whisper, the pressure of my admission heavy in the air.

Caleb's jaw tightened, the realization of my words hitting him like a tidal wave. "Oh, Twy. You don't think you're... We'll work it out together. I'm here now. You don't have to worry."

"I have a doctor's appointment in the morning. Hopefully it's a false alarm. Rory is going to take me; I don't want Mom to know what we suspect yet. She's going to kill me if I'm pregnant."

"I'll take you to the appointment tomorrow. I'll call off work. Will your parents let me stay on the sofa?" His words, sincere and steady, offered me comfort amidst the current of my worries. In his presence, the fear that had been quietly gnawing at me seemed a little less daunting.

"She didn't seem to mind last time you stayed over, as long as you stayed on the couch. They know it's a long drive to San Clemente."

THE NEXT DAY AT THE DOCTOR'S OFFICE, THE STERILE SMELL of antiseptic hung in the air. It was a stark contrast to the comfort of Caleb's presence beside me. We sat together in the waiting room, his hand clasped mine as a silent promise of support.

"Twyla Cameron," the nurse called out.

As my name was called, I felt a flutter of nerves. Caleb gave my hand a reassuring squeeze before I stood up. "I'll be right here, Twyla. No matter what."

The examination room was clinical and cold. Dr. Maybe was the same person who delivered me, who stitched me up when I fell off my bike, and so much more. As usual, his words were professional and precise, cutting through the silence with the sharpness of reality.

The sway of his white lab coat reflected a certain weariness. His smile held kindness, yet his demeaner revealed a professionalism that kept me at a distance. "Twyla, let's discuss your last menstrual cycle," he questioned, settling onto a stool as he flipped open a well-worn chart.

As Dr. Maybe probed into my health, I found myself stumbling over the details of my last period again. The questions felt invasive, and the awkwardness of discussing such intimate matters made my cheeks redden.

"Let's run a blood test to rule out anemia," the doctor said with a tight expression on his face.

I rolled up my sleeve as he drew some blood, the antiseptic scent of the room filled the air, as I perched on the frigid examination table. When it was all over, I found Caleb in the waiting room, his wide eyes searched mine for answers.

"They said I can call on Tuesday to get the results. It takes a few days."

"Okay, all we can do now is wait and see. Let's go grab some food on the way home."

"I don't have an appetite right now."

"You need to eat. You're looking so frail. Is there

anything you've been craving? What about one of those hot fudge cakes you like so much?"

"I could try to eat some ice cream, no pickles though." I laughed at my feeble attempt at a joke. "There's a Bob's Big Boy around the corner."

"I'm happy to see you haven't lost your sense of humor. Let's grab a bite to eat."

As we settled into the booth, the hum of conversation and the clinking of silverware surrounded us. Caleb ordered the blueberry pancakes while I had the ice cream cake. Tension hung thick in the air like a heavy fog.

"If the test comes back positive, I want us to get married and raise our baby together, I've always wanted to marry you. It may have to be sooner than we planned, but your dad can't say no if you're pregnant." Caleb declared.

"I'm not looking forward to telling my parents, Mom always talks about me becoming a teacher. If the test is positive, I'll have to leave school, and she'll be devastated."

"*If* we have to tell them. This could be a false alarm."

"You're right," I said, though deep down, I was certain the test would be positive; I could feel it in my bones. A tightness formed around my throat, and a warm swell of emotions threatened to overflow.

"Twyla, no matter what happens, we're in this together. You're not alone." Caleb's hand intertwined with mine, and at his touch, I could feel the tightness slowly dissipate. But the 'what ifs' kept circling in my mind like vultures.

As we left the restaurant, my heart pounded against my

chest and the drive home was quiet, each of us lost in our own thoughts, the unknown future stretched out before us like a winding road, shrouded in fog.

THE NEXT DAYS WERE THE LONGEST OF MY LIFE. CALEB stayed by my side most of the weekend, until Monday morning came, and he had to work while I went back to high school. The hours dragged on until it was finally Tuesday, and I made my way to the school payphone during lunch.

"Doctor Maybe's office," the receptionist answered on the other end.

"This is Twyla Cameron calling for my test results."

"Yes, Ms. Cameron, the test came back positive. We'll need to set up a follow up appointment and get you on prenatal vitamins."

The moment the words hit my ears, it was as if time slowed down, each syllable hit me in the very pit of my stomach. A coldness swept through me, as I tried to find my voice again.

"I-I'll call back this afternoon to make that appointment." I stammered before I hung up to call home.

"Rory, I need you."

"I'll be right there."

Once again, I made my way to the nurse's office to notify them I wasn't feeling well, and my sister was coming to pick me up. My mind was swimming, and I couldn't face Honors English class right now. What was the point? Pregnant girls weren't allowed to attend high school and I'd be forced to drop out soon enough.

"Rory, we need to talk," I murmured, as I climbed into her lemon-yellow truck. I swallowed, my heart hammered against my ribs like a ferocious drum. "The test came back positive, I'm pregnant."

I could see the flicker of fear in my sister's wide-eyed surprise, yet she tried to appear calm. "Are you sure? I mean, maybe the test was wrong."

"It's not some cheap drugstore test," I shot back. "It was a medical test. I'm sure."

We were submerged in a silence as thick as molasses.

"I was hoping it was a false alarm. What are you going to do now?" Rory finally asked.

"I think I'm going to keep it," I confessed. My fingers nervously twisted the hem of my skirt as I sought solace in the familiar texture. "I need your support now more than ever. I'm not looking forward to telling Mom."

Rory's gaze softened as she looked over at me. "Let me know when you plan to tell her, so I can leave town. She's going to blow her top, you know."

"Thanks for the support, sis."

"I'm only teasing, I'm here for you, no matter what. You know that is true." Abruptly, Rory turned the wheel, directing us away from home.

"Rory, where on earth are we headed?" I must've looked like a deer caught in the headlights.

"We're going to our favorite place in the world, we both need a breather. I mean, your life is about to change, and I want us to remember how things were before this all went down." Rory reached over and squeezed my hand as she started heading up the winding roads of the mountain ahead.

Soon we arrived at the Mt. Baldy Ski Lodge.

"I'll grab us some to-go cups of cocoa. You wait here and pop the tailgate down."

Soon we were wrapped in the warmth of steaming Styrofoam cups of cocoa, our cheeks reddened with the crisp air, the rich liquid warmed us from within. The silence around us was thick but oddly soothing.

"You know you have options." Rory delicately broke the silence.

"I know, but I can't see myself having an abortion. I mean, I'm scared and all, but this life growing inside me is a part of Caleb. I do love him. He wants to marry me."

"Are you sure you're ready for that? What about adoption? Remember Christina Silva? She got pregnant last year and went away for her pregnancy to some place out of state. Later, she gave the baby to a loving family who keep sending her pictures and updates."

"I thought Christina was off to some fancy school back east?" I quizzed, baffled.

"Nope. That's what her mom told everyone to hush the

town gossips. I don't know why people act so shocked, everyone I know is having sex outside of marriage," she ranted, the feminist in her getting the best of her.

"Well, you've always been open-minded. Most folks around here are still holding on to traditional beliefs."

"Traditional? I prefer to call it antiquated," she retorted.

"Whatever you want to call it, I'm going to be dealing with it in spades when I start showing."

"Well, it sounds like you made up your mind and I say to hell with what everyone thinks. I'll pick the biggest fight with anyone who even looks sideways at you, sis."

"I know. You're right, it's my life. I wish people would see beyond the old-school gossip and understand that times are different now. That we're all trying to do our best." I sighed, the weight of this decision and the societal pressures washed over me. "But no matter what, I need to do what is right for me and this child."

THE FOLLOWING WEEK I FOUND MYSELF PARKED OUTSIDE the family home in Redlands Caleb's hand, rough but comforting, engulfed mine in a silent pledge of partnership.

"Are you ready for this?" Caleb asked,
"Are you sure we need to do this now? Maybe we should wait until I start showing?" With the shared whisper of our impending parenthood looming over us, the thought of

facing our parents now seemed more daunting than ever before.

"We've decided on what we're going to do, and we need to let your parents know, Twyla. It's time to step into our new roles. And remember, we're in this together. You won't have to face anything alone." His words, firm and reassuring, matched the firm grip of his hand, anchoring me amid the wave of anxiety.

Hand in hand, Caleb and I walked up to my familiar door, summoning the courage to reveal the secret we'd been keeping. Once inside, we found my parents sitting in the living room, their expressions a blend of curiosity and concern. Caleb and I exchanged a glance, a silent acknowledgment of the journey we were about to embark on together. Dad, with his greying hair and kind eyes, looked up from his newspaper, sensing the weight of our presence.

"Twyla, Caleb," he greeted, setting aside the paper. Mom, ever perceptive, studied us with a gentle furrow in her brow.

Caleb took a deep breath, his voice steady yet tinged with vulnerability. "We have something important to share with you," he squeezed my hand in reassurance. "Twyla and I have made a decision about our future."

Dad's gaze shifted between us, and trepidation etched across his features. "We know you two want to marry, but you need to wait until Twyla is finished with school."

"It's going to need to be sooner than that, sir," Caleb ran a hand through his dark blonde hair.

I cleared my throat. "Mom, Dad, Caleb and I are going to have a baby."

I choked the words out, barely holding back my tears, a delicate confession, as we braced ourselves for their reaction. Dad stood up, his expression reflected alarm. "A baby?" His eyes glistening with unshed tears.

A heavy silence blanketed the room. The impact of our decision sinking in as the room failed to resound with joy.

"Yes."

Mom broke the heavy silence, her words slicing through the air like a sharp knife. "You're only seventeen. You're too young to be facing this kind of decision. It's not the right time. You might have to consider… ending the pregnancy. You both have your whole futures ahead of you," she said, her voice red with frustration, her face etched with a deep sadness.

Dad also wore a pained expression. I felt their expectations crushing down on me, their dreams for my future now clashing with the unexpected reality growing within me.

Caleb's hand tightened around mine, a silent anchor in the cyclone of emotions. His eyes met mine, and I saw the same resolve that lit up his face when he was about to race. We were at the crossroads of our youth, where dreams collided with unplanned twists, and the choices we made would shape the rest of our lives.

"No, ma'am, we've talked it over. We are getting married and having this baby. We have known for a while that we want to spend our lives together. It's going to be sooner rather than later. I love your daughter." Caleb stood firm as he looked my parents directly in the eyes.

The unspoken grief and concern were thick in the air, casting a shadow over what is usually a traditional moment of joy. Dad's heart looked broken, and Mom looked like a volcano ready to burst.

"I'm sorry I let you down," I said in a small voice.

"I know it's a shock, and Twyla *is* very young, but I'm going to be cutting down on my racing and working for my dad's tree business. I'll be taking it over one day, so you don't have to worry about Twyla. I'll provide for her, and our child."

"Well, if that's the decision you two are adamant about, we'll need to go to Vegas and have us a wedding, right away. Mom and I are here to support you, Twyla." A single tear trickled down my father's weathered skin. I could see he was trying to put on a brave face, but he still looked devastated.

"Ellis, we need to talk about this more. We can't let her run off to get married and have a baby." The volcano that was my mother erupted.

"What are we going to do? Force her into having an abortion or adoption? We can't do that if she wants this child. I don't see what options we have? My mom was only eighteen when she had my oldest brother."

"I wanted a better life for Twyla. She's going to be an English teacher one day, but a baby will derail everything," Mom began, her frustration evident. She paused, then started again, "This is just like—" but abruptly cut herself off. Taking a deep breath, she announced, "I need to take a walk and cool down. I can't deal with this right now," and stormed out the front door. Her sudden departure left a palpable tension in her wake. Dad, Caleb, and I remained in the living room, stunned by the intensity of her reaction.

"What was she going to say? *What* is this like?" I questioned.

"Don't fret about her, she'll come around," Dad reassured, his words struggling to mask the uncertainty written across his face. "Give her some time. You know your mom, she's quick to erupt but she always comes around, once she cools down."

Caleb's hand found mine once again, the unspoken promise of unity resonating between us.

In the subsequent days, we found ourselves engulfed in endless talks, wedding arrangements, and the discussions of the opportunities the future held. I hoped we were ready to navigate the labyrinth life would throw at us, but I couldn't help but notice the tension that had taken residence over my parents. It made me wonder if there was something deeper to their unease, something they weren't sharing with me.

I heard them whispering in hushed voices, deep into the late hours of the night, and soon, I found myself yearning for the upcoming month when Caleb and I would be married, and I could escape from under the weight of their unspoken tension.

PART TWO
Twilight Silverson

You still have a lot of time to make yourself be what you want. There's still lots of good in the world.

— S.E. Hinton, The Outsiders

CHAPTER 16

Always and Forever

LAS VEGAS, NEVADA

APRIL 1977

Twilight Silverson
Seventeen Years Old

*I*t's all happening. My wedding day had arrived. The day I had dreamed about and imagined in meticulous detail, was unfurling before me in a cascade of moments too surreal to grasp. I was seventeen and about to step across a threshold that would irrevocably alter the course of my young life.

"Twyla, you're so fortunate you aren't showing yet. Your wedding photos will be exquisite," Susan's voice erupted as we entered the Silver Bells Chapel in Las Vegas.

Smiles from loved ones enveloped us, and my teen pregnancy remained safely concealed beneath the flowing gown.

Although Susan's words were meant as a compliment, they served as a stark reminder of the delicate balance I navigated between adolescence and adulthood.

Amidst the sea of well-wishers, my gaze landed on Caleb. Dressed in a powder-blue tuxedo, he embodied youthful elegance of the seventies, his long hair flowed freely through an image so handsome it made my heart flutter like a tiny hummingbird.

"Ready to take on the world?" Caleb whispered, his voice filled with determination. As we exchanged vows, a rush of contentment swept through me, like a comforting breeze on a warm summer evening. Caleb's hand in mine felt safe as he gazed into my eyes.

"Absolutely, together, always and forever," I replied as we stepped out of the chapel and into the bright Las Vegas sunlight, a shower of rice fluttered around us.

Caleb seized the moment to address our family and friends. "We're still finding our way through life. We might not be perfect, but our love is real, and we're grateful for your support today," he said, scanning the faces around us. "We're grateful to start this journey with our loved ones by our side. Join us at the Sands Casino for a night of celebration."

"Snag 'em young, bro. Raise them how you want," taunted one of Caleb's older brothers with a mischievous grin. The edgy jest echoed around us. Mom shot him a dirty look, and Cody had the good sense to look embarrassed by his comment.

"Don't mind him, he's always saying the wrong thing at the wrong time. You'll get used to it." I swallowed my disappointment, and I vowed not to let a brash comment ruin my wedding day. I needed to embrace this new chapter, and there was no turning back now. Caleb gently squeezed my hand, his gaze offering reassurance.

The jovial mood regained momentum, and we celebrated our union with a simple dinner and reception in a small events room at the Sands Hotel and Casino. As the evening unfolded, I hoped that together, we would navigate whatever challenges came our way, building a life rich in love, laughter, and cherished moments.

The night whirled by in a blur of laughter, dancing, and heartfelt toasts. As Caleb and I swayed together during our first dance as husband and wife, I felt a mix of belonging yet apprehension about becoming a mother so soon in life. Knowing Caleb and I would embark on the adventure of parenthood helped me push my worries out of my mind.

Caleb leaned in, his whisper barely audible over the music, "We've got this, love. You, me, and our little one on the way. We can do this." His words were sincere and encouraging. With our decision firmly made, there was no looking back—only the path ahead, urging us forward.

AFTER OUR VEGAS WEDDING, WE MOVED INTO A SMALL duplex Caleb rented in San Clemente. It was a modest space with secondhand furnishings and reflected the California Seaside style. The walls, painted in a faded shade of avocado green, were bare except for a small, framed photograph of us atop horses on our first date in Ensenada, Mexico.

"It may not be much, but it's walking distance to the ocean. Don't fret. You can put your stamp on this place soon enough."

"It's fine, Caleb. It has… potential." I tried to sound upbeat. "I had hoped our child would have a yard to play in."

"We'll get there one day; this is just a stepping stone to bigger and better things." It was sweet of your niece Lacey to give you her little black-and-white TV," Caleb quickly added, steering the conversation away.

'Yes, she's always thinking of others. It did catch me off guard that Mom wouldn't let me take my bedroom furniture, though," I responded.

Caleb, curious, asked, "And why do you think that is?"

"She mentioned she didn't want to break up the corner set," I replied with a shrug, feeling a sting in my heart. Our relationship had been tense ever since the confrontation over my pregnancy decision.

"Still, they covered the wedding and reception costs. That's promising, right?"

"I suppose."

"Plus, I'm confident about winning my next race. Then

we can shop for some new items," Caleb said, attempting to lift the mood with a note of optimism.

"You're right… and our little peanut will have her very own room. Should we paint it yellow? I'm thinking of a *Winnie the Pooh* theme." My spirit lifted as I thought of decorating the nursery.

"Whatever you want. I'll help you paint it. Want some scrambled eggs?" Caleb made his way to the kitchen.

"Let me clean everything up first and I'll make the eggs. You finish unloading the groceries."

"Deal," he replied.

I started to scrub the worn laminate counters. I pushed aside any anxious thoughts about how we would afford to furnish this place and buy everything we needed for a new baby. Things would soon come together, I had to be strong now for the life growing inside me.

CHAPTER 17
Love Grows
REDLANDS, CALIFORNIA
NOVEMBER 10TH, 1977

Twilight Silverson
Seventeen Years Old

"Seriously, Twyla? Another hotel on Park Place?" Caleb groaned as he handed over a wad of Monopoly money, his eyes darted between the board and his dwindling cash pile.

Friendly banter and competitive jests filled the room, setting a steady rhythm as we huddled around Randall's living room coffee table.

"All's fair in love and Monopoly." I was winning and held up my colorful bills with a triumphant grin. "You're just sore because I've got the best real estate."

Randall, ever the strategist, piped up from across the

table. "If I were you, Caleb, I'd start worrying about Twyla's empire. She's got more properties than a tycoon."

"Easy, you guys. It's just a game. I don't want a repeat of last week's fight." Maya was nestled in an armchair with a mug of hot cocoa. She had already gone bankrupt, never able to charge the rest of us rent when we landed on her properties.

"It wasn't a fight per se," I interjected, trying to downplay last week's intense game. "More like a spirited debate over the rules."

"Yeah, spirited until Twyla here decided to launch a hotel at my head," Caleb added, but his eyes were laughing, betraying the seriousness of his words.

"You two need to behave, or go straight to jail, do not pass go and no two hundred dollars," Maya laughed.

The warmth and humor were a clear contrast to the cool drumming of the rain against the windows. As the laughter faded, a sudden, sharp pain seized me, and I grabbed my belly in surprise.

As I tried to catch my breath, another sharp pain began. I gasped, clutching the edge of the coffee table. Caleb's smile faltered, his eyes meeting mine with sudden concern. "Twyla, what's wrong?" he asked, his voice cutting through the laughter like a knife.

I tried to speak, to reassure him and myself that it was nothing, but another wave of pain washed over me, more intense than the last. The Monopoly pieces blurred before my eyes, the colorful bills and property cards melding into a whirl of colors.

"I think I'm starting labor," I managed to whisper, the words sounding foreign and surreal even to my own ears.

"We need to get to the hospital now." Caleb sprang into action. He grabbed our coats and Bronco keys while Maya scrambled to retrieve my purse. The room erupted into a flurry of movement, each gesture precise and purposeful, as I attempted to time the moments between my contractions.

"Will you let the rest of the Camerons know?" Caleb's voice cut through the urgency, directed at Randall.

"Sure thing, just take care of my baby sister," Randall replied with a determined nod.

As we rushed out into the night, the reality of the moment struck me like a bolt of lightning. I was on the brink of bringing a living human being into the world. I eased into the passenger's seat of our little Bronco, and we surged forward toward Palomar Medical Center and toward our future as new parents.

"How far apart are the contractions? Will we make it all the way to Laguna Hills?" Caleb asked.

"They aren't too close. We'll make it."

An hour later, we arrived at the hospital, the glowing lights of the entrance beckoned us forward into the unknown as another painful contraction wracked through my petite frame.

"She's only seventeen," I heard the nurse whisper to the doctor.

"Twyla, we're here, baby girl. We got here as soon as we heard." It seemed like moments later Mom and Rory came to be by my side. "Caleb, you go wait outside in the waiting room. We'll take it from here."

"Can't he stay?" The sweat dripped down my face as I felt a pang of fear at the thought of Caleb leaving me.

"The men usually stay in the waiting room," the nurse advised. "He can come back when this is all over."

"I'll be right down the hall if you need me." Caleb looked at me apologetically.

"Ellis is out there with some cigars," Mom added.

The next few hours passed in a whirlwind of pain and anticipation. Each contraction felt like an eternity, gripping me in its relentless haze of pain and medication. Mom and Rory hovered nearby; their reassuring presence provided solace amidst the agony of childbirth.

As the medical staff bustled around me, I couldn't shake the nagging feeling of being unprepared for what lay ahead. I tried to calm my nerves by focusing on the rhythmic sound of the hospital monitors and with one final push, Celeste Starla Silverson made her way into the world. Her cries echoed through the room. My anxiety slowly dissipated in a cloud of maternal instincts as I held my baby girl in my arms for the very first time.

"She's as beautiful as her mom, but look, she has my hands," Caleb admitted.

"Would you like to hold her?" I gazed up at him.

"You bet I would." He cradled our newborn daughter

with a tenderness that warmed my heart. In that moment, I saw a glimpse of the father he would become—a man devoted to his family, unwavering in his love and support. "My little sea star," he softly whispered.

We had affectionately nicknamed our baby during the last trimester and in her tiny form, I saw the embodiment of our love, a testament to the bond that bound us together as a family.

"I've read that most babies are born with blue eyes, but I think hers have a hint of green," I said, managing a smile despite my exhaustion. As I spoke, I noticed Caleb's gaze on our daughter, filled with an unmistakable depth of love. Having grown up with several younger siblings, Caleb seemed to approach fatherhood with a natural ease, applying the same effortless grace he brought to every challenge that came his way.

"Whatever color they end up, I think she's the most beautiful thing I've ever seen."

Suddenly, Celeste, with her tiny fists grabbed onto her dad's finger. "Did you see that? She's already advanced!" Caleb exclaimed.

Having navigated the challenges of childbirth, I now felt a newfound strength coursing through me. The pain and apprehension of labor gave way to a profound sense of peace and overwhelming love for my growing family. Her presence marked not only the beginning of motherhood but also a transformation within myself, into a fiercer and more protective version of the girl I once was.

A FEW WEEKS LATER, I HEARD THE RUMBLE OF DAD'S TRUCK in our driveway and ran out to greet him in front of our duplex.

"Hey, you two, I've missed you so much. Where's Mom?" I noticed Rory sitting in the passenger seat.

"Mom couldn't make it today. She wanted to stay back and make sure the pool company was doing their job. You know how she can be," Rory awkwardly explained.

"Well, come inside. I made coffee." We entered my cozy duplex and sat down around my secondhand couch. "How's the construction going? When will the pool be ready?"

"It should be done next month. Your mom is already planning a pool inauguration party, and everyone is invited." Dad chuckled.

"That sounds like Mom," I replied. "Always wanting her family close."

"I wish you'd consider taking over the house on Harvard Street, it's not too late. The renters gave their notice, and it'd be a perfect starter for you and Caleb. I'd like you to be closer to us, Twyla." Dad looked at me with a hopeful expression, but his voice was filled with concern as he looked around our tiny home.

I took a deep breath, conflicted by the prospect. The idea of returning to the familiar streets of Montclair held a certain allure, but the life Caleb and I were building in San

Clemente felt so free and independent. I was proud of the fact we were making it on our own.

"Dad, it's not that simple." My voice was tinged with hesitation. "Caleb and I have started a life here, and we have our independence. Moving back to Montclair? I don't know if Caleb will go for it."

Dad nodded understandingly, though a trace of disappointment flickered on his face. "I want what's best for you, for all of us. It's not just about the house; it's about being together as a family. Your sister is eager for you to move closer and it's not too far from your husband's wood yard business in Orange County."

"That's right, sis. I need some help planning my wedding." Rory held up her ring finger and wiggled it at me with a big smile on her face.

"I was surprised when you called to say Mitch had proposed, but you know I can still help plan your wedding, no matter where I live. I'm just a phone call away. Now let me see that ring." Mitch was the stable manager at the San Dimas Canyon Equestrian Center where Rory had been working this past year.

"Don't change the subject. Won't you consider taking over the Montclair house? We will be so close," Rory pressed. "Mitch owns a place not too far from there we'll practically be neighbors."

"I'm so happy for you, sis, but now isn't the right time to move. I just got this place looking presentable. Let's not argue about it. My mind is made up."

"Maybe we can talk about this when Caleb is here? Any word on how he's doing in the semi-final today?" Dad asked.

"Not yet, he's going to call home tonight."

"Will you let him know about my offer tonight?"

"Yes, Dad. I'll talk to him. I promise. Now do you want to hold your new grandbaby?"

Dad's eyes widened as he exclaimed, "She's the biggest newborn I've ever seen! How much did she weigh?"

"Nine pounds, nine ounces." I replied, a touch of pride in my voice. "She was too big for the newborn clothes from my baby shower. I had to exchange them all for three-month sizes."

"I'll never figure out how someone as petite as you give birth to such a big baby." Rory looked astonished.

"I'm not sure either, especially with the constant morning sickness I had."

"So, how is it being married and having a newborn?" Rory pressed.

"It's not always easy, but I'm managing. Celeste is a good baby, which helps when Caleb's away balancing his racing with his job at the wood yard." *I get lonely sometimes*, I silently added. Without a job or driver's license I longed for more companionship in the day, maybe moving closer to my family wouldn't be such a bad idea. I planned to talk to Caleb about it when he called.

"Maybe Caleb should slow down on racing and spend more time at home," Dad advised.

"He plans to, next year. He's almost through with this season and has a real chance at the world championship this year. He'll start reducing his races afterward," I explained, hoping what I said proved to be true. There was a moment of silence as my mind drifted back to Mom's obvious absence. "I know my news had come as a shock at first, but Dad, you and everyone else seemed to support our decision. Is Mom mad at me?"

"Don't worry, she's probably upset her little Twyla isn't becoming a teacher," Rory chimed in.

"She'll come around. She's not mad, it's just difficult for her." Dad looked down.

"There's something I wanted to discuss with you both, but since Mom isn't here, I'm not sure if I should wait."

"Spit it out, Twy," Rory cut in.

"I've been studying for my GED, and I want to pursue a career as a hair stylist," I shared with zeal. "I've always loved hair and makeup, and I want to start beauty school when Celeste starts preschool. I know it's a way off, but do you think it's a good idea? Caleb will reduce his racing to watch Celeste while I'm at cosmetology. What do you think?"

Dad, turning pale, dropped his coffee mug, splashing a bit of coffee on to the table. After a while, Rory asked, "Dad, are you okay? You look shocked."

"Yes, I'm fine… That's an excellent idea," he stuttered, visibly emotional. "I… believe it's your calling. I'll even cover your classes and tools. Let me know how much you need," he said, his eyes moistening.

"It's a hair stylist position. Not a vow to become a nun or anything," Rory joked.

"I'm dealing with allergies today. Now, tell us more about cosmetology school." Dad said as he regained his composure.

After Rory and Dad departed, I felt a pang of loneliness. Caleb was off racing for the weekend, leaving me to my thoughts and the company of Lacey's little black-and-white TV. I put Celeste to bed and settled down to watch television. Exhaustion had been catching up with me; Celeste's feeding schedule had interrupted my sleep. As I drifted off in front of the TV, Dad's stunned expression haunted me. Why had the news of my career aspirations as a hairstylist affected him so deeply?

The shrill ring of the phone interrupted my thoughts. It was Caleb, and his voice burst with triumph. "Twyla, you won't believe it. I nailed the semifinal. We're heading to the championship in the spring."

A smile played on my lips as I imagined the furniture shopping spree we had planned with the prize money. "That's amazing, Caleb. I can't wait to celebrate with you."

"Hey, Twy, hold up a sec," he said, his tone shifting. Curiosity enveloped me as I waited for him to continue. "I overheard some of the other racers talking. There's this guy, a fellow racer, and he's in a tight spot. His son needs surgery on his knee, and he was trying to win the prize money for the procedure."

"What did you do?" I replied.

"Jeff needs the money more than we do, and I hope you understand," he confessed. The impact of his decision was evident in the earnestness of his voice.

"Wait, you gave away all of the prize money?"

"Yes," Caleb affirmed. "I gave it to him without thinking it through."

Warmth permeated my chest. This was a side of Caleb I hadn't seen before—a hidden selflessness that transcended the racetrack. "Oh, Caleb. I'm proud of you. It reminds me of how Mom said everyone always helped each other during the Great Depression. That's how they survived. It was a nice thing to do."

His response was simple yet profound. "So, you're not mad?"

"I was looking forward to a new sofa, but you did the right thing,"

As we talked, furniture shopping became a distant thought. In late-night conversation, our connection deepened. The unspoken understanding between us grew, and I found myself falling even more in love with the layers of Caleb that went beyond his rugged exterior.

"Caleb, I told Dad about my plans to become a hair stylist,"

"That's brilliant, Twy, I know you are going to be

amazing at that and it's good for you, to have goals. I'll help however I can." I could hear the smile in his voice.

"I hope so, Caleb. I miss you when you're gone racing so many nights. By the way, your father called earlier today. He wants you to call him as soon as you're back."

"Oh, him? I'm not talking to him."

"Why, Caleb? What's happened."

"I'll tell you about it when I get home. Let's just say my dad isn't the man I thought he was."

"I'm sorry things aren't going well between you and your father. I'm sure you'll work it out."

"I'm not so sure, but look, I don't want to get into it while I'm away. I love you and I'll tell you soon, but let's not talk about it now. Alright?"

"I understand. Good night, Caleb. I love you, too." We said our goodbyes, but as the night stretched on, a subtle, nagging sensation bothered me. What had his father done to upset him so much?

I struggled to fall asleep after our phone call. Now wide awake, my mind whirled with thoughts that wouldn't settle. After Caleb's news, I realized I'd forgotten to bring up moving back to my hometown. Moreover, the situation between Caleb and his dad lingered in my mind, unresolved. Amidst these swirling thoughts, one question kept coming to mind: Was Caleb hiding something from me?

CHAPTER 18

Dancing Queen

HOLLYWOOD, CALIFORNIA
JANUARY 10TH, 1981

Twilight Silverson
Twenty-One Years Old

T urning twenty-one was a significant milestone, and I was ready to celebrate in style at the famous Gazzarri's nightclub on the Sunset Strip. It had been four years since my last girls' night out. During that time, I had devoted myself entirely to my family—watching Celeste grow more each day, while Caleb was evolving into a fantastic father and provider. Despite their joy, I felt a part of me was incomplete. I hoped that a night out, combined with embarking on a new journey into cosmetology school, would help fill the void I'd been feeling.

"Are you ready for your first legal drink?" Rory interrupted my thoughts with her usual upbeat questions.

"This is long overdue, sis," I responded as I pushed my thoughts of Celeste and Caleb aside for the night.

Our small group entered Gazzarri's and it felt like I'd stepped into a neon-lit dream. It seemed alive with energy and the promise of unforgettable memories. The eighties were in full swing, and the crowd was a mosaic of subcultures: glam rockers in white leather and tight pants, hardcore punks with defiant stares, and disco bunnies in shimmering outfits. On the Sunset Strip everyone spoke the universal language of music.

The dance floor was the epicenter that drew us in and I'd heard musical icons like Van Halen and Stevie Nicks had made their mark here, their flamboyant and rebellious spirits forever etched into the music of my generation.

"Time for the ladies to get out and have some fun. I've been busting my ass at the courthouse and I'm ready to let my hair down." Susan took a large sip of her cocktail. She was an embodiment of sophisticated cool; Her dark, edgy style accentuated her high cheekbones, deep auburn hair and fair skin.

We found a booth tucked away from the dance floor's chaos and settled in with laughter and music blending into a chorus for our celebration.

As we clinked glasses, Rory's laughter cut through the air. "Twyla, this is your night. Let's make it legendary."

"Absolutely. We'll boogie our asses off." Maya, always up

for a good time, raised her glass. "To Twyla. Our Dancing Queen." Her deep, soulful eyes shined, and her thin frame sparkled in her bellbottomed jumpsuit. A voluminous cascade of curls framed her bronze face in a style that was undeniably eighties. "Happy Birthday, Twy."

Our energy soared higher with every passing moment, and, at the peak of our revelry, a familiar face emerged from the shadows. Keith Simpson, our old paperboy, strolled towards us, dressed in a white suit and gleaming smile.

"Twyla Cameron." He grinned, his voice a low hum. "Well, if this isn't my lucky night." Keith's gangly body had continued to fill out nicely, his eyes sparkled with mischievousness.

I chuckled in surprise, the years melted away as our eyes locked. "It's Twyla Silverson now." I held my left hand up and wiggled my ring finger.

Keith's mullet and pierced ear screamed rebellion, and his snakeskin boots looked expensive. "That's what I heard, and where is Mr. Wonderful tonight?"

"The men are at home while we celebrate Twyla's twenty-first." Susan nudged me mischievously.

"Hi, Keith. What have you been up to since high school? I heard you live out here in Hollywood now." Rory raised her eyebrows.

"Mind if I join you ladies? I'll buy a round of drinks in honor of our birthday girl." Keith scooted into our booth with a crooked smile directed at me.

"Make yourself at home," Rory retorted. "You always have." She added, under her breath.

"I'm a Production Assistant on the *Beverly Hospital* set. It's a nice gig. I live in Hollyweird now." Keith leaned back. "How about you, ladies?" He spoke to all of us but kept his eyes on me.

"I'm a mom now. I have a little girl named Celeste. But I'm starting school to be a hair stylist soon."

"That's bitchin' news, Twyla. Congratulations on both counts," came his warm reply.

Rory chimed in, "Susan's working as a stenographer at the courthouse, while Maya and I are living the stay-at-home mom life. I occasionally lend a hand at the stables, too."

Keith, however, seemed to bypass Rory's contribution, his interest piqued by my news. "We're always on the lookout for fresh talent on set. Perhaps I should recommend you?" His focus narrowed in on me, the intriguing offer hanging in the air.

"I'm still living in San Clemente. It would be too far."

"But Dad has been talking about signing the Montclair house over to you. He'd like you closer to the rest of us. Won't you reconsider it?" Rory asked.

"I'll think about it, but I'd like to wait until Celeste is in school before I commit to something like that," I said with a forced smile.

"I'll reach out next year if you'd like?"

"Sure, but enough talk about work. Let's get back to

our girls' night. Nice to see you." I dismissed Keith as I grabbed Rory's hand, and we made our way to the dance floor.

"That's a unique opportunity you tossed away," Rory yelled over the music.

"Working with Keith in Hollywood might not sit well with Caleb. He still has a thing for me. Couldn't you tell?"

"Do you always do everything your husband says?" Rory laughed.

"Let's keep it light. It's my one night off from being a mom. I've decided I'm going to convince Caleb to move to Montclair. Tackling a new job in Hollywood would be too much, right now."

"Caleb's away a lot on racing weekends. Being closer to your family makes sense. He's got to see that," Rory persisted.

"Enough serious talk for one night. Let's dance and be free." I shot Rory a stern look as Maya and Susan joined us on the dance floor. We formed a circle, each one of us trying to outdo each other with our energetic dance moves. The pulsating beats, neon lights, and sisterly banter created a magnetic pull and a memorable night.

A FEW WEEKS LATER I SWUNG OPEN THE FRONT DOOR TO our small duplex. I couldn't contain the triumphant smile spreading across my face.

"Guess what, Caleb? You won't believe it." I called out, breathless with delight.

My husband looked up from the scattered mess of half-packed boxes, curiosity lighting up his face.

"What's going on, Twy? You look like you won the lottery," he said, setting aside the shirt he was folding.

I couldn't hold it in any longer. "I passed my GED today, on my first try."

His smile widened, and he dropped the shirt. "No way. That's incredible. I knew you could do it, but on the first try? You didn't even have to study too much. That's my girl. You've got your driver's license and GED all in the same month. I'm proud of you."

I nodded, the grin on my face threatening to split it in half. "Yep, every single section. And you know what that means? Cosmetology school, here I come."

Caleb's face broke into a slow grin. "That's nice of your dad to offer to pay for everything. Are you sure this is the right career choice? I mean, your writing is so good."

"Absolutely. Maybe one day I'll even own my own salon. I still love to write, but I just can't see myself going back to college with Celeste so young. I can get my cosmetology license a lot quicker than I can a college degree."

"You can do anything you set your mind to. Maybe I'll retire and become a house husband," he joked.

"Right, you'd be out racing dirt bikes in the desert all day," I joked.

We shared a hug, and I scooped up little Celeste, who

had been playing with her toys on the floor. She looked up at us, sensing the joy in the room, and I showered her with kisses. "We're going back to the house on Harvard Street, my little sea star. Back home. I can't wait for you to start going to school with your cousin."

"I'm glad you're happy and it's not too far from the family wood yard."

"Thank you for being on board with all of this, it's a lot of change." I looked up into his piercing blue eyes.

"I'm sorry I resisted for so long. Our little sea star deserves her own backyard to play in and it will happen a lot faster if we accept your parents' help," Caleb took my hand in his. The room felt warmer, our small family wrapped in the security of our plans and the love that bound us together. Celeste giggled, oblivious to the specifics but sensitive to the happiness that enveloped her.

"You're going to love living on Harvard Street. It's a big step, but you won't regret it. San Clemente has gotten so expensive. Montclair is still affordable and it's growing like crazy. They have everything there that we have here."

"You drive a hard bargain, Mrs. Silverson," Caleb teased.

"It's going to be good for us, and I know we'll have the life we've always dreamed of."

CHAPTER 19

I Love a Rainy Night

MONTCLAIR, CALIFORNIA
SUMMER 1981

Twyla Cameron
Twenty-One Years Old

"Hurry. Let's get all of this unloaded before everything gets soaked!" Caleb shouted to our makeshift moving crew. The urgency in his voice mirrored the impending crescendo of raindrops as they collided with the pavement.

Caleb, Rory, and her husband Mitch, moved like a well-choreographed team. They passed carefully packed boxes from hand-to-hand. The summer rain couldn't dampen the spirits of our merry group. We were soaked to the bone as we sprinted back and forth from the moving truck to the house, trying to beat the rain's relentless advance.

As the last box found its place, Caleb surveyed the front yard, raindrops glistening on his unruly hair. He threw me a triumphant grin. "Mission accomplished, Twy. I guess it helps we don't own much furniture."

"We'll make this place feel like home soon," I said as I settled onto the front porch swing with Celeste on my lap. The rhythmic pitter-patter of raindrops added a soothing melody to the atmosphere. "I adore a warm rainstorm. You guys didn't mind getting a little wet?"

"Not at all. I'm over the moon to have you back in the neighborhood. And speaking of moons, I've got some exciting news for you. Mitch and I have a bun in the oven. I'm due in November."

"Oh my gosh, sis, sit down. You shouldn't have been working so hard." I leapt up from the porch swing and motioned for Rory to take my seat.

"Congratulations, you two." Caleb clapped Mitch on the back.

This unexpected announcement created an electric sense of new beginnings. The future was here and as I stood on the front porch, a sense of warmth and contentment washed over me.

"I never would have expected we'd be moving in the rain in June and my best worker would be a pregnant woman."

"Now, the house has the christening of a summer rainstorm and future cousins for Celeste to play with." Caleb laughed.

The banter continued as we shook off the rain, but in the storm, we found joy in turning a house into a home.

"Let's order pizza after we get the dining table set up, and maybe the men can partake in a little wacky tobaccy? I just got some Acapulco Gold from my neighbor," Mitch chimed in.

"I don't want any smoking with Celeste in the house. I don't like it," I snapped at Mitch. I didn't fully approve of my new brother-in-law's behavior, and although he was nice enough, his drinking and smoking occurred a little too often for my liking.

"You heard the lovely lady, but I will spring for those pizzas as a thank you for your help moving and how about a Coors?" Caleb interjected as he sensed my discomfort.

"Happy wife, happy life." Rory looked pointedly at Mitch. "And although I won't be drinking, I did bring you a housewarming gift," Rory pulled out a bottle of Boonsville Strawberry Hill wine.

"Fancy, sis. It looks like we'll be having wine and pizza for dinner." I smiled at Rory and couldn't help but feel like we'd made the right choice by moving closer to my family. I hadn't realized how much I'd been missing my sister. Despite my apprehension about her husband, I was looking forward to seeing more of Rory and her new baby.

IN THE MONTHS THAT FOLLOWED, I EMBRACED THE SUBURBAN rhythm, settling into our new home. The familiar surroundings of my childhood neighborhood offered comfort, and living closer to my relatives filled the sense of closeness I had missed while living in San Clemente.

"Good morning, sea star. Today's a big day for both of us. It's not only your first day at your new preschool, but Mama is starting a new school too."

"To learn how to cut hair?" Celeste questioned.

"That's right, now let's get you dressed in your favorite red coat and boots, so we aren't late on our first day."

I buckled Celeste into the second-hand Ford Pinto that Caleb had recently fixed up for me and we took the brief drive to Chicken Little Preschool. Holding her hand tightly, we entered her classroom, I fought to keep my nerves hidden. It was my first time leaving her with anyone outside the family, and she seemed so vulnerable. However, my anxiety faded as the room's vibrant colors and the sound of children's laughter surrounded us.

I looked around at the other parents. They were all five to ten years older than me, and I unexpectedly felt the weight of my youth.

Miss Salazar, with her bright smile and crinkled eyes, walked up to us and crouched down to meet Celeste eye-to-eye. "Hello there. You must be Celeste Silverson. And this must be your older sister, right?"

I opened my mouth, ready to correct her, but Celeste beat me to it. "Nope. She's my mama," she said, her chin jutting out defiantly. "She's the best. She can do cartwheels and everything."

I couldn't help but laugh, surprised and proud all at once.

Miss Salazar's eyebrows shot up, then she smiled. "Oh, I see. That's quite impressive. You must be very proud of her."

I knelt beside Celeste, wrapping her in a quick hug. "And I'm super proud of you," I whispered, feeling her squeeze back.

She placed her small hand on my arm and pulled me closer. "You know how Grandma Dawn goes by her middle name?" she whispered in my ear.

"Yes. I've heard the story of how Grandma changed her name many times."

"Well, now that I'm starting big girl school, I've decided that I'm going to go by my middle name, too. I feel more like a Starla."

"Starla and Twyla. I love it." I smiled. As I stood there, holding my daughter's hand, I knew I had nothing to worry about. I was raising a determined daughter, and her confidence reflected the tenacity that ran in our family. "If that's what you've decided then, Starla it is. Would you be able to make the appropriate changes?" I looked up at Mrs. Salazar.

"Of course, come with me, *Starla*, and you can come

meet the other children." Ms. Salazar held her hand out for her to grab hold.

I kissed my daughter goodbye and I ventured into West Covina to start my first day of cosmetology school.

Hair dryers buzzed while excited chatter echoed through the halls. The scent of styling products lingered as I weaved through a crowd of aspiring stylists, on the hunt for Room 101. Drying my damp palms on my jeans, I looked for an open seat in the crowded classroom.

The instructor soon addressed the class. "We are going to start with the proper way to hold your scissors, so pair up with the person next to you. I want you to critique each other."

As I rummaged around my hobo bag, I couldn't seem to find my scissors. Perspiration formed at my temples.

"Twyla, where are your scissors? This is your first day, and you don't have your most important tool." Mr. Garcia zeroed in on me – his impatience showing on his face.

"I... I don't know. I had them a minute ago."

The blonde next to me must have sensed my distress, she flashed a quick, reassuring smile. "Here they are... they were hiding right here next to your bag. They must have fallen out."

The instructor's stern expression softened.

"Thanks for covering for me, but won't you need them. I must've left mine at home," I whispered when Mr. Garcia moved onto the next student.

She flashed me a mischievous grin, showing that the scissors were actually her spare pair. Her clever act of kindness saved me from the instructor's wrath and spared me embarrassment on my first day.

"I'm Kaity. Don't let old Mr. Garcia intimidate you. Underneath it all he's a big teddy bear, but you don't want to get on his bad side on the first day."

"Nice to meet you, Kaity. I'm Twyla."

"That's a bitchin' name!" she exclaimed.

I quickly discovered that Kaity hailed from a large Puerto Rican family. After her mom had left when she was just thirteen, she took on the responsibility of raising her five siblings, which explained her loud and authoritative manner.

"I can't wait to start cutting hair and making my own money. My dad finally remarried and I'm free to start my own life. Free at last! Let his new wife take care of all my siblings, I deserve this." Kaity declared, her enthusiasm contagious.

"I became a mom at seventeen. I know what it's like to want to spread your wings and do something for yourself," I knowingly replied.

"You and I are going to be good friends, I can just feel it," Kaity confidently shot back.

As the days rolled by, Kaity and I became inseparable. Her Puerto Rican flair added a unique vibrancy to our routine, and I found myself marveling at her ability to transform any ordinary day into a good time.

One day, Mr. Garcia caught our attention. "You two," he began, with a smile that hinted at both admiration and amusement, "have a rare synergy. Your creativity and teamwork are exactly what this field is about. I'm going to start calling you the dynamic duo," he laughed.

His words only fueled our passion further, reminding us that in the realm of hairstyling, our artistry could truly flourish without limits.

"He's not wrong," Kaity remarked.

"It's a lot harder than I imagined, but I'm enjoying every moment of it." I continued working on my mannequin head.

It had been five years since I attended any kind of school, and I was soaking everything up like a sponge. I wondered if Starla was enjoying her preschool class as much as I was enjoying my new venture. I hoped she was making friends with the other children.

However, my elation for my new career path was abruptly undermined one day when I returned home from a particularly challenging lesson. I opened the door, smoke lingered in the air, a stark contrast to the hope I had been feeling. I found Caleb and Mitch together, lounging in the living room, surrounded by a haze of marijuana smoke. I felt my spirits take a sharp nosedive at the sight of the two stoned men.

"Caleb, seriously? Starla is asleep in the other room. All this pot smoke is bad for her."

"Babe, chill. It's only a little weed. I've got the ceiling fans on, no smoke is in her room. You are being a little too uptight about this." Caleb smirked, seemingly impervious to my discomfort. I shot him a look that could freeze time.

"We haven't lived here that long, and now you're smoking pot with Mitch, with Starla home? I'm not going to live with a drug addict."

"Relax, Twy. You're overreacting. Weed is not addictive... We're just having some brotherly bonding time. If it bothers you that much, we'll keep it in the garage. Besides, I found your little birth control packet, so I guess we both have our own little secrets." Caleb's voice dropped.

I squeezed my eyes shut and pinched the bridge of my nose, struggling to control my temper. "I'm starting my own career, and I'm not ready to be tied home to another baby yet. I may not ever be... and I definitely don't want to have any more kids with a pothead, I'm leaving," I ran to our room to grab Starla and an overnight bag.

"You knew I've always wanted a big family." He raised his voice.

"I was seventeen when we first discussed that. Things change, I'm older now and I'm not going to let you make all the decisions anymore. I'm a partner in this marriage, I deserve an equal say."

"What exactly *are* you saying." Caleb looked shocked.

"You don't know what it's been like being a teen mother, everyone judging you and looking down on you. It was harder than you'll ever know. But I refuse to discuss it now with you in this state. I'm going to my dad's house. I think we need a breather." I responded.

"Don't run home and tell your daddy about this. It's not a big deal."

"I'll come back when you realize this *is* a big deal. My opinions are important, too, and should matter to you," I said. Holding Starla in my arms, I gave Mitch a stern look and brushed past him with determination as I raced out the door.

The porch light cast a flickering glow on the rain-soaked street as I hesitated for a moment, glancing back at the home I had hoped would be a sanctuary.

"Fine, go run home to Daddy." Caleb's voice called after me, the rain muffling his words, but I pressed forward for the half hour drive to my parents' house.

Twenty minutes later, I approached my parents' house, the echoes of the argument lingered in my mind. I hesitated at the door, Starla nestled in my arms, her innocence a vivid contrast to the complexities that unraveled around us.

The door creaked open, revealing Dad's dream house— a place of comfort, yet now a temporary refuge from my tempest of emotions.

The single-story ranch house was an embodiment of my parents' contrasting styles. Inside, the rough-hewn beams and leather furniture spoke of Dad's rugged spirit, while the handsewn curtains and clusters of wildflowers Mom kept in dainty vases, scattered throughout, brought a touch of cozy, homely charm. Each room was a blend of practicality and warmth that reflected the essence of their combined tastes.

"Twyla, what's wrong? Did something happen to Caleb?" Dad greeted me with concern etched across his face.

I bit my lip, holding back tears, finding solace in my dad's arms.

"The only man a girl can count on is her daddy," Mom proclaimed after hearing what had gone on between Caleb and me.

"You did the right thing, Twyla. You must stand up for what you believe is right, especially for Starla. I'll go talk to Caleb tomorrow, and we'll get everything fixed up. He deserves a second chance. If your mom left me every time I messed up, well... let's say that marriage isn't all sunshine and rainbows, and you'll make it through this storm."

"I hope so, Dad, but I'm not sure if Caleb and I want the same things anymore."

"You'll find a way to make it work, but boozing and drugs aren't good for a young family... I know that much. Now get some sleep. Things always look better in the morning." Mom made her way into the spare bedroom and placed some extra blankets on the bed. I tossed and turned all night. I'd never known Caleb to be a big drinker and he never used marijuana around me. What had changed?

The next morning, the world outside mirrored the wave of emotions within me. The rain had stopped but it was a deary morning, with heavy clouds hanging low, painting the sky a somber grey. Starla played with her toys on the living room floor, oblivious to the weight of the night's events. The scent of coffee filled the air.

In the quiet moments of morning, my mind became a battleground of conflicting thoughts. The path ahead appeared foggy as I sipped my coffee. I wondered if Caleb would accept me now that I'd developed my own opinions that might go against what he wanted. Up until now, we'd agreed on most things. This was our first huge disagreement.

A knock on the front door interrupted my thoughts and echoed through the halls of my parents' home. I exchanged a worried glance with Dad as he got up to answer it.

"Look who we found out sitting in his Bronco on the driveway," Susan had Lacey in her arms and behind her was Caleb. His eyes were red, worn with fatigue, and shadows clung to the hollows beneath them.

Caleb's gaze met mine, wistfulness swimming in his tired gaze. His presence brought forth a collision of emotions— unfinished conversations lingering in the air.

Dad, ever the mediator, broke the tense silence.

"Caleb, come on in. We were having a little chat. Twyla, why don't you get him a cup of coffee? Susan and I were going to take Lacey to get her first big girl bike at Toys"R" Us. We'll leave you kids alone to talk."

I nodded, rising from the comfort of the couch, happy to have something to busy my trembling hands. The aroma of coffee wafted through the air once again as I poured Caleb a cup, the silence thick with unspoken words.

Caleb looked at Starla playing nearby. His gaze lingered on the innocence of our daughter; a poignant reminder of the stakes involved.

"I… I messed up, Twyla. I shouldn't have let things escalate like that. I care about you and Starla more than anything. I don't want to lose my family."

He choked the words out, a fragile bridge spanned the divide between remorse and reconciliation.

"Sometimes we say things we don't mean, especially in the heat of the moment. But what matters is what we do next. Caleb, I'm not a quiet teenage girl anymore. I want things, I have opinions and I need you to realize that we are a team, not a dictatorship." The words spilled out, a declaration of my newfound confidence and the firm stance I needed in this relationship.

"I get it. I won't bring that stuff into the house again. You know I love you. I took a break from racing so you could chase your dream. Your wants matter to me, even if I'm not the best at saying it."

"I'll meet you halfway. I don't want to lose our family either." I responded as the morning sunlight finally broke through the clouds and filtered through the curtains. Caleb made his way towards me and enveloped me in a gentle hug.

"Let's promise to never fight like that again, " he whispered, the weight of our argument still heavy in the air.

"I hate fighting too. How about I make you some eggs? You look exhausted."

"I tossed and turned for a few hours and ended getting up in the night and driving here, I was trying to build up the nerve to face your dad when Susan found me out in my Bronco. "

"My dad is more understanding than you think. He and Mom went through their ups and downs, but always found a way to make it work."

As the afternoon unfolded, Dad, Susan, and Lacey returned from their outing with a huge teddy bear for Starla. Lacey giggled as Dad wrestled with the stuffed animal, and even Caleb couldn't help but crack a smile. "Ellis, you're going to get yourself beat up by a bear," he quipped.

The tension from the night before had been erased within the comfort of family love.

Mom returned from feeding the horses and chickens, seemingly unaware of how close my marriage had come to ending. "I hope you'll all stay for spaghetti and meatballs tonight," she declared, as she looked at me with a wink. "Your favorite, Twyla."

"Of course, if it's alright with everyone else." I looked at Caleb.

"I'll never turn down Mom's famous spaghetti and, besides, I'm an expert at teaching kids how to ride their bikes. I taught all of my younger siblings. What do you say?" Caleb then turned to Lacey.

Lacey's eyes lit up with excitement. "Really, Uncle? Can we go take the training wheels off now?" she asked, eagerness bubbling in her voice. And so, we spilled into the front yard, the scene unfolded with the sound of Caleb's patient instructions and Lacey's triumphant laughter as she learned to pedal on her new, big girl bike.

"Thank you for doing this, Caleb. Daniel's off consulting for that project up north and I know he'd be glad you stepped in." Susan placed her hand on Caleb's arm.

Later that night as we sat around the dinner table, bowls full of Mom's spaghetti, our conversation flowed easily. I knew Caleb must have had a momentary lapse in judgment and decided to let it go for the sake of our future.

THE FOLLOWING YEARS UNFURLED LIKE A WINDING RIVER, I graduated from cosmetology school, and Kaity and I both landed jobs at the local Supercuts. Her father had a friend who vouched for us, securing us positions as new hires.

Caleb resumed his racing career, and with my earnings from hairstyling, I found a neighborhood girl to watch Starla while I worked, part-time.

Things weren't always easy, and our disagreement about

having more children remained a sore spot between us. Caleb and I both avoided the topic, but it crept up every now and then.

One morning I was in the salon early discussing it with Kaity, when the chime above the salon door tinkled, announcing the entrance of a familiar face.

I glanced up and there he stood—Keith Simpson, memories of our past flooded back, and I was genuinely happy to see him. "Keith? Is that really you?" I couldn't hide the surprise and happiness in my voice as I greeted him, momentarily forgetting the hairspray and gossip of the salon.

"Twyla!" Keith's surprise was evident in his voice, as if my name unexpectedly sprang to his lips. Time had sculpted his features, transforming the shaggy hair of his youth into a neatly styled undercut, short on the sides and longer on top. It accentuated the sharp contours of his face—a few wrinkles around his eyes and a more chiseled jawline contributed to his more mature appearance.

A warm smile softened my features, and I tried not to laugh. It was obvious he had orchestrated this not so chance meeting. "Keith. It's been a while. What brings you to town? Are you still working in Hollywood?" I gestured toward the empty chair and decided to play along with his charade. Although Keith could be a bit of a wannabe, I knew he was a good person inside.

"I'm here for the holidays, visiting my parents. I'm now an assistant director on the set of *Beverly Hospital*. Thought

I'd swing by for a trim, I didn't know you worked here. You look amazing. How's the married life treating you?" Keith asked.

I motioned for him to sit, setting aside my tools. "Caleb and I are doing well. Congratulations on your promotion. You've come a long way from paperboy to assistant director," I ribbed him.

Keith laughed, the lines on his face revealing the passage of time. "Yeah, it's been a journey. But hey, that's a good thing, right?" As I draped him with a protective leopard print cape, and I noticed his eyes scanning the salon in a calculated way. "Actually, Twyla, I'm glad I ran into you. We are always in need of a talented stylist."

"Thanks for thinking of me, but I'm not sure I'm ready for all of that."

"Mom mentioned you've built up quite a name for yourself. We always need someone on set to work magic with hair—someone like you."

I raised my eyebrows, the suggestion catching me off guard. "Did your mom mention I worked here?"

"Okay, I'm busted. I knew you worked here when I made the appointment. We're short staffed on the set right now and I thought, why not pay Twyla a visit?"

"I'll think about it."

"I know it's a big leap," Keith continued, his gaze unwavering. "But Twyla, you've got talent, and I can vouch for you."

"The offer is attractive, I won't lie. I need to talk it over with Caleb, though."

A slight spark of excitement churned inside me. The opportunity to work on a famous soap opera was thrilling, but my ties to Montclair were strong, I was comfortable here, maybe too comfortable. Was I ready to chase success in Hollywood?

CHAPTER 20
Live To Tell

FALL 1986

Twilight Silverson
Twenty-Six Years Old

The years slipped by as they so often do, with each day melding into the next, until Keith's once tempting offer faded into the background, lost amidst the daily hustle of motherhood and work.

Starla was ten years old, and it made family camping adventures not just possible, but more enjoyable. Caleb, ever the doting father, had built her a small red and blue go-kart, igniting endless joy in her youthful heart.

"We'll make a racer out of this girl yet," he would joke, his eyes sparkled with pride as Starla zoomed around the desert, her laughter filling the air.

As autumn ushered in its chill, a sudden call from my brother Randall in the dead of night marked the beginning of a new, unexpected and unwanted chapter. "Randall, what's wrong?" I clutched the phone tightly.

There was a pause, filled with a tension that stretched across the miles. "It's Dad, Twyla. He's sick. Very sick."

"I know he has pneumonia. I've been making him chicken soup and taking it up to the house every weekend."

"No, Twy, he's in the hospital. He had an episode in the night. Mom had to call an ambulance. The doctors have found a spot on his lung. I'm here with them now. I don't know how to tell you this, but they think it's cancer." Randall's voice broke, and I could almost see him, trying to hold himself together. "Can you come up to the hospital? Everyone is coming."

I sank onto the nearest chair, my mind reeling. "Cancer? But how? He's always been the picture of health."

"I know, that's what we all thought. I bet it's all those years working around the paint and drywall. They are talking surgery, it doesn't look good."

The words echoed in my head and a pit formed in my stomach.

"I'm on my way." I hung up the phone and hastily put on a pair of jeans.

"Honey, I've got to go. Can you watch Starla? Dad needs me." I gently shook Caleb awake.

"What's going on? You look too upset to drive. I'll take you." He got up, a concerned look on his face.

"I don't want Starla there. Dad just found out he might have cancer. Everyone's going to be emotional, and it's going to be a lot to handle for a little one." My voice broke on the word cancer. I could hardly say it, let alone comprehend how everything had changed. Caleb emerged from the bedroom. His gaze a mask of concern as he looked at me.

"I understand. It's almost daybreak. I'll drive you up to the hospital and take Starla for an early bite to eat. How bad is it?"

"They are saying he may need surgery. I'm going to take a leave of absence from work. I need to be there for Dad." I wiped at the tears streaming down my face. The drive to the hospital was a blur, with Caleb trying to offer comforting words, while I was too lost in my own turmoil to respond.

Caleb pulled into a parking spot and killed the engine. "I'm here for you, Twy. Whatever you need."

As I walked up to the hospital, the automatic doors opened with a swish, ushering in a chapter I wasn't sure I was prepared for.

As the days passed, Dad's resilience became increasingly evident. Despite the grim prognosis from the doctors and the removal of his diseased lung, he defied the odds and lived another year and a half. His spirit, tempered by the hard years of the Great Depression and enlivened by the rich Cherokee blood that flowed through his veins, refused to succumb easily. In him, the indomitable spirit of a warrior emerged, battling the intruder with a resilience that spoke of his deep roots and unyielding strength.

However, as all battles do, this one reached its inevitable conclusion. Late one evening, the phone rang, shattering the quiet. 'The doctors said it's time for goodbyes,' Susan's trembling voice marked the end of Dad's brave fight and the beginning of our final farewell.

"I'll be right there, Susan." I replied.

It had been Susan's week to stay and help. She and I took turns staying at the house, helping Mom with Dad's care.

"I'm going to the hospital. You stay here with Starla." I grimly told Caleb the bad news.

"I'm sorry, Twy. He put up a tremendous fight. Are you sure you don't want me to come?"

"No, stay here with Starla. I'll feel better knowing she's home, safe and sound. I'll call you later." I grabbed my keys and made my way to Loma Linda.

My hands trembled as I arrived at the hospital and soon found Randall in the hallway smoking a cigarette, a grim look on his face "Dad wants to see you alone. He's been asking for you."

"You shouldn't smoke out here."

Randall flicked the cigarette away with a tenacious look on his face. "Rules never were Dad's thing, and right now,

they aren't mine. He's asking for *you*, Twyla. Go see him."
His voice, though laced with heaviness, carried the charac-
teristic rebelliousness that Dad himself would have
appreciated.

"Hey, my sweet pea. There's something I want to tell
you," his voice was barely a whisper, his skin pallid and
waxy, his hair now pure white but still thick despite the radi-
ation treatments he had endured. I made my way to his
bedside, my body tingling with electricity, feeling as though I
might pass out."

"I'm here, Daddy. Do you need anything?" I stroked his
forehead with a damp cloth.

He hesitated as if he were looking for the right words. "I
want your Mom to move into that house I've been refur-
bishing across the street from you, keep her close to you.
She's going to need you to lean on. Take care of each
other."

"Yes, Daddy."

"There's one other thing… I love you, dear, you've
always been my best girl." He paused again, like there was
something more he wanted to say.

His eyes, once so full of life and grit, now gazed at me
with a depth of emotion that words could hardly convey. I
squeezed his hand softly, fighting back the tears that threatened to overwhelm me. "I love you, too, Daddy. More than
words can say."

He nodded, a faint smile playing on his lips. "You've

grown into such an incredible woman, Twyla. You're stronger than you know. You're a Cameron don't ever forget that."

At that moment, Mom came into the room. "Dad needs his rest. The doctor will be coming to check on him soon."

His grip on my hand weakened, but his gaze held mine with an intensity that spoke volumes. It was as if he was imparting all the knowledge of his years in that one final look, a silent expression of the love and pride he held for me. "Take care of each other."

I nodded, unable to speak through the lump in my throat. "We will, Daddy. We'll be okay."

Mom moved to his side, her hand gently holding his. Their love remained as evident as it had been in their younger days. It was a love that had been the cornerstone of our family, unwavering and true.

As Dad closed his eyes, a sense of tranquility washed over him. It was as if he had found some peace, knowing that he was leaving his tight knit family united, and we'd be there for each other through the grief.

Exiting the room alongside Mom, I was engulfed by devastation and a profound emptiness, as though my heart had fractured into countless pieces. The sorrow that permeated my being, mourning the loss of a man who had been both my hero and my guide, was overwhelming and all-consuming,

Randall, Buck, and Rory were waiting outside, their

expressions a combined solemness. Together, we gathered in the hallway, wrapped in our own thoughts, yet united in our love for the man who had shaped our lives.

"Where's Susan and Bobby? They should be here."

"Susan said her goodbyes and went outside to get a breath of fresh air. Bobby is on his way. He was in Palm Springs with his family. He'll be here any minute."

"I'm here. Where's Dad?" Bobby came running into the corridor, with Susan close behind.

"He's gone," Buck somberly replied.

"No!" Bobby exclaimed as he fell to his knees, the other siblings all gathering around him to offer support.

My brother's anguished cry echoed through the sterile corridors, slicing through the heavy silence that had settled over us.

As Mom entered the room, a quiet resilience reflected on her face. "We'll make it through this." Her words, simple but profound, reminded us that even in the depths of despair, we were not alone. Together, as a family, we would navigate the uncharted waters of loss and emerge, somehow, still intact, still united.

BACK HOME, CALEB AND STARLA SHARED MEMORIES OF DAD, their voices sounded distant, muffled by the growing void inside me. I tried to join in, to cling to the warmth of their reminiscences, but my heart was sinking into a deep, dark place. I sought sanctuary in sleep, a reprieve from the reality that consumed me. I was always tired; no amount of sleep could make me feel rested.

In the days that followed, I found myself going through the motions, a shell of my former self. The routines of daily life, once comforting, now felt like chains, binding me to a reality I no longer felt part of. The brightness of the past seemed like distant stars in a rapidly darkening sky.

THE MONTHS AFTER DAD'S DEATH WERE THE DARKEST OF MY life and seemed to drag on in a never-ending haze of depression. Every moment of solitude was a descent into tears, a reminder of the dark abyss that had swallowed me whole.

One morning, Caleb approached me with a gentle suggestion, his voice tinged with concern. "Twy, I know you're hurting, and it feels like a part of you has been torn away. But you need to think about yourself and your family. Maybe going back to work could help you get out of this funk. Being alone at home all day isn't doing you any good." He ran his hand through his hair, now neatly trimmed and a far cry from the untamed tresses of our younger days.

His words, though well-meaning, stung like salt in an open wound. I couldn't help but feel a surge of resentment. "The salon's moved on without me, and frankly, I don't have the heart to return there. It's as if everyone expects life to continue as if nothing's changed. I can't do that." I slumped down on the sofa.

Caleb persisted, his face full of earnest concern. "You don't need to go back to Supercuts. There might be other opportunities out there. Something new could be what you need right now."

I remembered that offer from years ago. "Keith Simpson mentioned a job a while back. I'm not sure. It's in Holly-wood. A world away," I said in a small voice, my mind grappling with the thought.

"It's only a thirty-minute drive. Perhaps reaching out to an old friend could be good for you. I heard Keith lost his dad a while back, he might relate to what you're going through."

The idea sparked a faint glimmer of possibility in my mind. I was surprised at Caleb's encouragement; he had seemed uneasy about Keith in the past. I could see the depth of his desperation, his longing to bring back the woman he knew and loved.

"I'll try to find his card," I said, more to myself than to Caleb. His suggestion, a lifeline in my sea of sorrow, was evidence to how much he yearned for the return of the vibrant woman I once was. With a quiet promise to myself and to him, I decided to make the call.

"Hi, Keith. It's me. Twyla."

"Hello, Twy. What can I do for you?"

"Well, I've been considering that job offer from a while back. Are you still working on that soap opera?"

"Indeed I am. Let's grab coffee tomorrow and talk about it more. Are you free around ten am? I can meet you at Porto's in Glendale?"

"I'll be there."

THE NEXT MORNING DAWNED WITH A SENSE OF PURPOSE I hadn't felt in a long time. I dropped Starla off at school and drove to Pasadena, the familiar streets unfolded before me like the pages of a book I hadn't read in years. The Cuban deli was bustling with the morning crowd, the air thick with the aroma of coffee and baked goods.

I spotted Keith at a booth by the window, his face lit up as he saw me. "Twyla!" he exclaimed, standing up to greet me. Keith headed towards me in his white jeans and snake-skin cowboy boots, I could see he still had his ear pierced. His hug was warm and genuine, a reminder of the friend-ship we once shared.

"Hey there, stranger."

"How are you?" I gave him a quick hug and took a seat at the booth.

"I'm doing good. How's the family?"

"Doing good, considering."

"Your dad was a great guy. He was always good to me.

I'm sorry for your loss." He reached across the table and squeezed my hand.

"Caleb thought it might be good for me to get back to work." I stirred my coffee and waited for it to cool.

"He is right, you must keep yourself busy after something like this. You don't want to be home alone with your thoughts. That's how I coped when my dad passed."

"I was sorry to hear about your father."

"It's been a few years now. You don't stop missing them, but you somehow learn to carry on. Even Mom's moved on. She already remarried and relocated to Monterey."

"Do you like your stepdad?"

"He's loaded so she'll be taken care of, and he makes Mom happy. That's what's important. Listen, I spoke with the styling department, and we could use another good stylist. It's a great group of people, you'd fit right in." Keith smiled.

"Yes, I appreciate you giving me this opportunity and I think I want to take it. I've got to do something. I can't go on like this."

"Good decision, this will be good for you. A chance to stretch your wings. It's a classic show, but there's been a revival and it's creating quite a buzz. You'll love the dynamic energy on set."

"Sounds exciting," I said, my voice still betraying a hint of hesitation.

Keith leaned in, his tone becoming more serious. "But

there's something you should know before jumping in. Hollywood's pace is a whole different world compared to Montclair. It's fast, demanding, and sometimes relentless. It's not only about talent; it's about keeping up with the speed and pressure."

"Fast paced, huh?" I replied.

"Yeah, it can be overwhelming at first. But don't fret, I've seen your work. You're adaptable and quick on your feet. I'm confident you'll fit right in. Thought you should know what you're stepping into."

I felt a vibration at my waist. I glanced down at the pager I wore ever since Dad got sick. The small screen displayed a number I did not recognize. I stared at the pager.

"I have to go. It could be Starla's school," I stammered, standing up abruptly. "I'll call you about the job, but I can start ASAP if you want to pass on word," I said quickly, leaving money on the table for my untouched coffee.

"See you soon, Twyla. Here's the new hire packet. I'd hoped you'd take the position and had HR print it out." Keith jumped up and handed me a manila envelope.

"Bye, Keith, and thank you." I gave him a quick hug before shooting off to find my car in the busy parking lot.

As I reached my parking spot, my sense of unease grew. I tossed the envelope onto the back seat and thought, 'What could be happening now?' The unknown number on my pager felt like an ominous sign; with so much bad news lately, I dreaded receiving more.

Was Starla okay? Was there some emergency with

Mom? The pressure of recent events had left me on edge, always anticipating the next crisis.

As I drove, I couldn't shake the notion of apprehension. Could I fit into such a world at my present state? As I hurried to the nearest pay phone, a sense of foreboding gnawed at me. I inserted the coins with shaky hands and dialed the number flashing on my pager.

"Hello, Mount Baldy Lodge," answered a voice, brimming with the kind of calm that only comes from being nestled in the mountains.

"I received a page from this number," I said, trying to keep my voice steady from this rising worry.

"One moment, please. There's a young lady here who asked to use our phone," the voice replied, a shadow of concern laced their words.

A brief silence filled the line, and a familiar voice, slightly slurred and unmistakably husky, came through. "Twyla, it's Rory."

My heart skipped a beat. "Rory? What's happening? Are you okay?"

"I drove up here to clear my head, but now my car won't start. I'm stranded." Rory's voice wavered, a cocktail of frustration and helplessness.

"Stay put, Rory. I'm on my way. Just need to make sure Caleb can pick up the kids. Which class is Jason in again?"

"He's with Mrs. Dryden. Twyla, I'm sorry, I didn't mean to—"

I cut her off. "It's fine. I'll be there in twenty minutes. Don't go anywhere."

I hung up the phone and a sense of urgency propelled me forward. I called Caleb's work and left a message before jumping in my brown Pinto.

Gripping the steering wheel as I raced up the familiar winding roads, I wondered, was this more than a simple car breakdown? Something seemed amiss with my sister, and I was determined to find out what.

CHAPTER 21

My Prerogative

MT BALDY, CALIFORNIA
FALL 1988

Twilight Silverson
Twenty-Eight Years Old

T finally reached the lodge, nestled among the tall pine trees; its beauty magnified by the wild, untouched solitude that can only be found in wooded areas. Memories flooded my mind, each one a precious moment spent here with Rory—from the winters filled with laughter and playful snowball fights to that long-ago day when I first learned I was pregnant.

Once inside, I spotted Rory sitting next to the stone fireplace. The warm glow of the fire cast flickering shadows across her flushed face, highlighting her shaggy blonde hair.

"Rory, are you okay? Where's Mitch?"

"He's at work. I needed a break from being a wife, a mom, and from all this sadness. I was driving home from the school drop-off and found myself up here. In our happy place."

"Oh, Rory, you had me worried."

"I'm sorry, I just miss Dad so much. I hiked around for a bit, then my car wouldn't start. I came in here to call you and one drink turned into two." She enveloped me in a hug as she started to cry.

"Why didn't you call Mitch?"

"I needed my sister. I wanted it to be just us two again. Like old times. Mitch doesn't understand what I've been going through, nobody does. I think I'm a little tipsy." She wiped her damp eyes.

"It feels like no one really gets how tough it's been without Dad. I think I need a drink, too. Where's the waiter?" I took Rory's hand and guided her to an empty booth. Rory got the waiter's attention and ordered a few more drinks and some appetizers. We reminisced about our childhood. "Remember the time Dad caught us smoking?" Rory laughed despite her tears.

"He really blew his top," I added.

"But he never told Mom. She would have killed us."

As the afternoon unfolded, the warmth from the fire and the comfort of our shared memories brought a sense of closeness that only siblings could understand. The lodge held so many memories for us, and it felt like a cocoon, a reprieve from the harsh realities waiting back home.

We continued to drink and reminisce until evening was upon us, eventually a seventies cover band took the stage. 'Come on." Rory drunkenly pulled me up. "Dad wouldn't want us to be so sad all the time. 'Life is for living,' like he always said."

The music from the live band flowed through the lodge as they seamlessly blended the groovy sounds of disco with the soulful tunes of Motown. The air was infused with the beats of *Stayin' Alive* and *Superstition*, which had us moving together to the songs of our youth. Rory, clad in her tight jeans and off-the-shoulder t-shirt, wore her wild beauty effortlessly. Despite her eyes, red from tears, and her words slightly slurred from the evening's grief, she remained as mesmerizing as ever.

At twenty-eight, the angular lines of my youth had soft-ened into curves, accentuated by tight high-waisted Jordache jeans and a hot pink crop top. My platinum blonde hair, teased into rebellion, was barely contained by a matching pink banana clip. Though I stood at a modest five-foot-four, not nearly as tall as Rory, my penchant for platform shoes and fearless dance moves always managed to capture both attention and admiration.

"This is exactly what we needed." Rory shouted over the blaring music. She pointed up toward the heavens above, and with a sad smile on her face, we attempted to dance our grief away. The evening unfolded into the escape we so desperately craved, a brief interlude from the mourning that had enveloped our lives. "It's been tough on everyone, but I bet Dad's up there, cheering for us to start living and laughing again," she said, her words a mix of hope and defiance against the pain.

THE NEXT MORNING JOLTED ME AWAKE, MY HEAD POUNDING and my mouth parched as if I'd wandered a desert in my sleep.

"What happened last night? It's all a blur. Did we even call our husbands to tell them we were staying?"

Rory jumped up and ran to the bathroom, I could hear her retching into the toilet, a wave of panic washed over me. I fumbled for my purse, my hands trembled, searching for my pager. There were ten missed pages from Caleb. I was in big trouble.

"Rory, did we even think to call our husbands last night?" I called out, my voice laced with anxiety.

Rory emerged from the bathroom, her face pale and her lips chapped. "I don't remember, Twyla. Everything's a haze."

I felt a knot tighten in my stomach. How could we have been so irresponsible? We were mothers, wives–we had people who worried about us, depended on us. And yet, here we were, waking up in a lodge room with no recollection of the night before, we were acting like carefree sorority sisters rather than the responsible mothers we were meant to be.

We needed to get back, to face the consequences of our actions. I quickly called home, my heart racing with each ring.

"Hello?" Caleb's voice came through, tinged with unease and anger.

"Caleb, it's me. I'm sorry. We're at Mount Baldy Lodge. Rory's car broke down, and... things spiraled from there," I explained, my voice trembling.

Silence hung on the line for a moment, heavy and expectant. His voice charged with ambivalence. "You couldn't pick up a phone to let me know where you were? I've been frantic, calling everyone, trying to track you down. What were you thinking?"

"I'll explain everything when I get home."

After I dropped Rory off at her house, I arrived home to find Caleb waiting with bloodshot eyes. Starla, now eleven and rapidly growing taller, nearly matching my height, ran towards me. She threw her arms around me in a tight hug, her legs long and slender, hinting at the young woman she was becoming.

"Mama, where were you? We were so worried."

"I had to help Aunt Rory with something, sweetheart. It won't happen again. Go read in your room for a bit while Daddy and I talk, okay?" I gently nudged her with a reassuring smile.

Caleb's gaze was accusatory, his face red with anger. "You reek of alcohol and cigarettes. Were you with Keith last night?"

"That's ridiculous, Caleb. You can call Rory and check."

"I know Rory was with you, but was *he* there, too?"

"You were the one who encouraged me to contact Keith. And no, he wasn't there. I accepted his job offer because *you* thought it would be good for me," I replied, my patience wearing thin.

"Call him back and decline. You can't take that job. It was a dumb idea." His face was red with fury.

"I won't do that. I've told you before, you don't make all the decisions anymore. We should decide things together. Look, I'm sorry about last night, but you've got to trust me."

In a sudden fit of rage, Caleb kicked the TV screen. It shattered and sent glass flying across the room. The sound of Starla crying from the other room pierced the air.

"Now you've scared Starla. Control yourself, or I'm leaving," I yelled, my own anger rising.

"Don't let the door hit you on your way out," he shot back.

I hurried into Starla's room and grabbed a few essentials before rushing to my car.

"Where are we going, Mommy?" Starla asked, her voice shaky.

"To Hollywood, sweetie. We're going to visit Aunt Susan and Uncle Daniel for a little while." I answered as I tried to sound calm. I started the engine, my heart heavy with uncertainty and anger.

"Will Lacey be there, too?"

"Of course, she will, and she'll be so happy to see you."

Caleb had every right to be upset, but couldn't he have shown a bit more understanding? Dad would have known exactly how to mend things; he always had a knack for it, and the realization that I'd never again seek his advice or hear his comforting southern drawl shattered my heart. As I made my way to LA, it dawned on me that I was on my own in navigating this.

"OF COURSE, YOU CAN STAY HERE. THE STUDIO IS ONLY TEN minutes down the road, but you and Starla will have to share the sofa bed. Let Caleb see what he's missing, and he'll be begging you to come back." Susan tapped her long red nails against the kitchen counter.

"That's the thing, I'm not sure if I want to go back. I'm only twenty-eight, but I feel I've lived an entire life-time already. Lived without living, I'm tired of it," I declared.

"Things haven't been the same since Dad died, it's like he was the anchor that kept us grounded. Life will settle down soon, sis. Mark my words."

I wasn't sure I wanted things to settle down.

I was angry.

Angry that Caleb wanted me to move on so quickly.

Angry that God took my dad at such a young age.

And angry I'd have to go through the rest of my life without a father. It felt good to feel something other than despair. Maybe this was the universe's way of nudging me out of my comfort zone. A fresh start was what I needed.

It was intimidating, but I felt a small spark inside at the thought of taking control of my destiny.

I watched Starla, who was quietly coloring at the kitchen table. Her innocence and resilience in the face of change were inspiring. She'd adapt, lots of parents split up these days.

Susan poured us both a cup of tea and sat down next to me. "You know, you've always been the one to play it safe, follow the rules. But there's a whole world out there beyond what's been planned for you, beyond what Caleb expects from you. Maybe it's time you explored it and figure out what *you* want out of life, while you're still young enough to start over."

Her words resonated with me. "Sometimes I feel like I can't breathe, I never mentioned this to anyone, but I had a miscarriage right before Dad passed. I feel so bad, because I wasn't sure if I was ready to have more kids, then I lost it. I never told Caleb. It would have broken his heart."

"Oh, Twy. That's a lot to process on your own. Why didn't you reach out?"

"Everyone's been so upset about Dad, I didn't want to add to it."

"I'm here for you, sis, and you can always confide in me. Let's get Daniel to stay home with the girls, and you and I can go to Barney's Beanery for a drink, and some more girl talk. It's good to have you here." Susan took my hand in hers.

"Only if you promise not to talk about babies or husbands. I just don't want to think about it right now."

"You have my word." She put her hand over her heart to make her point clear.

"Let me call Keith and find out about a start date before we go." I tried to ignore that small voice in the back of my mind telling me to go home and fix things with Caleb. I shook off the notion. I needed to clear my head. I'd spent my whole life trying to please everyone else, maybe it was time to start pleasing myself. I deserved this.

CHAPTER 22

Shut Up and Dance

HOLLYWOOD, CALIFORNIA
WINTER 1988

Twilight Silverson
Twenty-Eight Years Old

The relentless thud in my head was in cruel harmony with the bustling energy of a hospital set. Navigating the hallways, I gripped my hair-stylist kit like a lifeline. The glaring studio lights were an unforgiving reminder of last night's overindulgence in alcohol—a decision I was now deeply regretting.

Crew members rushed about, lugging equipment, fine-tuning lights, and arranging cameras with precision. My gaze landed on the iconic nurses' station—the very heart of the show. Actors were on the set running through their lines with dedication.

It's all happening.

I did my best to appear composed and professional, but the queasiness in my stomach was making it difficult.

"Rough night?" Keith's voice cut through my foggy state. I turned to see him eyeballing me with an amused yet concerned look. His charismatic smile, usually a source of comfort, now felt almost too intense against the backdrop of my discomfort.

"Something like that," I managed to mumble, my voice betraying the remnants of last night.

With an understanding nod, Keith responded. "Come with me." He led me to a small corner office and reached into his bag, he pulled out a small baggy with white powder inside. "Might help you get through the morning, this is a big opportunity. You've got to be on top form."

"Drugs, Keith? I'm not sure. What even *is* it?"

"Only a little cocaine, it will give you a burst of energy. I put my neck on the line by getting you this job. You look like hell. This will sort you out. It's an immediate hangover cure." Keith pulled out a small mirror and credit card, he deftly arranged the powder into a thin line and handed me a little straw.

I'd always been the good girl and had never even tried marijuana, I was home being a mother while all my friends were out experimenting with drugs and alcohol.

"I'm not sure," I murmured, the very idea unfamiliar and daunting. "I've never even come close to trying marijuana." A knot of apprehension tightened in my gut, a physical manifestation of my internal turmoil.

"Come on, everyone's doing it. It's going to be fine, I promise you. You're in Hollywood now. It's time to see what you've been missing," he coaxed, his words a siren call to abandon my reservations and dive into the unknown.

Maybe it was time for me to start experiencing new things. I quieted the warning alarms going off inside my head and snorted the powder up quickly. My eyes watered and my nose burned. Gradually, I experienced a burst of energy and a brief escape from the relentless headache. Almost immediately, I was enveloped in a sense of euphoria from the sudden increase of dopamine, my mood instantly lifted.

"The Hollywood life is tougher than I anticipated."

Keith chuckled softly. "Now you look like the bright-eyed Twyla I remember. You'll do great. You can keep the rest of this in case you need it, I can always get more. Coke is everywhere in Hollywood these days." He shook the small baggy in the air.

"Thank you for this opportunity, I really appreciate it," I managed to say as I tucked the small baggy away, a mix of gratitude and apprehension swirling within me. The reality of my choices, the stark contrast between my past life and the one I was stepping into, hit me hard. I was far from the small-town girl who dreamed of making it big. Here, in the pulsating heart of Hollywood, I was playing by a whole new set of rules.

"There's someone important I'm having lunch with; we're trying to write him back onto the show. Would you stop by around noon to say hello? Make sure you are looking your best."

"Of course, Keith, and thanks again."

As he walked away, I wiped my nose, I felt a newfound confidence and determination as I headed towards the hair and makeup area. Despite the less-than-ideal start, I vowed not to let it overshadow my first day.

With each step, I felt a growing determination to turn this challenging beginning into a successful start in my Hollywood career. I needed my own income, if I was going to make it as a single mom.

The rest of the morning flew by, the head stylist showed me the ropes and let me work on some of the extras to get a feel for my talent.

Before I knew it, lunchtime arrived. I caught a glimpse of myself in the mirror, gave my platinum hair a playful fluff, and refreshed my look with a swipe of bubblegum pink lip gloss. With a renewed sense of confidence, I navigated my way through the bustling set towards Keith's office, ready for whatever the afternoon held.

"Come in, Twyla. There's someone I think you should meet," Keith said, his words laced with a playful tone. I entered the dimly lit office and time seemed to slow. There, in the flesh, was Blackie Greenfield, the epitome of Australian charm and rock 'n' roll charisma. His muscular frame was casually poised, every inch of him radiated a captivating intensity.

His hair, a perfectly deliberate mess that struck a balance between carefree abandon and calculated allure. It framed his face in a way that hinted at an unbridled spirit inside. His brown eyes were the eyes of a storyteller, a soul with stories only music could tell.

"Blackie, meet Twyla, our talented new hair stylist," Keith introduced, his voice bridging our two worlds. "Twyla, this is Blackie Greenfield."

A warmth bloomed in my cheeks as I offered a tentative hand, my voice a fragile whisper. "It's an honor to meet you. I love your music."

His handshake was firm yet gentle, his smile warmed my heart. "The honor is mine, Twyla. I've heard great things."

"Are you thinking of coming back to the show?"

"Maybe, if the script is interesting enough." He looked pointedly at Keith.

We engaged in small talk, skirting the boundaries of formalities and genuine interest. However, his gaze quickly shifted to the small notebook tucked into my leopard print stylist belt. Its worn edges a stark reminder of the countless hours I'd devoted to spilling my heart onto its pages.

"What do you have there?" he inquired, nodding towards the notebook with a gentle curiosity.

"It's my notebook. I write poetry. Just as a little hobby," I said, feeling a little embarrassed as blood rushed to my cheeks.

"May I?"

With a hesitant nod, I handed Blackie the notebook, my heart a silent drum of nerves. He treated each page with reverence, his eyes scanned the words I had poured my soul into.

"Twyla, these are really good," he said earnestly, his voice a warm echo in the cool air. "Your words, they speak of a tortured artist inside."

I was floored. The words of Blackie Greenfield, a legend whose own lyrics had etched themselves into the heart of the eighties, filled my soul with light.

"Would it be alright if I jotted down this poem, maybe put it to music? You could make a pretty penny if the label releases it." He leaned back onto Keith's desk.

"That would be an honor," I managed to say. "You can have it. I have that one memorized." I ripped out the page and handed it to him.

"Cheers, love. This was a bit of an unexpected turn," he offered, flashing that movie-star grin, then shifted focus to Keith. "Shoot that script over to my manager, mate. I'll let you know my take on it. Gotta bolt now."

"Do you realize what just happened? Looks like you made quite the impression on Blackie. He doesn't take to everyone like that. Here I am trying to show off our new sexy hairdresser, and you're pushing your poetry on a mega rock star." Keith's eyes were huge with disbelief and something else, perhaps envy?

"That's not exactly how it happened," I defended myself.

"Make sure you keep your songbook hidden from now on. Around here, people get weird if they suspect you're self-promoting instead of focusing on work."

"Got it, Keith. I didn't realize that would cause an issue, nor did I know Blackie Greenfield was who you intended for me to meet. Thanks for making the introduction," I replied, my voice tinged with the frustration Keith's words had sparked.

"Well, that's what I get for trying to show off. I am happy for you, and it just took me by surprise. Don't get mad."

I nodded, the reality of the surreal turn of events slowly sunk in. My simple, heartfelt poem, born from the struggles of my childhood, was now in the hands of Blackie Green-field, a global rock icon. The thought sent a thrill through me, maybe this Hollywood life was just what I needed.

Keith nudged me again, his smile didn't quite reach his eyes. "Twyla, you better brace yourself. This could be the start of something big."

"We'll see, Keith," I replied, catching the faintest glint of something complex in his gaze—was it concern or a silent rivalry with Blackie's sudden interest in me? "It's hard to imagine. It's Blackie, and I'm, well, I'm just Twyla. I'm a nobody, he's a famous singer songwriter. I have a hard time believing he needs my little poem to create a hit."

"You shouldn't undersell yourself. You have a lot to offer."

I gave him a small, appreciative smile. "Thanks, Keith. I guess it's a lot to take in all at once." I didn't quite know how to take his reaction. Keith seemed to switch from hot to cold at a moment's notice and it left my head swimming. He's changed so much from that awkward paperboy I once knew.

"Just take it one step at a time. Hey, do you want to grab some lunch? I thought I was going to have lunch with Blackie but now it appears I'm free."

"Thanks, I'm not really hungry. I'm just going to grab a tomato juice and get back to my station," I responded.

"As you wish." Keith looked a little disappointed, but I wasn't sure I was comfortable with all this extra attention. I didn't want my coworkers to get the wrong idea.

I turned towards the styling station, my hands instinctively reached for my tools—the brushes, the scissors, all neatly arranged in my stylist belt.

As I returned to my work, my attention seamlessly transitioned to the strands of hair gliding through my fingers, to the characters whose stories I helped bring to life with each snip and style. My face glowed with the happiness of new adventures and the buzz of mingling with celebrities I'd admired on TV and radio energized me. I hoped I'd made a good first impression.

It was all happening.

"You won't believe the first day I've just had, Kaity, I met all the stars of the show, and everyone is so beautiful, there must be something in the water here. I even met Blackie Greenfield!" I had finished my first day at work and had to tell someone about my exciting day. Daniel and Susan weren't home yet, so I called my old friend from Cosmetology school, Kaity.

"You're just as beautiful. Now, what was Blackie like? Is he coming back to the show?"

"I'm not sure, I think they are talking about it. He was meeting with Keith, and he's beautiful, Australian, and a rock star in every sense of the word. What else is there to say?"

"Tell me everything he said. I just love him."

"He saw my notebook and asked about it," I giggled at the memory.

"You still carry that thing around?"

"Writing is my escape. You never know when inspiration will hit. Anyway, he even asked to look at it and guess what?"

"What?" she replied.

"He took one of my poems, said it might make a great song."

"Now you're pulling my leg," she gasped.

"No, hand to God, it happened," I squealed.

"I hope he's paying you for it."

"He said I could make a lot of money, if the record company is interested."

"No contract? Oh, Twy, you're too trusting. Hollywood is going to eat you up. Maybe you should come home." Kaity's voice reflected concern.

"There are too many memories of Dad in that old house. You know that's the house I grew up in?"

"I know. Maybe you and Caleb can sell it and move somewhere else?"

"I don't know if Caleb and I want the same things anymore. This has been brewing for a while. I love him, but I don't know if I'm in love with him." I wrapped the phone cord around my finger, my thoughts drifted to the life I'd lost.

"I'm no expert, but I do know love takes work." Kaity held a certain sadness in her voice.

"Enough about me. How are things in your love life? Any new men?"

"No, I'm as dry as the Sahara Desert." She laughed.

"Why don't you come out here and I can show you around? I'm a free woman now. Maybe I could introduce you to Keith. He knows everyone in Hollywood."

"I'm game for that, girlfriend, just name the date and time. See if you can get Blackie to come along. I'd eat him up with a spoon." She laughed.

"That's crazy, Twy. Time really does fly. Give me a buzz when you've got a date for our night out, I'll be up there in a flash."

As I hung up the phone with Kaity, I pulled out my phone book to look up Keith's number. This is exactly what Kaity needed.

THE NIGHT OF OUR GET-TOGETHER ARRIVED QUICKLY. AS WE stepped into the Rainbow Bar and Grill on that bustling Thursday night, I was instantly transported back to that time when Rory and I sneaked in as underage minors. I was so timid before, afraid of my own shadow, clutching onto Rory as if she were my lifeline in that smoky sea of noise and laughter. But things were different now. I was different.

The dimly lit interior, with its dark wood walls, emitted a warm and inviting rock 'n' roll atmosphere. The once overwhelming sounds of clinking glasses and raucous conversations now complimented my newfound daring spirit.

We moved through the crowd with a sense of ownership, a long way from the wallflower I had once been. My laughter mingled freely with the eclectic assortment of patrons, from weathered rockers to starry-eyed dreamers. I found Keith at the bar, wearing his tight jeans and snakeskin boots as he sipped an apple martini.

"Keith, this is Kaity, my friend from cosmetology,"

"Nice to meet you, Keith."

"Hi, Kaity. I think I met you once before, at the Supercuts." Keith took her hand in his and kissed her on the cheek. This was going to be a great night.

The bar buzzed with the energy of a typical Los Angeles evening. The aroma of pizza permeated the air and blended with the sounds of clinking glasses and lively conversations.

"What would you ladies like to drink?"

"Two glasses of sparkling," I responded.

"Okay, Miss Fancy Pants."

"I'm only drinking champagne from now on. Life should be a celebration. Every day."

"Two glasses of bubbly it is." Keith went to the bar to order our drinks while we checked in with the hostess.

Throughout the night, Keith's attention seemed to flit back and forth between us, but his focus lingered more and more on me. His subtle touches, the way he leaned in when I spoke, and the lingering glances he gave me didn't go unnoticed. It was flattering, but also a bit overwhelming, given my recent doubts about Caleb and my own future.

Kaity took it all in stride. She laughed at Keith's jokes, engaged in the conversation, but I could tell she saw what was happening. As the night progressed, we made our way to the nightclub next door, Keith was over talking to the bartender when Kaity leaned in close to me, her voice scarcely a whisper.

"Twyla, I think Keith's still got a thing for you," she said with a knowing smile.

I looked over at Keith, who was currently animatedly telling a story to the bartender and felt a heavy sense of trepidation. "I'm starting to realize that, too."

Kaity shrugged, her smile full of mischief. "Well, if he has a brother, feel free to send him my way."

We both laughed, the tension easing a bit. The night unfolded with more laughter, dancing, and moments where I caught Keith watching me with an intensity that made me wonder what it would be like to be with him.

Later, as we took a break from the dance floor, he pulled me aside. "Twyla, I'm having a great time tonight. I'm sorry about overreacting in my office that day you met Blackie. It was fine you gave your poem to him. I know it wasn't contrived. I just didn't want the higher ups seeing something like that happen."

"I understand and thanks again for the introduction."

"Do you think we could go on a real date sometime? Maybe just the two of us? I heard you and Caleb aren't together anymore."

"How?" I asked, a bit surprised.

"My mom called me the other day. You know she still keeps in touch with the gossip circle in Montclair."

I hesitated, my mind a tempest of thoughts about my marriage, my new life, and this unexpected turn of events. "Maybe, Keith. I need some time to think. Let's have some fun tonight and not take things too seriously, okay?"

"Fun is my middle name. I have a little nose candy if you care to partake."

I hesitated but remembered this was the new me, the one who enjoyed living on the edge.

"Okay. Let's go to the bathroom."

"I didn't know you had this hidden wild side." Keith followed close behind.

"This is the new me. I'm done being the good girl, always putting everyone else first. After Dad passed, well let's say I realized life is short, and I haven't really lived yet." I bit my lip as I looked back at my old friend.

Soon we found ourselves crammed into a tiny bathroom stall, Keith's grin matched the glint in my eyes as he handed me his small mirror with a line of white powder.

"To old friends and secret rendezvous."

"To old friends and breaking all the rules," I replied as I snorted the coke up my nose and felt that immediate rush of endorphins. I leaned against the bathroom stall as Keith snorted his line.

The clandestine thrill of it added an unexpected layer of thrill to our bathroom meeting.

As we stood there, side by side, I could feel the radiating warmth of Keith's presence. His arm brushed lightly against mine, sending shivers down my spine. I turned to look at him. We'd bonded over what it was like to lose a father as a young adult and the forbidden nature of our rendezvous had intensified the connection, igniting a spark of desire that had laid dormant beneath the surface.

Without a word, he gently cupped my face in his hands. The world faded away as his lips met mine in a soft, lingering kiss. It was a kiss brimming with years of friendship, longing, and unspoken feelings he'd kept at bay.

My heart raced as our lips moved together in perfect

harmony. The taste of his martini lingered on his tongue, mingling with the excitement of our forbidden kiss. The rush of breaking the rules and the undeniable attraction Keith had for me culminated in this lustful encounter.

As we pulled away, our eyes locked once, and a smile formed on Keith's lips. "I've wanted you so much, Twyla," he whispered.

I smiled back, my heart brimming with confusion. Why now was I feeling drawn to Keith? "Don't go falling in love with me. I'm not looking for anything like that."

"I've always been in love with you, Twyla. Haven't you realized that by now?" He twirled a lock of my hair through his fingers.

"No, Keith, it's too soon. I'm not ready for another relationship. Let's keep things light, okay?"

"As you wish." He looked a little deflated.

"Now, shut up and dance with me." I laughed as I grabbed Keith's hand and dragged him out of the bathroom and onto the dance floor.

The rush from the cocaine and buzz from the champagne combined to create an electrifying energy. The dance floor was a sea of vibrant lights and pulsating music, beckoning me to surrender to its rhythmic embrace.

We lost ourselves in the music, our bodies moved in perfect sync. Our cocaine-fueled chuckles echoed in the air. We spun and twirled; our laughter harmonized with the beat of the music. I felt young, alive and invincible.

In that moment, it didn't matter that we were breaking

the rules or that we now worked together, I *wanted* to break the rules.

EVERY LAST ONE OF THEM.

THE NEXT DAY, IN THE EARLY MORNING HOURS, I STUMBLED back into Daniel and Susan's apartment. It was just before five am. Kaity had found her way home hours earlier, not wanting to come to the after-hours party Keith and I had gone to in the Hollywood Hills.

"Well, is this the first time you've ever sneaked in? Because you're terrible at it. What's all that clatter?" Susan grumbled.

"Sorry, I dropped my purse on my way through the door." I slurred my words.

"I know you are trying to spread your wings a bit, but the kids have school today and the grownups have work. I think it's about time you got your own place. Your new lifestyle is too disruptive. Partying on the weekend is one thing, but this midweek stuff won't fly with Daniel."

"Sorry, sis. I'll check with the apartment manager later today and see if anything has opened up."

"Good idea. You know, Caleb came by while you were out partying. You need to stop ignoring him and figure out what you two are doing."

"Caleb was here?"

"Yes, he took Lacey and Starla out for ice cream and left you those." Susan motioned over to a dozen red roses.

"Well, I'm not going back. I can't go back to that house… to that marriage. It's too stifling."

"You need to figure yourself out. Tell Caleb what's bothering you." Susan tapped her fingers on the countertop. "Nothing good will come from this living between two worlds. Either file for divorce or go back to your husband. You guys can sell the house and find a new one."

"I'll think about it, sis, but now I'm going to shower and get ready for work," I said, trying to hide the turmoil in my heart.

"Caleb also left this for you." She handed me an envelope.

> Twyla,
> I hope this message finds you well. It's been a while since we talked, and I've got a lot to say to you. First off, I ain't the best with fancy words or saying what needs to be said, but I need to try.
> I know I haven't been the easiest guy to live with, and I've done some things . . . I've been too controlling and selfish, at times. I took you for granted, and that's on me. But I want you to know, I'm going to change.
> I'm seeing a marriage counselor now, working on sorting out my stuff. And I've been reconnecting with

my spirituality, I shouldn't have stopped going to church. It helps keep me grounded.

I let my anger get the best of me that day, but it will never happen again. I want to get back on course and maybe find some redemption... a way to be a better man.

Our home is so lonely without you and Starla. I miss you both every day. I'm ready to do whatever it takes to make things right again, even if it means eating a little humble pie. I know things have changed since the passing of your dad, but I still love you—I'm always here for you. I hope you'll consider giving us a chance to fix what's broken.

With love and a whole lot of regret,
Caleb

As I read the letter, thoughts of my troubled marriage and uncertain future weighed on my mind. I tossed the letter onto the table and headed for the shower. The warm water cascaded over me and served as a brief refuge from the chaos of my life, but it couldn't wash away the confusion and pain that had taken root.

Midst the steam and solitude, I realized that the decisions I made in the coming days would shape my destiny. The choices between love and independence, reconciliation, and separation, all loomed ominously over me.

Little did I know that fate had an unexpected twist in

store, one that would rock the foundation of my already unstable life.

CHAPTER 23

Tainted Love

HOLLYWOOD, CALIFORNIA
SPRING 1989

Twilight Silverson
Twenty-Nine Years Old

Days turned into weeks and weeks into months as we adapted to our new Hollywood lifestyle. I rented my own apartment and fell into a rhythm of working all day and partying most nights. Starla spent a lot of time over at Susan's or Lacey would stay over with us and they were soon as close as sisters.

The city's vibrant energy coursed through my veins, and every day felt like an adventure waiting to happen. As I navigated the ups and downs of my new life, Keith and I became more entangled and, although we still maintained separate apartments, we spent most of our time after work together.

After sharing that kiss in the bathroom stall, slipping into a relationship with Keith came naturally. His vibrant personality and access to the city's best parties made every day exciting. However, Starla couldn't stand him. Despite being only twelve, her determination was as solid as an ox. Once she formed an opinion, convincing her to change it was almost impossible.

Now I needed to share the news that I knew would disappoint her.

"Hey, sweetie." My voice was filled with trepidation. "I need to talk to you about Easter."

Starla closed her book, her brow furrowing in frustration. "What is it now, Mom?"

My heart ached as I hesitated, "This year, things are going to be a little different for Easter. Dad wants to take you to San Diego to spend the holiday with him and your grandparents on his side."

"But we always spend Easter together with the Camerons. Grandma Dawn has that big egg hunt and I'll miss my cousins." Agitation reflected on Starla's face. Her green eyes flashed with fury.

I nodded, my own tears welling up. "I know, sweetie, and I wish we could keep that tradition. But, um, this year, I have something important to do, too."

"What is it, Mom? What's so important?"

I took a deep breath, "I'm going to Monterey with Keith Simpson to meet his parents."

The frustration in Starla's eyes quickly turned into anger and hurt. "What? You're bailing on me at Easter to be with him? You are like, the most bogus mom ever. How could you change so much? I want everything to be how it was before. I hate you!" she screamed, her voice fused with anger as she bolted from the room, dashed into her bedroom, and cranked up her tunes to maximum.

My heart ached as I sat there quietly stunned, I knew that my decision was difficult for Starla to accept, but I hadn't expected this. I hoped, that in time, she would learn to understand.

EASTER WEEKEND ARRIVED QUICKLY, AND I WAS MEETING Keith's mom and stepdad at a fancy restaurant in Monterey. Amidst the plush surroundings, the air seemed to hum with unspoken expectations.

Keith's Mom Barbara, with her perfectly coifed hair, leaned in closer to me. "You know, dear, I can't help but wonder if we might hear wedding bells in your future." Her words filled the air like a heavy perfume enveloping the space around me. Her face was flushed with the Bloody Marys we'd been drinking, and she seemed a bit tipsy.

Barbara, Keith, and his stepdad Marc exchanged

knowing glances, and the conversation naturally transitioned towards the future, making me feel like an unwitting extra in a yuppie romance flick. Feeling the pressure, I called the waiter over and ordered another Bloody Mary, hoping the alcohol would dull the anxiety I felt. This was going all wrong.

Marc chimed in. "Yes, and once you settle down, the pitter-patter of little feet will surely follow." His gaze drifted towards my empty glass.

"I'll have another one of these spicy Bloody Marys, please." Then I turned to Keith's mom. "Well, Keith and I will have to discuss that. My divorce isn't even final yet."

"It shouldn't be too long," Keith assured his mom.

Just then the band kicked in, synthetic beats created the perfect soundtrack for the night, I saw an opportunity to escape the scrutiny of Keith's parents. The front man, stylishly tousled hair and an oversized blazer, directed his charm my way. My head pounded with the aftereffects of day drinking and I looked for anything to help detract from more talk of marriage and babies.

"We should dance." I pulled Keith up onto the dance floor.

"What's going on with you? You seem so nervous, and you might want to slow down on those Bloody Marys," Keith questioned.

"What's with your parents and all the baby talk." My words were slightly slurred, earning me a less-than-pleased look from Keith.

"Maybe you should have a glass of water or an espresso." Keith motioned towards the table. The lead singer caught my eye and winked.

"This next song goes out to all those females who find themselves wanting to run away," the band announced before breaking into the song *Tainted Love*.

"Keep dancing with me. I love this song."

"Stop making a spectacle of yourself. I see you flirting with the lead singer of the band." Keith's face was as red as the Bloody Marys we'd been drinking, as he pinched my arm.

"Ouch, I did nothing to deserve that," I muttered, a wave of discomfort flooding my soul as I confronted a disturbing side of Keith that I didn't care for. As we navigated our way back to the table, Keith maintained a tight hold on my wrist, his grip firm and unyielding. I noticed the lead singer observing us, his eyes reflecting a mix of concern and sympathy. I managed a feeble shrug in his direction before sinking back into my seat, my head swimming from the alcohol I'd consumed.

Maybe I'll slip away to the bathroom and do a line of coke. That would clear my head. I thought to myself.

"I'm going to the ladies' room. I'll come right back."

Keith looked at me with a distrustful look in his eyes. "See that you do."

Once in the bathroom, I splashed some cold water on my face and pulled out a mirror, quickly snorting up a small line of coke that I'd carefully laid out. I returned to the table feeling a bit brighter but still tipsy.

"What did I miss? Not more talk of babies, I hope."

"What has gotten into you?" he said to me before turning to his mom. "She's never like this."

Keith attempted to regain control of the situation with hidden pinches under the table. The stings couldn't dull my spirit; I tried to maintain my composure and drink some coffee, but as Keith's parents continued to talk about our future together, I found myself going back to my Bloody Mary. The world around me blurred into a haze. With each word they spoke, the sensation of dread grew in the pit of my stomach, pushing me further from seeing a future with Keith and into a perfect storm of unease and confusion.

"Maybe we should take Twyla home. She seems to be a lightweight." Barbara chuckled.

"Good idea, Mom. I'll go get the valet to pull the car up. Meet me out front in five minutes." Keith made his way to the valet stand in front of the building while his parents tried to help me sober up.

We found Keith in front of the glitzy restaurant, now a blur in designer threads and frosted tips, he guided me into his mom's sleek blue Mercedes. The ride was strained and silent, the city lights reflected off the polished exterior. My head throbbed, and my stomach rolled in discomfort.

"Enjoy your fun now, darling. You won't be able to drink once the babies start coming." Barbara turned towards me and batted her big fake eyelashes.

Without warning, I vomited all over the pristine interior of the new Mercedes. Barbara's expression turned from one of amused tolerance to shock and dismay, while Keith's face reddened with embarrassment and anger.

"For God's sake, roll the window down and have her stick her head out, in case she does it again," Marc ordered.

With my head out the window, the city lights passed by, and a realization dawned on me. Keith just wasn't for me. I wanted fun and freedom while he wanted a wife and baby.

The next morning, I awoke with my head spinning.

"Do you have any Tylenol?" I asked as I shuffled into the kitchen, finding Keith and his parents already enjoying cappuccinos and croissants.

"Good morning, bright eyes. How about a little hair of the dog?" Marc suggested, nodding towards the Bloody Mary mix on the counter, leftover from the day before.

My stomach rolled as I waved off the offer. "No, thanks, and I'm sorry about the car. Day drinking isn't really my thing, it turns out. I'll pay to have your Mercedes cleaned."

Barbara was surprisingly amiable despite my embarrassing behavior. "Nonsense, my dear. It's normal to be a bit nervous around your future in-laws."

Keith, however, didn't seem as forgiving. His tone was tight as he suggested, "Why don't you take a shower? I'll bring some toast to your room."

After showering and settling down with the toast Keith brought, I tried to ignore his strained expression as he watched me eat. He leaned against the bedroom door, his posture rigid.

"We have lunch reservations at the carvery in two hours.

I expect you to be ready, and let's avoid a repeat of what happened yesterday. No alcohol or cocaine, okay? Last night was a bit gnarly." His words carrying an unspoken strain of expectation.

"What did you tell them? What's with all this talk about babies and marriage? It's too much."

"Well, I was planning to give you this at lunch today," Keith whipped out a little black jewelry box and tossed it on the bed. "But I guess my plans have been ruined now, haven't they?"

"Keith, I can't marry you. I'm not ready for that. I thought we were keeping things light and casual."

"I was trying to do that, but I love you. I want you to be my wife. Won't you at least look at the ring?" He motioned over to the tiny box lying on the bed.

"It's beautiful," I managed to choke out the words. It was an oval cut diamond with a halo of pearls. I detested pearls.

Keith didn't know me at all.

"I can't accept it. I'm not ready for this. My divorce isn't even final, and you want me to jump into another engagement?"

"We've known each other since I was twelve. I've always loved you. I lost you once to Caleb and I'm not losing you again."

"Do you even know why Caleb and I split up? We started to want different things. He wanted more kids and couldn't accept that I didn't want a big family, not with him and not with anyone."

"That's what broke you up?"

"Partially, he couldn't seem to understand why I didn't want to have more babies and things became tense. My dad's death made it all worse." Having spent over a decade striving to be the perfect wife and mother, I wasn't ready to start all over with Keith. He was another man who wanted to plan my whole life out for me, without considering my feelings and desires. Silently, I vowed to escape this relationship.

"Well, if that's how you feel, perhaps it is best for us to part ways. I know I want kids, *my own kids*. I guess I misread the situation."

THE NEXT DAY THE CAR RIDE TO THE AIRPORT WAS SILENT, an unspoken tension hung between us. Seated on the plane, I turned to Keith. "We need to talk, but I don't even know where to begin."

He exhaled deeply. "I know. This weekend was rough. And Easter lunch was painfully awkward. How did things go so wrong? I thought we were on the same page."

"And I thought we were just having a bit of fun. I didn't know you were about to propose," I said, sensing the weight of our situation. "I thought you knew where we stood. You and Starla can hardly be in a room together, and after what you said yesterday, I don't see the situation improving."

Keith met my gaze with a mix of regret and understanding. "I've been thinking about that, too. I could have phrased it better. I want to be a dad to Starla, but I want kids of my own too. Preferably more than one. If you don't want that, it's best if we parted ways. I got over you once, I can do it again. I think."

I leaned back, closing my eyes briefly. "Splitting up is going to be the best for both of us, Keith. Let's try to keep things friendly. We still work together."

"Of course." As the plane soared back towards LAX, the space between us felt more significant than ever. I truly hoped we could put this behind us and continue to work together without animosity.

As the city lights welcomed me back to la la land, the realization that some divides are too vast to bridge settled heavily upon me, marking the end of one chapter and the uncertain beginning of another.

CHAPTER 24

Steal My Sunshine

HOLLYWOOD, CALIFORNIA
SPRING 1990

Twilight Silverson
Thirty Years Old

"Oh, let her go. She'll be safe," I found myself saying, a blend of assurance and hope in my voice.

Susan shot back, skepticism lacing her tone, "Palm Springs? But they're only seventeen."

The conversation unfolded amidst a backdrop of a girls' spa night, with Daniel away, the air was brimming with the laughter and conversation that comes from watching movies, painting nails, and sharing slices of pizza.

A year had passed since the Monterey debacle, a time defined by clarity and growth rather than chaos. After splitting from Keith, I immersed myself in my career, exploring the realms of styling and fashion that initially drew me to Hollywood. I focused on discovering myself independently, without a man's guidance. This journey was about more than professional advancement; it was about unveiling the true Twilight Silverson, free from any man's influence over her desires and decisions.

Everything was looking up. My relationship with Starla had started to heal post-Keith. We still had our moments, but we were able to talk them out instead of Starla yelling and running off.

Parting ways with Keith had left us on good terms, and as an unexpected bonus, I found my reliance on coke dwindling. I was almost completely drug free but had a couple of relapses in moments of weakness.

Caleb and I, too, found a new rhythm in our co-parenting life. Our divorce still wasn't final, and we had worked towards a more respectful and understanding partnership.

It was a year of living deliberately, of making choices that aligned with my deepest truths and aspirations. The path ahead was mine to shape, and I stepped forward with confidence, unburdened by the need for approval or direction from anyone else.

"Did you hear me? You seem a world away." Susan interrupted my thoughts.

"Lacey is a senior now. Remember, I was already a mother at her age. I wish I had done more things like that before jumping into marriage. They'll be fine." I took a sip of my tea.

Susan sighed, the weight of future worries momentarily pressing down. "Okay, but just wait till Starla turns seventeen. You'll understand the worry."

"Twelve is already a challenge enough," I chuckled, trying to lighten the mood. "She acts as if she's twenty-one."

We shared a knowing look, aware of the unique blend of wisdom and naivety in such young souls. "So, who's going to break the news to Lacey about Palm Springs? You or me?"

"Lacey, the coast is clear." I called out.

"Yes, Aunt Twy?" she responded with an innocent smile from the hall.

"You can go to Palm Springs with your friends, but you must call home every day. Understand?"

"Yes, Mom, and thank you." She squealed. "I'm going to go call Emma and let her know."

"I hope I don't regret this," Susan sighed.

"What are we going to do for spring break, Mom?" Starla chimed in. "We missed Easter together last year and I want this year to be extra special."

"Have you been awake this whole time?" I questioned.

"Nobody can sleep with you two jabbering on," Starla teased. "Well?"

"Well, what?"

"Spring break, Mom. What are we going to do?" Starla asked again.

"Your Uncle Randall and Aunt Rory are taking their families to the Colorado River for some jet skiing. It was supposed to be a surprise, but would you like us to join them?"

"I would love it. You're coming too, right, Mom?"

"Well, your dad might come up for the weekend, but don't go getting any ideas. We are trying to get better at this co-parenting thing."

"Mom, don't you miss Dad at all? Why did we have to move here? I had friends back home, I miss Kaya, and I was doing great in school," Starla's voice cracked, the upheaval of her life spilling into her words.

"Starla, honey, this was a great opportunity for us. It was our big adventure; Hollywood is a place where dreams are made. I know it's hard, but sometimes we have to take chances in life."

Starla's eyes flashed with hurt. "But what about my dreams, Mom? My life? You dragged me out of school in the middle of the term. Do you even care about how I feel? It's been a year and a half and I just don't fit in here."

"Of course, I care, Starla. But I couldn't continue with how things were going back home. You'll understand when you're older, you'll see."

"I know you were so sad about Grandpa, but I thought you'd get it out of your system, that this was some kind of midlife crisis and you'd miss our old life and want to go back."

"Midlife? I'm only thirty years old, honey."

"No duh, Mom," Twyla retorted.

Sensing the argument about to escalate, Lacey slipped effortlessly into the role of peacemaker, more like an older sister. She diverted our attention from the brewing storm with a casual request. "Aunt Twy, could you do my second piercing?"

"Pierce your ears?"

"Yeah, let's make tonight exciting. You're good at everything, Aunt Twy. Starla and I can have matching piercings. Do you want to do yours, too?" she asked her younger cousin.

"That would be radical!" Starla exclaimed.

The suggestion clearly diverted Starla's attention from her complaints, and I silently mouthed a "Thank you" to my perceptive niece.

"Girls, Aunt Twy's ear piercing party is about to commence."

I scavenged through my sewing kit for the sharpest needle I could find and sterilized it with some alcohol from under the bathroom sink.

"Who needs a piercing gun? I've got everything we need right here."

"I'll go first," Lacey bravely proclaimed, her expression a mix of exhilaration and a tinge of fear.

"Hold still, darling. Aunt Twy's going old school." With a swift motion and a gentle hand, Lacey's ear was pierced. "Voila. One ear down. You're officially half a cool kid now."

Starla was next. She sat there, calm as a summer sea. "And… done." I declared. Starla blinked in surprise.

"That's it? I didn't even feel it. Mom, you're a natural."

Susan piped up, "Alright, my turn. Let's do this."

Piercing Susan's ears was a challenge, mostly because we couldn't stop giggling. Finally, it was my turn. Standing in front of the mirror, I held the needle with a steady hand. "Who says you can't teach an old dog new tricks?"

We spent the rest of the night admiring our new piercings, laughing over our boldness, and snapping pictures to commemorate our daring escapade. Starla declared it the best spa night ever. And honestly? I couldn't argue with her.

THE FOLLOWING WEEK WE ARRIVED IN LAUGHLIN, NEVADA. Randall had switched from dirt bikes to jet skis and had recently bought a secondhand ski boat. As we pulled into the Edgewater Hotel, there sat Caleb on the bench outside.

"Dad!" Starla ran over to him and jumped into his arms.

"I thought you weren't coming until Friday?" I asked.

"Well, I had a little surprise for Starla." He led us to the parking lot, where attached to the tow hitch of his Chevy truck was a brand-new WaveRunner Watercraft.

"Is it for me?"

"It's a three-seater. It's for all of us."

"How did you afford this, Caleb?" I enquired.

"Well, I heard how much Randall and his family were enjoying coming to the river, and I decided to sell my dirt bike."

"But what about your racing?"

"All those racing weekends away weren't good for our family. This is something we can all do together."

"Are you giving up racing?" I gazed deep into his eyes with shock.

"I've already been a world champion, several times. I'm stepping aside, passing the torch to the young bucks. I'm feeling it more in my old age."

"You're only thirty-three."

"Yes, an old man in the world of motocross. I'd rather go out on top, I'm getting my priorities in order."

I tried not to smile, but I'd be lying if I said I wasn't impressed with this new selfless version of Caleb. He seemed so humble and like he'd truly grown over the last two years.

WE SPENT THE NEXT WEEK IN THE CLEAR WATERS OF LAKE Mojave, and most evenings the families got together to have dinner at the casinos. We were all having the time of our lives until devastating news came crashing into our world in the form of an early morning phone call.

"Twyla. Thank God. It's Susan. Lacey is missing."

"What do you mean missing?" I questioned.

"She hasn't been checking in for the last few days. I called the hotel in Palm Springs where she and her friends were supposedly staying, and Lacey wasn't with them. Can you come back and help me? I need you."

"Of course, sis. Did you call the other parents of the other girls she was going with?"

"Yes, that's the thing. The other girls went to Palm Springs as planned, but Lacey and her boyfriend decided to go to Rosarito Beach."

"Mexico?" I replied.

"Yes, Emma spilled the beans when her mom questioned her."

"Oh my gosh, sis. When was the last time anyone heard from them?"

"It's been two days. Daniel is down in Mexico looking for them as we speak. I stayed back by the phone in case she called. I want to go help Daniel look for her. Will you come back and man the phone for me?"

"I'm on my way." I quickly woke up Starla and told her to pack her things. I knocked on the door that separated Caleb's hotel room from ours and quickly explained the situation.

"I'm driving you," he immediately insisted, his voice firm and leaving no room for argument. The urgency in his eyes matched the pounding of my heart. Within minutes, we were packed and rushing down to the car, the early morning air crisp and tense around us.

"What about your truck and the WaveRunner?"

"I'll get Mitch or Rory to drive it home. I already left the keys with the front desk. They were helpful when I explained the situation."

"Good idea."

"You know, I have some connections down in Mexico from all that time I spent down there racing. I'll drive Susan down and get in touch with my men in the area."

"Okay, Caleb. Thank you."

The sun crested over the desert expanse as we headed west and we made it back to Hollywood in record time.

"Any word?" I asked Susan as we entered her apartment.

"Not from Lacey, but Daniel called. He said the police had found a body that fits the description of Kyle, Lacey's boyfriend. His parents are on their way to identify the body," Susan said, her body racked with tears.

"Sis, we'll find her. Caleb has connections in Mexico— he knows some federales. He's going to drive you down today and help you look," I comforted my sister, trying to sound strong, but inside, my heart was breaking.

"Thank you, Caleb. Can we go now?" Susan regained her composure.

"I'm ready whenever you are."

THOSE NEXT FEW HOURS WERE THE MOST TERRIFYING OF MY life. I stayed by the phone at Susan's apartment in case

Lacey was somehow able to call home.

"Mama, will we ever see Lacey again?" Starla cried.

"We have to keep the faith. She'll turn up safe and sound."

"But shouldn't we be out looking for her, too?" she persisted, her eyes wet with tears. I wrapped my arms around her, pulling her close, feeling her body tremble against mine.

"Daniel, Susan, and Daddy are already on it, and they're doing everything possible. Right now, our job is to be here just in case Lacey or anyone calls with information. We need to stay strong." Starla nodded, wiping away tears as she settled next to me. The phone was our constant companion as we waited for the call that would bring our world back into balance.

The weight of the unknown pressed down on us, but together, we held on to hope, a flickering light in the over-whelming darkness.

"I'm scared, Mommy. It's like having a nightmare, only I'm awake."

"Maybe you should sleep with me tonight? You know that we are safe here, and nothing is going to happen to us."

The shrill ring of the phone interrupted our conversation.

"Listen very carefully. I want you to go to my brothers and ask them to chip in some money." It was Caleb speaking on the end of the line.

"What's going on? Is there any news?"

"Yes, and it isn't good. The body that's been found was identified as Kyle. He was tied up and shot execution style, but there was no sign of Lacey. Only a note with a phone number in his pocket asking for money."

"Oh no!" I tried to keep calm so I wouldn't scare Starla, but the coldness that crept into my heart was like nothing I'd ever felt. How could something like this happen to sweet little Kyle, Lacy's happy-go-lucky boyfriend. He was so young. They both were.

"Trafficking is big here, but money talks. I have my friend putting the word out that the family has money to buy their daughter back. You need to get as much money together as you can and wire it to me. It's our biggest chance to find Lacey. The more time that passes, the harder it will be."

"Call me back in a few hours. I should have everything we need for the wire transfer by then," I said, keeping it straightforward and focused on the task at hand. I was barely holding things together, but I had to be strong for Lacey and Starla both.

My hands shook as I called all of Caleb's and my siblings, apart from Randall. After everything he'd been through in Vietnam, I felt nervous about calling him with this horrible situation. I pulled together a thousand dollars, but I didn't know if it would be enough. Finally, I dialed the hotel in Laughlin where Randall was staying.

"I just spoke with Rory. She told me everything. How much do you have?" he asked.

"Two and a half thousand."

"I'll match it."

"Thank you, Randall. I love you, brother."

"Don't worry about it, just find our niece. Do you want me to come be with you?"

"No, stay with your family, I've got things covered here. When they find her, I'll be driving down to wherever they are," I explained.

"We are all packed up and heading home. Call me there as soon as you hear anything, no matter what time, and I'll drive with you down to Rosarita. You and Starla shouldn't make that long of a drive alone. It's not safe, especially if the news is bad. You'll be upset."

"Hopefully the news is good, Caleb is optimistic. He has a connection down there with the police force. I'll call you as soon as I hear anything."

"Caleb's a good guy. Maybe it's worth giving him another chance, you know, for the sake of your family. When he was here, he mentioned how much he's been working on himself. He's ready to do whatever it takes to make things right," he continued, his voice earnest.

"I'm starting to realize what a mess I've made of my life. When Dad died, it was like I wanted to do anything to fill the void, even drugs. I guess I went a little off the rails."

"It's not too late to get back on track, you know."

"This kidnapping has stirred up so many old memories from our time in Pomona—the violence we faced, how Mom and Dad always stood together to keep us safe. I hadn't let myself think about those days for a long time, but now, everything's rushing back. It made me realize I want to be just like our parents were for us, to better shield Starla from the ugliness of the world. I see now that I can do that best with Caleb's support. I've really messed things up, haven't I?" I sighed, feeling the weight of my words.

"Sometimes it takes a tragedy to open our eyes and see what we want out of life. Now that you've seen the other side, is it all worth it?" he asked.

"I'm asking myself that same question. I thought I'd missed out on so much, now I'm realizing what I had. I think I made a terrible mistake," I answered.

"Better to figure that out now than later," Randall responded.

"Thank you, big brother. How did you get so smart?"

"Let's say my life reached a turning point when I let go of the past and started focusing on everything I had to be grateful for. I've been in therapy; did you know that?"

"I didn't, but I'm happy for you. They should have had that available right when you came back from Vietnam."

"As Dad always said, better late than never. Now try to rest. You'll need your strength for whatever lies ahead."

I hung up the phone, Randall's words echoed in my heart. As the stillness of the night enveloped me, reflections of my past life with Starla and Caleb surfaced. The laughter, the tears, and the simple, everyday moments we shared stitched together.

In the quiet, I confronted a stark realization: the life of a hotshot Hollywood stylist, the noise, and chaos of fast living was never truly my dream. It was a distraction to numb the pain from the loss of Dad, but it never aligned with my core values. I longed for the safety and authenticity of the life I had left behind, where fame and fortune didn't dictate the rhythm of my days.

In just one night the allure of Hollywood's glamour had faded, revealing a hollow reality behind the relentless parties and superficial connections. The scene, once captivating, now felt empty and wearisome.

Where had that little girl gone who dreamed of being a teacher?

A new thought abruptly entered my mind, *"It's never too late to follow your dreams,"* and in that moment, I knew the road to redemption, however difficult, was still an option. It was time to emerge from behind this Hollywood dream and live the life that had been waiting for me the entire time. I scribbled a poem out while I waited for Caleb to call.

> In the silence of the night, true dreams unfold,
> A life of laughter, tears, tales untold.
> Hollywood's glare, once a siren's song,
> Now fades to whispers of where I belong.
> Home's gentle call, in my heart, takes hold.

LATER THAT NIGHT, WHEN CALEB CALLED, I GAVE HIM THE info for the wire transfer.

"Good work. I have another thousand to chip in. Six thousand dollars should be attractive to the kidnappers. My connection has been in touch with them… and he's hopeful we'll get her back."

"Thank you, Caleb, I mean it."

"Hold on a sec while I give Daniel the transfer information. I want to talk with you more."

"How is Susan?" I asked when Caleb came back to the phone.

"She's a wreck. Let's pray this works. How is Starla taking all of this?"

"She's upset. She was fond of Kyle… all of this is a lot for a twelve -year-old to deal with."

"I know, Twy, it puts things in perspective. Either way, things are going to be rough. Lacey could be sold or worse, and we will never see her again, even if we find her, and she'll be traumatized. Something like this… Well, it's too much for a little girl to deal with. I kept thinking, what if it was Starla. How can I protect her from this kind of violence?"

"I've been doing the same. I haven't been putting Starla first. Caleb, I want to change that, for us to fix our family. I realize how much she's going to need her parents right now. Starla needs you. *I need you.* It will be better for everyone if we are together after this, whether we get Lacey back or… " I burst into tears.

"I'm doing everything I can to find Lacey, but Twy, Susan has told me what's been going on with your drinking and drug use. I want to know if you are ready to put all that aside, that's not you. Will you go to rehab? My insurance will cover it, I've already looked into it."

"Let's talk more about it when you return, but yes, I'm ready. I've already been clean for months… There's just one thing…

"What is it, Twy?"

"I'm not sure if I have the strength to go back to the house on Harvard Street. There are too many memories."

"Is that what this was all about? I'd sell the house in a heartbeat to get you back. We can rent an apartment until it sells. Come back to me and we'll figure things out together. I want to fix things. I realized I was trying to keep you in a box, and it wasn't fair. I know that now."

"You don't have to say another word. We've both been selfish. I spent the first half of our marriage giving my all to everyone. I put everyone's needs ahead of my own. When Dad died, I felt something inside me die too. I went from one extreme to the next. I need to find a balance. I think we can do that, together."

"You have no idea how happy that makes me, I love you, Twy, but I need to go now. Daniel's back with the money. We are going to take it to my federales friend."

"Do you trust him? What if they take the money and run?"

"I trust him, Twy. I haven't told you this, it's a long story, but he's my half-brother. I found out a few years back. Dad had a girlfriend down here, and he knocked her up. The old man told me one day when he was drunk, it slipped out. All those fishing trips he took, he was seeing his mistress. That S.O.B."

"Oh, Caleb, why didn't you tell me? Is this the secret you've been keeping? I sensed something had been upsetting you."

"I had been meaning to tell you, but the timing never felt right. I discovered his existence shortly before your dad fell ill. Initially, I wanted to gauge the kind of man he was before introducing him into our lives. Then, with your dad's passing, it seemed too cruel to add to your grief. Diego is great, I can't wait for you to meet him, hopefully under less dire circumstances. I'd better go tell him how much ransom money we have. I'll call you back as soon as we hear anything."

I hung up the phone, awestruck by this new development. Caleb had a secret brother. What a shock that must have been for him. I couldn't imagine him dealing with it all alone.

"Mama, did they find Lacey?"

"Not yet, baby, but if anyone can do it, your dad can... and when this is over, we are going to be together again."

"Can we be a family again like before?" She looked up at me with hopeful eyes, her voice barely above a whisper.

"It's going to be even better than before. I know what I want now."

"I love you, Mom." Starla jumped into my arms. Everything from the last few years seemed to be forgiven. She was an adolescent and on the brink of womanhood, but still a little girl in so many ways.

"I'm sorry I broke up our family. I'm going to spend the rest of my life making it up to you." But Starla didn't hear me. She'd fallen fast asleep in my arms. I kissed her forehead and placed her in bed before going back to wait by the phone. I must have fallen asleep as well because the next thing I knew, a shrill ringing jarred me awake.

It was Caleb, his voice urgent and laced with relief. "Twyla, they found Lacey. She's in a hospital near the border. She's banged up but alive."

Tears of relief flooded my eyes. "Is she... is she okay?"

"She's stable, Twy. She's being airlifted to Rady's Hospital in San Diego. The US police are meeting us there. They're taking samples from her to see if they can identify the kidnappers one day."

The strain of the past days concern lifted, replaced by a new concern for what Lacey had endured. "I'm on my way," I said, my voice firm with resolve.

"We'll meet you there. And Twy... we might finally have some answers."

I hung up, a mix of emotions swirled inside. Relief, fear, and a burning desire for justice. As I headed out, I knew our lives were forever changed, and the road ahead was uncertain. But for now, Lacey was safe, and that was all that mattered.

CHAPTER 25

Nothing Else Matters

SAN DIEGO, CALIFORNIA
SPRING 1990

Twyla Silverson
Thirty Years Old

The sunrise drive to the hospital seemed to take forever, my mind raced with a thousand thoughts. I'd called and informed Rory of the news and asked her to tell the others.

I arrived in San Diego nearly three hours later, to find Caleb and Susan waiting in the lobby, their faces etched with concern and relief. I hugged Susan and she didn't let go for a long time, a silent acknowledgment of the ordeal we'd endured.

"I should have never convinced you to let her go,"

"It's not your fault, sis. Nobody could have foreseen this happening. One minute they were a young couple on a spring break adventure; the next, their hotel room was invaded by gang members looking for a quick score. It was a wrong place, wrong time situation. Lacey begged for her life. She said her parents would pay a ransom." Susan's voice was calm but carried the gravity of the reality we were facing.

"She's a smart girl," Caleb responded. "It probably saved her life. I know my brother and his team are working hard to catch these monsters."

"Let's go see her now. She's been asking for you, Twy."

Together, we made our way to Lacey's room.

My gaze rested on her, and my hands clenched. The stark bandages wrapped around her head contrasted sharply against her pale skin, a visible indication to the ordeal she had endured. Her eyes, once sparkling with life and mischief, now held a depth of pain and fear that words couldn't capture. She lay there, looking small and fragile in the hospital bed. Clearly, the mental scars would take longer to heal.

I took her hand gently. "Hey, sweet girl," I whispered.

Lacey managed a weak smile. "Hi, Aunt Twy."

The room was infused with an unspoken bond, a connection strengthened by the trials we'd faced over the last three days. Caleb stood beside me, his hand rested reassuringly on my shoulder, a symbol of the new beginning we were embarking upon.

Starla, usually so full of energy, stood quietly, her gaze fixed on Lacey. After a moment, she moved closer, and reached out to hold Lacey's hand. The cousins, so different yet so alike, united in a silent gesture of support and love.

"Lacey," Starla whispered, her voice steady but tinged with emotion, "you're the strongest person I know. We're all here for you. You're not alone, not now, not ever." Her words, simple and sincere, infused the space with a warmth that only heartfelt truth could bring.

Without warning, a doctor entered the room. "We have a therapist here to talk to Lacey. Her parents can stay if she wants them to."

"Yes, I don't want to be alone," Lacey cried.

Susan rushed to her side as we cleared out of the room. It was going to be a long road ahead, but I knew we'd face it together.

Navigating our way to the elevator, my daughter's gaze lifted to mine, her expression a vivid reflection of the tumultuous emotions we'd ridden over the past few days. "Can we go home now, Mom?" she asked, her voice soft yet hopeful.

I looked at my daughter and at Caleb, a profound sense of gratitude and love enveloped my heart. "Yes, sweetheart, we can go home. Our *real* home," I replied, my voice steady and full of conviction. I had been so afraid of all the memories waiting for me, but now I realized those memories were a part of who I am. They shaped me, brought me to this moment. "With you two by my side, I can face anything. I know that now."

Caleb gently squeezed my hand, and I felt a new connection building within.

As we entered the lobby, the murmur of a disturbance grew clearer. My heart jumped as I recognized the central figures of the commotion: Mom and Rory, in a fervent conversation with the hospital's receptionist. Rory's hands moved expressively, punctuating her urgent pleas. "Please, we need an update on Lacey Cruz."

Mom stood by her side looking like a volcano ready to erupt. Her words flowed like a barely contained stream of lava. "This is my granddaughter we're talking about. We need an update on her condition, now."

"Mom. Rory." My voice cut through the tension as we reached them. They turned, and their expressions shifted from stress to relief.

In that instant, amidst the sterile hospital backdrop, the embrace that followed was more than just a physical connection. Rory, Mom, and I—our hug was a fusion of hope and family support that transcended words.

"Lacey is going to be fine. She has some recovery ahead of her, but she's alive. The trauma specialist is talking to her now. They are in room 20A. You might want to wait in the hall until they are done with the counselor."

"It's so nice to see you all together. Thank you, Caleb. Thank you for helping get my granddaughter back." Mom moved toward Caleb; she only came up to his chest but somehow seemed to envelop him in her arms. "I'm glad you're here to help. You'll always be part of the Cameron family, you know that." Mom rubbed his back as they embraced.

"Where are you three off to?" Rory interrupted with a knowing look on her face.

"Home. We are going home, *together*."

"Well it's about time! We've missed you back home."

"Call me when you guys get home. We have a lot to catch up on." I gave Rory's hand a squeeze. My sister and I had grown apart in this last year. She was always supportive, but I knew that she disapproved of my new lifestyle. Somehow, I had a notion we'd be closer than ever again soon.

"Are you ready?" Caleb looked at me, full of love.

"Let's go."

On the drive home, the world seemed different – more vivid, more alive. We were not the same people who had left on spring break just a week ago. We were stronger, closer, and more determined to cherish each other. Lacey's brush with death had woken something inside me. I needed to be here for my daughter, to set a good example for her and above all, protect her.

The dark cloud had lifted from my head, and I was ready to face a new dawn.

"Mom." Starla's voice broke through my thoughts, her emerald-colored eyes shined with a mixture of faith and wisdom beyond her years. "It's not just the house that makes us a family. It's us. We are together now, and nothing else matters."

"You're right, my love. Home isn't just a place; it's where

our family is together. And that's where we're heading now
– home, to our new beginning."

CHAPTER 26

Sweet Dreams

MONTCLAIR, CALIFORNIA

SPRING 1990

Twyla Silverson
Thirty Years Old

Turning onto Harvard Street, I saw our family home and felt a whirlwind of emotions. Excitement for new beginnings mixed with apprehension about revisiting childhood memories. It was a bittersweet symphony of past and future combined.

Caleb, ever attuned to my shifts in mood, gently took my hand, grounding me with his touch. "You okay?" he inquired, his voice a soft anchor in the sea of my tumultuous thoughts.

"Just a lot of memories," I admitted, the words barely

scratching the surface of the emotions that swirled inside. I tightened my grip on his hand, grateful for the connection.

Nearing the front porch, a lone package caught my attention, resting against the door as if guarding the threshold to the past. My name was etched on it in bold, unmistakable letters.

Caleb's curiosity was piqued as he noticed my name. "Looks like you've got mail," he remarked, his eyebrow arching in intrigue.

I picked it up, feeling its weight.

The package contained three items: a cassette tape, a check, and a letter from Blackie Greenfield.

Dear Twyla,

I hope you don't mind. I got your address from the HR Department at Beverly Hospital. I am writing to share some exciting news with you.

First off, I've got to say a massive thanks to you. When you showed me your poem, I was deeply touched by its depth and beauty. The words you penned hit me in a way that felt like pure fate.

I felt compelled to transform your powerful words into a song, a melody that could carry the essence of your message to more hearts. After much work in the studio, your poem has come to life in a way I believe you'll be proud of. The song has been accepted by the record company, and they are as enthusiastic about it as I am.

Enclosed with this letter, you will find a check. This is your share of the advance from the record company. I believe in giving credit where it's due, and your poem is the soul of this song. Should the song do as well as we anticipate, you will continue to receive royalties for your contribution.

I want you to know your words have touched not only me but everyone who has worked on this project. You have a remarkable gift, Twyla, and I feel honored to have played a part in bringing your vision to a broader audience.

Warm regards,
Blackie Greenfield

"How did they know to send it here?" Caleb asked.

"I must have mistakenly put this address when I filled the HR paperwork. Maybe subconsciously I knew I'd be back."

"There are no mistakes. This *is* your home." Caleb smiled down at me.

"Can we play it, Mama?" Starla asked, her face brimming with enthusiasm.

"Of course. Bring your tape player over here," I replied with a smile.

Starla came back into the living room, her small hands carefully holding the portable cassette player. With an eagerness in her eyes that I hadn't seen for a while, she gently inserted the tape into the slot and pressed play. The opening strums of Blackie's acoustic guitar filled the air, each note resonated through the house, wrapping us in a warm, melodic embrace. His voice soon joined the melody, rich and clear, breathing life into the words I had written, so long ago.

TITLE: "TWILIGHT'S HIDDEN TRUTH"

VERSE 1:

    In the streets of Hollywood,
    There's a girl, they call Twilight,
    She's a shining star, the brightest light,
    In the hours darkest night.
    Unafraid her love takes flight.

CHORUS:

    Why can't I find a woman like Twilight?
    In her strength, my guiding light.
    In her dreams, she shines so bright.
    Let's run away tonight.

VERSE 2:

    Now she talks with a whisper,
    But there's a mystery within her

That keeps me warm at night.
In the land of broken dreams,
She's more than she seems.
A girl that shadows fear,
I long to keep her near.

BRIDGE:

Her spirit, wild and true,
In a land of broken dreams,
She's more than what she seems.
Every night, every day,
She hides her pain away.

CHORUS:

Why can't I find a woman like her?
In her strength, I see the light.
In her dreams, she shines so bright.
Let's run away tonight.

VERSE 3:

Her past, a whisper of pain,
A memory, a ball and chain.
Yet she marches on unseen,
In Hollywood's streets,
A beauty queen.

Every night and every day,
It doesn't take the pain away.

BRIDGE:

In a world of right and wrong,
Her passion, a fiery song.
In the hours darkest night,
She's a shining star, the brightest light.

CHORUS:

Why can't I find a woman like Twilight?
In her strength, my guiding light.
In her dreams, she shines so bright.
Let's run away tonight.

OUTRO:

Twilight, where could you be?
You're a mystery, to me.
For a woman like Twilight,
You could never hold her tight,
Her spirit shines too bright.

CALEB WRAPPED HIS ARMS AROUND ME. "THAT'S INCREDIBLE, Twyla. I always loved your poetry and now the world can know how talented my wife is."

Starla peered at the check. "Whoa, that's a lot of zeros. What are you going to do with it?"

A newfound determination filled my soul. "I'm going to chase a dream that's been with me since childhood," I declared. "I lost track of it for a while, but I'm going back to school. I'll start with Chaffey College, and we'll see what happens. Writing has always helped me through so many things, and I want to teach others how it can help them, too. It's time to realign with my true calling."

"Are you thinking of teaching a writing class or something?" Caleb had a proud look on his face.

"That's exactly what I'm thinking, maybe even a professor. I know it's going to be a lot of work, but with this money, I can afford the education and time I need to get there."

"You should do it. I'm behind you a thousand percent," he responded.

Starla hugged me tightly. "That's so cool, but what about your job in Hollywood?"

I smiled, a sense of peace washed over me. "Hollywood was an experience, but it wasn't where I belonged. Teaching, guiding others to learn and grow, that's where my heart lies. I had an English teacher that inspired me so much when I was in junior high. I want to be that for someone else. This song has reminded me of the power of writing, how it's been part of my salvation."

Caleb's understanding smile was comforting. "Your

God-given gift with words, your patience, and yes, your tenacity, make you a natural teacher. It's exactly where you're meant to be. We'll work out the logistics. What matters is you're following your heart."

I looked at my family and found a sense of purpose and support that I'd thought had been lost. The house, once a symbol of my past, now stood as a beacon for my future. I was ready to start this new chapter, with my family by my side.

Epilogue

Twilight Silverson
Fifty Eight Years Old

The cabin was shrouded in the gentle quietude of early morning. Starla and I stayed up until the early hours, immersed in the tales of my past, the room heavy with emotions stirred by each revelation. We sat surrounded by the remnants of family history—journals, photographs, and the echoes of a life defying expectations.

"Good morning, dear. Can I make you a coffee? I'm sorry I kept you up so late with my tales from the past."

"Mom, your story and Grandma's story, they're both incredible. I had a hard time sleeping last night after all of that. I can't wait to start writing it all down. I had no idea about so much of it. Thank you for getting back with Dad. Those two years in Hollywood, I think I blocked a lot of it out," she said, her face reflecting a blend of sadness and understanding.

"That's why I always encouraged you to find yourself and experience the world before settling down with kids. I wanted you to have an adult life before getting married. Not that I ever regretted having you. You are the best thing in my life, and you've honored me with two beautiful grand-daughters and a wonderful son-in-law. I admire you so much. You're everything I wished I could have been as a mother."

"Don't say that. You've been an amazing mother. You've raised me to be strong, to persevere, and so much more. I don't know how you did it when you were just seventeen."

"I was young and selfish at times, I'm the first to admit. I didn't even know who I was or what I wanted out of life, when I had you. I guess we sort of grew up together." I reached out to squeeze her hand. "Sometimes, we lose parts of ourselves, and you've got to go on a journey to find them again. That time in Hollywood, it was tough for all of us, but it helped set up everything we have now."

"And you did it. You're a successful songwriter and you've been teaching those song writing classes at the college. I'm proud of you, Mom. Is there anything you can't do?"

"Lots, dear. I'm still a terrible cook." We both laughed and my heart swelled with appreciation for the connection we've forged throughout the years. It took a long time to earn her trust back, but we were closer than ever now, especially now that my daughter was a mother herself.

Starla started rummaging around in mom's cardboard box as she smiled to herself. "I can't wait to show Kaya and the girls some of these old pictures."

The atmosphere suddenly shifted as Starla, her eyes gleaming with curiosity, pulled out a slip of paper from the bottom of the cardboard box. "What's this?"

"It looks like a birth certificate," I replied. I held my breath in silent anticipation as she examined it, her eyes widening in disbelief. "Mom, why does this birth certificate say Twilight *Lockheart*?"

The room seemed to spin as the weight of the revelation settled upon us.

"I... I don't understand," I stammered, my gaze shifted between the birth certificate and my daughter's emerald, green eyes.

"And here's another birth certificate. It says Dawn *Cameron* and it says it was amended in 1966. What does it mean? Who's Twyla Lockheart? Why would Grandma leave this for us to find this way?"

"I don't know what it all means. I was friends with a Penny Lockheart in junior high, and Dad was friends with her uncle, Charles Lockheart. I wonder if it's all connected." The room pulsated with unspoken questions.

As a cloud momentarily eclipsed the sun, shadows enveloped the room, casting us in a suspenseful gloom. Our gazes intertwined, heavy with the realization that we had stumbled upon a mystery—a key poised to unlock long-sealed doors hidden within the intricate maze of our family's history.

"What does this mean, Mom?" Starla's voice quivered mirroring the uncertainty hanging in the air.

"We'll go see Grandma this morning and get to the bottom of all this."

Starla's look intensified and I watched her mind race with the implications of the discovery. "Grandma will tell us the truth, Mom. We must ask her in person. Maybe that's why she was adamant about giving us this box yesterday. She wanted us to find this birth certificate together."

"Get dressed and we'll go see her now." I agreed, my voice just above a whisper.

Starla squeezed my hand, her presence a comforting anchor in a world of confusion. "We'll figure this out together. Maybe there's a simple explanation."

As I nodded, my mind was a whirlwind of questions. Was I Dawn Lockheart? And why had my mother never mentioned this before?

The truth about my past, about who I was, became shrouded in mystery and I suddenly knew everything was about to change.

In the quiet of the morning, with mysteries unfolding before us, I realized that our journey was just beginning, and this one piece of paper would redefine everything we thought we knew about the past.

TO BE CONTINUED...

In the Fall of 2024 with *Twilight's Brightest Star*, the third installment of the *Winds of Change* trilogy.

amazon.com/stores/author/B0CK63T7X1

Thank you for picking up a copy of *Twilight's Hidden Truth: Winds of Change Book 2* and giving it a read. I would love your feedback so please feel free to leave me a review here: https://www.goodreads.com/review/edit/213346363

Authors Note

STORY BEHIND THE STORY

Although the 'Winds of Change' trilogy is fictional, its essence is deeply rooted in pivotal moments from my own life. It began taking shape in 2017, inspired by these key events, ultimately weaving a unique saga of family dynamics, personal growth, and the enduring power of love. As the trilogy unfolds, you will journey alongside characters whose lives intersect in unexpected ways, mirroring the complexity and beauty of the human experience. Through the lens of fiction, I was able to share some of my own personal experiences.

I want to share two integral moments that sparked the flame for this trilogy. The first occurred during the summer of 2017, when my vibrant 90-year-old grandmother defied the odds by surviving a heart attack. Her tenacity and resilience became a guiding light, inspiring elements of the characters and their journeys in the trilogy.

During this period, my aunt became Grandma's primary caregiver, with our family rallying around her in support. Despite the distance between my home in Temecula and Grandma's residence, I made frequent journeys to visit her, cherishing each moment together. Our bond has always been unique, especially as I am her only surviving granddaughter through the maternal line. Having lived just across the street from Grandma during my upbringing, I was further able to strengthen our connection. I treasured her contagious laughter and the profound stories she shared about her experiences during the Great Depression and World War II. At times, I even questioned if some of these tales were exaggerated for my benefit, though I later discovered they were not.

One day, shortly after her heart attack, Grandma asked me to locate a box at the top of her closet. It was brimming with notes, old photographs, and letters, entrusting me to fulfill her dream of writing a novel about her life in Washington State during those challenging times. Fueled by her encouragement, I started writing, completing the first two chapters and reading them to her before she passed away.

Her death left me bereft. I was unable to write more of the story for several years until one night, a vivid dream of Grandma as a young girl running through the fields inspired me anew. I wrote fervently, capturing her spirit and the essence of her larger-than-life persona.

The second life-changing event that year was set in motion upon receiving an Ancestry DNA kit from my husband for my birthday. Eager to uncover my heritage, I was shocked when the results revealed a family secret that turned our lives upside down. My mother's biological father was not the man who raised her, whom we had loved dearly, but the town barber, who was still alive.

After meeting him and experiencing his and my mother's emotional reunion, we were saddened by his passing just six weeks later, soon followed by Grandma June. These revelations reignited my need to write as a way to process the emotions that both my mother and I were experiencing. After that initial burst of inspiration, however, my writing was sidelined by the demands of daily life. For two years, I set it aside. But in early 2023, after contracting Covid, I rediscovered my passion for writing. During a week of quarantine, I completed the manuscript, with the words flowing from me with renewed energy and purpose.

While the first installment of this trilogy is a tribute to the indomitable spirit of my grandmother, this second novel is dedicated to my amazing mother, her sacrifices, and resilience in becoming a teen mother and overcoming other hurdles in her life. Especially her family's experiences when my uncle was drafted into the Vietnam War.

This event cast a long shadow over her family, drawing them into a collective experience of unease and shaping her young life. It's a chapter of history that deserves to be told, shedding light on the sacrifices made by so many individuals who willingly stepped forward or were drafted into the military. This novel seeks to honor their sacrifice and the complex emotions of the families they left behind.

Stay tuned for the third novel, *Twilight's Brightest Star*, which is loosely inspired by my own journey and explores how the choices of generations past shape the lives of those who come after them.

Through telling these stories as Women's Fiction, the goal is to illuminate the enduring resilience and unwavering hope that form the cornerstone of not just one family's legacy, but the shared legacy of women across the world.

RACHEL VALENCOURT

Recipe

MOM'S FAMOUS SPAGHETTI AND MEATBALLS

The Sauce Ingredients:

- 2 Tablespoons Olive Oil
- 3 Cloves of Garlic, Minced
- 1/2 Cup Finely Chopped Onion
- Salt & Pepper to taste
- 1/4 Cup Chopped Basil
- 1 Teaspoon Dried Oregano
- 1/4 Cup Chopped Fresh Parsley
- 1 (6oz) Can Tomato Paste
- 1 Large Can Pureed Tomatoes
- 2 Cups water
- 3 Tablespoons Grated Parmesan Cheese

Meatball Ingredients:

- 1 – 1.5 lb. Ground Beef
- 2 Tablespoons Fresh Chopped Parsley
- 2 Tablespoons Grated Parmesan Cheese
- 1 Egg
- 1 Cup Bread Crumbs
- 1/2 Cup Milk

INSTRUCTIONS

Prepare the Sauce:

1. In a large skillet, heat olive oil over medium heat. Add minced garlic and chopped onion, sauté until tender.

2. Stir in tomato paste, pureed tomatoes, water, basil, oregano, and parsley. Bring to a boil.
3. Season with salt and pepper to taste. Add optional red pepper flakes for some heat.
4. Reduce heat to simmer, cover, and cook for 2 hours, stirring occasionally.

Preparation:

1. In a bowl, combine breadcrumbs and milk. Let sit for a few minutes to moisten.
2. In a large mixing bowl, combine ground beef, chopped parsley, grated Parmesan cheese, egg, and the bread crumb mixture. Mix until well combined.
3. Shape the mixture into nearly, golf ball-sized meatballs and place them on a baking tray.
4. Cook the Meatballs: Heat olive oil in a large skillet over medium heat until shimmering. Working in batches, sauté the meatballs, turning frequently, until browned on all sides (about 5 minutes per batch).
5. Transfer the browned meatballs to the simmering sauce using a slotted spoon.
6. Let the meatballs simmer in the sauce for another 2 hours over very low heat, stirring occasionally.
7. Cook the spaghetti according to package instructions until al dente.
8. Serve the meatballs and sauce over the cooked spaghetti.
9. Garnish with additional grated Parmesan cheese if desired.
10. Enjoy Mom's famous spaghetti and meatballs.

This recipe is a delightful blend of hearty meatballs and rich tomato sauce, sure to evoke memories of home-cooked meals and family gatherings.
— Bon appétit.

Acknowledgments

To my wonderful husband, you've been my rock and soulmate since we first met. We've weathered every storm together and I'm thankful for your indulgence of my wild ideas and readiness for new adventures. You're the peas to my carrots, the perfect partner in this wonderfully complex life we've crafted. Our journey, with its ups and downs, showcases what love, patience, and humor can accomplish. Thank you for the love, laughter, and support on this grand adventure. I love you more than words can express.

To my incredible daughters, you are the greatest gifts life has given me. You infuse each day with wonder and a touch of chaos (the good kind). I'm honored to be your mother and grateful for the fresh perspective and excitement you bring to my world. I love you both deeply.

To my dear parents, our life has been an extraordinary adventure! From spontaneous midnight road trips to your steadfast support during my impulsive move to England, your unique mix of tough love and protective care has emboldened me to face the world. Thank you for the countless lessons, laughter, and endless love.

Shout-out to my cousins—Andrea, Anne, and Cindy—and to all my amazing ARC and Beta readers. Your support has been invaluable. The stories I write are a tribute to each of you. Thank you for being a part of my literary experience.

And to God in Heaven, thank you for Your strength, Your guidance, and even the timely reality checks. Through joys and challenges, Your light has been a constant guide, and I am forever thankful for this beautiful life.

To my faithful readers, this book exists because of you. I am grateful for each of you; your engagement has truly made a difference. A heartfelt thanks to all the book lovers whose enthusiasm for stories like mine keeps this adventure thrilling. Let's continue this journey page by page.

All my love and gratitude,

Rachel Valencourt

Editors
Ann Leslie Tuttle, Jenna O'Malley, Gail Delaney

Format Designer
Dawn Baca

Images

Section and Scene Breaks—Golden Border Ornament (*Edited*) by Yodafunkyo from Pixabay *Pixabay.com/users/yodafunkyo-9881052/ Pixabay.com/illustrations/golden-border-ornament-design-4203142/*

Chapters— Watercolor Flower @ Freepik *Freepik.com/free-vector/watercolor-hand-drawn-flower-set_4494785.htm*

Glossary
1970S AND 1980S TERMS

Greaser

- *A 1960s youth subculture distinguished by leather jackets, slicked-back hair, and denim jeans. Drawing inspiration from James Dean, Marlon Brando, and the British rock scene, greasers embraced a rock'n'roll ethos that crossed racial and ethnic divides. Typically associated with the working class and Rockabilly culture, the term "greaser" symbolizes a defiance of mainstream societal norms.*

Okie

- *Initially referred to residents of Oklahoma who migrated during the Dust Bowl; now describes any destitute migrant worker from the Southern Midwest, often used pejoratively.*

Bitchin'

- *Excellent or awesome; originally surfer slang, used to describe something very pleasing or high quality.*

Boogie

- *To dance enthusiastically, especially to disco or pop music.*

Bogus

- *False or ridiculous; used to describe something not genuine or to express disbelief in something as being false.*

Far Out

- *Used to express astonishment or admiration; amazing or unbelievable.*

Get Out of Dodge

- *To leave quickly to avoid trouble; refers to Dodge City's lawless reputation.*

Gnarly

- *Originally surfer slang for dangerous or challenging; now means something excellent or impressive.*

Groovy

- *Fashionable and exciting; used to describe appealing music, clothes, or events.*

No Duh

- *A sarcastic response implying that something is obvious or already known.*

Radical

- *Describes extensive or impressive actions; politically, used for extreme reform.*

About the Author

Rachel Valencourt is a former Flight Attendant and OG mom blogger turned full-time writer. When she's not crafting stories, she's fueling up on coffee and indulging her severe case of wanderlust, often exploring exciting new places with her family. She also loves getting lost in juicy novels, joining fictional characters on spirited adventures as bold as her morning espresso.

Rachel's debut novel *Every Night Has A Dawn* is a finalist for Best New Debut in the American Writing Awards, marking her as a notable new voice in Contemporary Literature. She now resides in San Diego with her British hubby, daughters, and a six-toed cat named Saffy.

Please join her mailing list to stay updated on the latest news and discover upcoming release dates.

http://eepurl.com/im5WFQ

Feel welcome to visit her website and explore her latest blog post. Rachel finds immense joy in connecting with readers, so don't hesitate to drop by and say hello.

https://rachelvalencourt.com

facebook.com/RachelValencourt

x.com/RDValencourt

instagram.com/rachelvalencourt

bookbub.com/authors/rachel-valencourt

goodreads.com/rachelvalencourt